A GRASP OF KASPAR

COMHAIRLE CHONTAE ÁTHA CLIATH THEAS
SOUTH DUBLIN COUNTY LIBRARIES

STEWARTS HOSPITAL BRANCH
TO RENEW ANY ITEM TEL:

Items should be returned on or before the last date below. Fines, as displayed in the Library, will be charged on overdue items.

Frances Lincoln Ltd
4 Torriano Mews
Torriano Avenue
London NW5 2RZ
www.franceslincoln.com

ISBN 978-0-7112-3116-0 (hbk)
ISBN 978-0-7112-3159-7 (pbk)

Printed in China

9 8 7 6 5 4 3 2 1

A Grasp of Kaspar

The old man stood and looked out north from the window of his library, out towards and over the great lake below. He stood very straight. He had long ago decided to allow himself no chair here, in this window. The impulse to sit and just muse on the prospect would be too strong. His eyes now scanned the low hills of Germany beyond the lake and were occasionally caught by vessels moving on the lake itself, but his mind was on news from Beirut.

Odd news from Beirut . . . he would have to act on it – nothing dramatic, some action quite small in itself, but an initiating touch of the master, setting the momentum and direction of later larger events and other people. Real agency must start with him. He willed it so.

Restlessly he moved over to the cello that leaned at one side of the window and with two fingers tapped a soft tattoo on its belly. He rarely played it nowadays but he loved the sonority of the thing, its power to enlarge by resonance, and he kept it more or less tuned. He gave a firm final tap with one finger and walked over to the fire.

It was dying down but he left it for a moment. The room was warm.

Above the fireplace was a large framed map, a curiously diagrammatic engraved map of the territory he had just been looking out at: *Les Cours de Postes par le Cercle de Suabe, l'an 1752.* From habit his eye fell first on the city of Ravensburg at the bottom centre of the map, but then it skittered up and ran wild over Swabia as he considered matters and persons. Yes, what was needed was a light initial touch and a suitable chain of suitable reactions . . . for this one must know how people would behave. And he knew he knew how people would behave.

With a familiar faint pang he thought briefly of, but not about, his daughter. Then of and about her husband. Then of his dead son.

He bent to choose a small applewood log from one of two bins by the fireplace – the other held pine-cones – and place it gently and precisely on the embers. Almost at once its bark flared up and soon some of the embers beneath it became more lively with this new draught. He added a couple more logs, larger ones.

Then he went across to his desk and his telephone to get to work.

I

October 12–16, 1956

1

'Just hang around the better bars and impend,' Charlie Livingston said, fluttering a hand in the air to show how. 'They'll line up to talk.'

He swivelled in his swivel-chair.

'Spiral in!' he went on, since Briggs was being slow to respond. 'Who works late? – that's sometimes interesting. Talk with local suppliers perhaps. And so on. But talk with your friends, that's the point really. You've friends in St Gallen, I know – you told me. All I want is the feel of things.'

'There are no better bars in St Gallen,' Briggs said dourly. 'St Gallen is not that sort of town – people go home to their stamp collections. What you need is a proper investigator. Try someone like Christopher Penney. Or there's that firm in the Stachus . . .'

'No, no, Will, we're old chums. DM 25 a day plus expenses.'

'Come clean, Charlie.'

Livingston leaned forward on his desk, rested his head on a hand, and frowned at Briggs.

'I love baroque organ music,' he said at last.

'Yes . . .'

'Wait! So does Florian Schulte – every couple of weeks we go together to one of the Thursday night recitals at the *Dreifaltigkeitskirche*. You know Florian Schulte?'

'No.'

'No? Well, Florian is the new generation at Schulte's, and Schulte's has been just about the sharpest private banker in Munich for the last forty, fifty years, probably longer. Solid but very active and more contacts than a mangrove. In three years Florian will be taking over from his Uncle Alois.'

'And you both like baroque music.'

'We do so. Anyway, afterward the two of us go on some place and have supper, share a bottle of wine – always Franconian: we're working our way through the Franconian vineyards. We talk music, not business. Registrations for Buxtehude – that was a topic on Thursday. Florian's views are rather primitive about that sort of thing, I may tell you.'

Briggs nodded and sighed.

'We don't talk business,' Livingston went on, 'that's an unspoken agreement, but agreed. Still, there's a couple of minutes between looking around for the waiter and the check and then getting up to find your coats, you know, and we may mention this or that of a general kind – where we've been, trends, just that sort of thing. It's important you get a sense of how it was.'

He looked down at his blotter and went on more slowly.

'On Thursday it began like this. I mentioned I had been in Ravensburg, looking over Ravensburger-Humpis Textilindustrie and getting their pitch. Florian raised his eyebrows and nodded and said nothing. I said, casually, they looked promising enough. In fact, I don't often push things that far with Florian, but he had raised his eyebrows. He just went on arranging bills back into his billfold and then, for heaven's sake, said something about what a shame it was Ravensburg had been so much damaged in the Thirty Years' War. But then, after he had put the bills away, he asked – and he doesn't normally do this – asked if I was thinking seriously about Ravensburger-Humpis. I said I thought I might be. Then Florian pursed his lips.'

'Oh, my!'

'Wait a minute. He pursed his lips like this, as if he was going to imitate a *Waldflöte* stop or something.' Livingston demonstrated solemnly, snickered, and at once became serious again. 'It was a signal, I swear. Then we got up and went out into the

Maximilianstrasse. But just as we were splitting up to go find our cars he asked if I'd had a look at the Ravensburgers' Swiss subsidiary at St Gallen. I said I hadn't. It's very small. Then he asked if I'd met with Kaspar Leinberger, who is the executive who deals with technical development there. I said I hadn't, as it happened: he had not been in Ravensburg. Then he said: "A pity, perhaps! A singular man." And then he said good-night, shook hands, and that was it.'

Livingston sat and stared blankly into the distance. He had thoroughly frightened himself.

'Look,' Briggs said, 'this is all a bit subtle for me. What's your problem? Ring up Florian Schulte in business hours and ask to consult him about Ravensburg, on a formal footing. Or if you're too fine-grained for that, just keep your money out of Ravensburg for the moment.'

Livingston dragged himself back from somewhere and glanced at Briggs. He got out of his chair with a jerk and walked over to a darkening window.

'You are being obtuse, Will,' he said, looking out. 'Point one: I cannot ask Florian what he meant. He already went a long way. He and I are friendly competitors in the investment business. You know very well that means information is our inventory. He was good enough to prompt me towards getting some information, myself. I can't ask him to hand over Schulte's information to Fremont Funds here. There's a sort of etiquette. I am surprised you have no sense of this.'

'Second point: I can't just not put money into Ravensburg. Some is more or less committed already and a hell of a lot more is in channels. With Dow Jones stalled two years running, will you imagine the pressure I am under from New York? German stocks are up ten per-cent this year already. In 1957 things will really take off here – every coupon-clipper in Florida, every damned orthodontist in Brooklyn knows that. And I am paid to find them a place on the escalator. And why not, dammit? It's a dollar-primed escalator. Well, there aren't that many of the good bets open to big-scale funds here in the south-east – not on our terms – and that crimp Ackerman in the Frankfurt office has a stockade round the south-west. I *need* Ravensburg if it's not kinky. If it is, I've lost a bit but maybe have a fortnight to save losing a pile – to say nothing of my job. That's how it is, boy.'

Livingston walked back to his chair, sat, re-arranged his grey flannel, and looked soulfully at Briggs.

'Help!', he said in a waif-like voice.

'Well, I don't know, Charlie,' Briggs said awkwardly. 'You want someone to go sniffing around Ravensburger-Humpis in St.Gallen. My friends there aren't to the point: they aren't business people. And me – what I know about in St Gallen is the fifteenth-century linen and fustian trades. I'm an historian. A thoroughly academic economic historian. I've no lines into what happens there now, at all. It's a weird closed-up community, you see. The old business families live inside their own clans.'

'The Ravensburg people won't be the old business families.' Livingston looked at his watch and took a blue folder from a drawer in the desk. 'Just do me one favour, Will. I've got to go now and huddle with a paper-maker from Augsburg. You stay here and have a quick look over this file on Ravensburg. It's their pitch plus some notes of mine. If you want anything else – directories or whatever – ask Sue. Tonight she'll be here till seven taking the New York calls.'

He was bustling about now, dropping papers into a brief-case and grabbing a tweed coat from a closet.

'When you've looked the stuff over, make up your mind. Leave me a note here or – better yet – call me at home later. I hope you'll go. I'd be grateful. But no hard feelings anyway. Hell! I'm late.'

'You're gambling on my curiosity.'

'Why not? So long, Will, and thanks.'

Livingston grinned a plucky grin and left. There was the

noise of a short burst of talk with Sue in the outer office and then the outer door slamming.

Briggs – a nondescript young man of medium height – got up and went over to the window Livingston had faced three minutes before. The *Englischer Garten* was sodden and sombre across the road. A few bent figures were making good time along the gravel paths, going to and from the university. There was a rapid and strangely regular glinting of reflected lights on a fast-running canalized stream. Children all gone home. No dog-walkers. It was very warm in the office.

Did he *owe* it to Charlie to look into these people? He wasn't a financial snoop. Charlie was a sort of friend, but the work Briggs usually did for Fremont Funds was a matter of mutual convenience, just occasional general reports on this or that industrial sector in Germany. It suited: the money was useful, naturally, but it also let him keep up some of the analytic modes he had once been taught. Charlie liked the reports; they were a bit external but they had the right collegiate cut and gave his own hunches tone. But this sort of thing . . . still, he would quite like to help Charlie out.

Did he want to go to St Gallen? Not particularly. A morose town. On the other hand, it would be good to see Maria and Klaus again, old friends and first-class people.

Did he really have any taste for poking about in a possible dark corner of a great textile firm? Well, very mildly, perhaps. A little. And perhaps he was more intrigued by Florian Schulte's pursed lips than he had got around to admitting.

He walked over and sat in Livingston's swivel-chair, and warily opened the Ravensburger-Humpis folder.

2

Next morning, then, found Briggs in his aged Volkswagen driving west out of Munich towards St Gallen. It was a day of hazy sun, ambivalent between early and full autumn, and presently his road bent more southward. He was driving rather slowly. This was benignly haunted ground for him.

In Briggs's mind central Europe was often a map with a late-medieval overlay, a diagram of old centres of manufacture, long-gone sources of materials, ancient roads. On this same road, or rather on a rougher and narrower road still underlying its modern metal, some of his ghosts had been purposefully moving bales and barrels along five hundred years before. It being late in the year, some of them would have been on the last trip of their season: the Alpine passes they laboured over to get to Lombardy, the Splügen pass and the Septimer, would be becoming awkward before long. They had been moving metal wares and linen south, silks and saffron north, all with great effort, on pack-horses and in small wagons. These had been hard and pushing men and their ghosts were strong.

Briggs came to Kaufbeuren, a small city now as a small city then, and he chose to drive through its centre rather than round the ring-road along the city walls. He drove through the narrow streets very slowly indeed. He knew a fair amount about Kaufbeuren and enjoyed his knowledge. Among other things, he knew that in the 1470s a linen-weaver and opportunist called – as it happened – Florian had lived in the Ganghoferstrasse there, and had played original games with letters-of-credit in Milan, games that had led to his being thrown out of the Weavers' Guild. They had known he was trying to do something new and that that was wrong. Conservative folk in Kaufbeuren, which was why the city had stayed small. He drove out of it.

Beyond Kaufbeuren the road ran from a sour flat terrain, drained now but not then, up into rolling hills, a great sheep country once. Briggs was aware of moving deep into an old textile zone. This was what Ravensburger-Humpis had come out of, he thought. Bigger scale now, but same principles: get a grip on the materials and the machines, and play the markets at both ends of the process. When wool had no longer offered profit, due to cheap imports coming up the Rhine, they had given up sheep and turned to flax and cotton; just as now, with cotton falling back and flax long gone, they were turning to synthetics, fast. The Volkswagen was soon chattering down towards Kempten, another small city, at the foot of greater hills.

The main point about Kempten was that this was where the cotton road had come in over the mountains from the south-east – from the Brenner pass and Venice and the Levant. Briggs's people had needed that Cypriot cotton to weave their fustian. But in the course of getting it they had also got cleverer. Along with the bales of cotton came a bundle of Italian tricks – ideas about partnerships, dry interest, analytical book-keeping, gearing-up, generally how to put florins to work. It was a period of commercial ingenuity out of which operators like Fremont Funds and the Schulte Bank were fairly straightforward developments. Briggs wondered if Charlie Livingston realised he was basically a late-medieval invention. He laughed and drove knowingly on through more wooded hills until the road began dropping down towards Lindau and Lake Constance.

Here some of his people would have been taking ship west to Konstanz itself, forty miles away along the great lake, with a mind to the long road through Geneva to Lyons, and then perhaps on past the Pyrenees into Spain. Last chance for forty easy miles by water here. One pack horse took two hundredweight at most, one lake boat took a hundred tons and sometimes more: thus the peninsular city of Lindau, once a functional port, now just a pretty fossil. Briggs drove past it and took the road along the east shore of the lake to the Austrian customs.

As he stopped the car and looked out his documents he felt hungry. He would eat something, he decided, in Bregenz – a faded Austrian resort he had little feeling for, but his last stage on the grand route to Milan. The old Lombardy road went southwards from here, along the unnavigable upper Rhine, past Chur, to the passes: whereas his own road to St Gallen diverged south-west, and from now on he would be going up a fifteenth-century by-road. It was a moment to put off. Besides, it was time to think in a preliminary way about the present and Ravensburger-Humpis GmbH and this was a good point to do it from. He drove into Bregenz, found a quiet beer-house on the water, and took a table by a window looking west down the lake – or down the quarter-mile or so of it that could be seen in the sunny haze. Waiting for his schnitzel, eating a roll and drinking beer, he directed himself to the problem.

This lake divided Ravensburg, ten miles north of it, from St Gallen, ten miles south of it. To the north in Germany Ravensburger-Humpis had a large plant and main offices in Ravensburg itself and half-a-dozen other spinning and weaving mills here and there in Swabia and Bavaria. To the south in Switzerland there was this one small unit in St Gallen.

Why? According to the papers he had worked through the evening before it had two roles. It produced certain fine textiles, including machine embroidery and lace, and it had a laboratory for developing and assessing textile machinery in general. Agency for the export of textile machines was a Ravensburger-Humpis side-line. This made fair sense.

It was also noticeable that a couple of the Ravensburger-Humpis grandees had houses in the neighbourhood of St Gallen. This was not in Livingston's file: Briggs had learned it last night from directories and phone-calls. Eberhard Vogt, the patriarch of the firm, had a country house near Arbon on the Swiss south shore of the lake; and the allegedly singular Kaspar Leinberger had a house in St Gallen itself. Leinberger, in charge of the technical side, was, it turned out, Eberhard Vogt's son-in-law.

As the crow flew, St Gallen would be well under thirty miles from Ravensburg – Westchester to Wall Street, say, or Haywards Heath to the Savoy Grill. But here the thirty miles included ten miles across the lake, and a frontier.

Well, there was one obvious explanation for the Ravensburgers having a toe in Switzerland – routine circumvention of tax. If a firm in a high-tax country like Germany had a subsidiary in a low-tax country like Switzerland, it could transfer some of its German product to its Swiss subsidiary at an artificially low book-price. The product need not be moved physically to Switzerland. It could be shipped direct from Germany to the United States or the Lebanon or wherever. The profit, however, went to the Swiss subsidiary and was minimally taxed. Chortles in Ravensburg. True, German tax officials learned all about this and much more elaborate under-invoicing exercises at their mothers' knees, or at least on the first day of their induction course in Wiesbaden, but never mind: delicately driven, it still worked. Besides, under the old 1931 double-taxation agreement Vogt and any other Germans could benefit individually from Swiss residence.

On the other hand, this really was rather pat and banal. If one had a more interesting reason for being in St Gallen, tax-dodging of a quite legal sort would make a convenient screen. And it could not have been the reason for Florian Schulte's reaction. It takes more than routine tax-avoidance to wring a moue from a banker.

The schnitzel had been greasy, the salad drenched. The coffee now was scarcely drinkable. And much too much seemed to be hanging on Florian Schulte having made a face like an organ stop. Briggs looked out along the lake again. An antique passenger steamer was coming into Bregenz harbour and, outside, a coxed four was racing along in a splashy spurt. He got up and paid his bill, used the occasion to move currencies about from pocket to pocket, and went out to the Volkswagen.

The shore road now ran out of Bregenz, across the upper Rhine, out of Austria and into Switzerland – a cluttered strip of shore here between lake and hills, though things opened out further along. But his own road soon veered up from the lake through orchards and pastures and he followed it up into the valley of the Goldach. Almost till misty eve of this short day he motored, arriving in St Gallen about half-past four.

Klaus and Maria Fleury lived inside the ring of the Old Town, on the top floor of a modest business building. At the front the ground floor of the building was a glossy lapidary's shop. Its windows displayed to the street big lumps of improbably colourful natural crystals, back-lit for effect. At the rear of the building was a small factory where half-a-dozen men manufactured eighteenth-century peasant-baroque wardrobes – a version scaled down a third for the modern home. Briggs took his bag and cut through an archway to the courtyard behind to fetch the key from the foreman folk-artist, who acted informally as Klaus and Maria's concierge. He was a conceited old man, uncannily like Woodrow Wilson in his looks, and nowadays he limited his exertions to dirtying-down and distressing the painted floral decoration on the product – a role with enjoyable possibilities for self-assertion over his men. These were now packing up for the day in a sullen silence. Briggs collected the key and climbed the three flights to the Fleurys' apartment.

Once inside their spacious and rambling garret, he dumped his bag and sat down in the big living-room to wait for Klaus and Maria, due any moment. It was a comic and marvellous room – a high but partly attic space with white sloping upper walls and, on two sides, big dormer windows. At some time these two windowed sides had been fitted out with wall-benches and three large tables of yellow pine. Somebody seemed to have wanted something like a country inn in a city penthouse. Two of the tables were used as working-tables nowadays and at the third table one ate. The Fleurys had just added bright vermilion curtains and cushions here.

Against this, the longer inside wall and such of the other wall as was not door or slope were lined with bookshelves from top to bottom, end to end. The books in these were real books, shabby text-books, battered paperbacks, tall facsimile manuscripts and thick library catalogues, austere statistical yearbooks, unbound offprints in clutches, political tracts and novels, incomplete runs of journals, scattered colonies of shining new books in five or six languages, some highly technical and some just humane, ring-books holding notes, a few stretches of sober old collected editions of an odd selection of authors: the Fleurys were people who used books without fuss.

But then, back over to the window side again, there was a theatrical view of the inner city – out over the steep, jumbled but immaculately tiled roofs of the Old Town to the great rococo abbey-church of St Gallen, now looming with its two curvy-topped towers in the mist and dusk. The room stood cheerfully for what was all right in St Gallen.

Briggs sat and let the light fade.

3

Within ten minutes there was a banging on the stairs. Briggs went to the door and helped a burdened Maria Fleury with her packages.

'Briggs! Willi! I'll just put these in the kitchen . . . and you put these on my work-table. You haven't switched lights on. Now how are you? Heavens! Quite gaunt and pinched. And how's Inka . . .? Oh, I have said the wrong thing, but it had to be got out of the way, didn't it? She was not one for you, perhaps, you know. Klaus felt that. But you know Klaus.'

Maria laughed. She was a small blonde woman with long hair pulled back into a roll. Her days were spent working in the Abbey library.

'Good! You've brought a bottle! Let's open it, shall we? Klaus will be here any minute. I've spent the whole day wrestling with just one secondary *scholium* – Walafrid Strabo, no less: you remember him – and I'm limp. Quite limp. How nice! It will be like the old days, with you moping in the spare-room again. Now I should warn you that Klaus . . . but here *is* Klaus.'

Klaus was a tall, dark, strong man with thick spectacles and the air of a bookish bouncer. Much of the time his brows were knitted in a semi-frown, as if part-puzzled and part-exasperated. That was deceptive: he was secretly placid, and professionally an effortless virtuoso in a kind of mathematico-economic high theory that left Briggs gaping.

They shook hands formally, and the three of them sat in one of the windows and talked about Walafrid Strabo, new equilibrium models, the state of the world, and the research and emotional problems of several friends, until they had emptied the bottle Briggs had brought and started another.

'We'll eat in tonight, out tomorrow,' said Maria suddenly. 'Come and help. Then Willi can tell us why he is here.'

An hour later Maria and Briggs had finished dinner and were sitting over their *Forstwein* while Klaus, who ate slowly, was still eating cheese. Briggs had sketched Livingston's problem.

'It is sad to see you as capital's lackey,' Klaus said. He was no more than half joking.

'Nonsense!', Maria said. 'Willi isn't a running-dog. He is a money-romantic. To Willi, money is communication, I think, like words, but more honest. For an economist, Klaus, you have very little feeling for money.'

Klaus tipped his head and chewed.

'"Movements of money and movements of mind"', Maria went on, and Briggs winced with recognition. 'Willi would say that if you know how money was moving – well, within and between Germany and Italy in 1517 or 1915, say – you know something about how people were thinking. And then you know something about how things happened. He is wrong, but that is how he sees it.'

Klaus swallowed cheese. 'But which people?'

'In the first instance rich people, who are anyway important in many great events', Maria pursued, 'and in the second instance those other people to whom you can plot rich people's relation in economic terms. Most people. Of course, Klaus, you would then say movements of money and movements of mind "can hardly be considered homologous, either as objective systems, or indeed as analytical constructions on behaviour". Oh yes, you would. But Willi would reply: of course they are not homologous. One must learn the language of money, the grammar within which a money operation signifies as a declaration of values and perceptions. Money is not a neutral medium, he would say, it has its own formal energies. And he would go on to argue – shifting his ground here, rather – that money is as much an aesthetic medium as words, almost a glass-bead-game. People play with it, enjoying their skill. So that when you know the financial forms of an age you have something like a literature, even like a cathedral – an art that embodies in its forms the mind of that age. And then you, Klaus, would quote Léon Walras on the proper limits of economics. You usually do.'

Maria laughed and finished her wine. Klaus was feeling in his pocket for his pipe and tobacco.

'A tax-evasive ploy,' he said. 'Probably it's just that. But do you know anything about the Ravensburg people?'

'Not much,' Briggs said. 'Eberhard Vogt, the chief, is sixty or so. He was a research chemist once, organic chemistry, and taught at Heidelberg for some years: he is "Professor Vogt". He went into textiles in the late 1930s – the connection being dye-stuffs presumably. He had been on the western front, a sapper, towards the end of the first War and in the second he was attached to the Reich Office for Economic Expansion, whatever that means. He has some sort of country house above the lake, down near Arbon. His wife and son both died in 1944, but there is a daughter, married to this Kaspar Leinberger. Leinberger isn't senior enough to be in the directories, but I rang up Otto Daucher at the *Münchner Allgemeine*.'

'Tcha, Otto!' Klaus was impatient, but Maria laughed again.

'How is Otto?' she asked.

'Still trying to liven up the financial pages.' Briggs had drunk enough to attempt an imitation: '"Leinberger, Leinberger, Kaspar Leinberger . . . Manager at Ravensburger-Humpis, just a technical man. Has a little development outfit, where he tries things out? Married Mechtild, the lovely daughter of Eberhard Vogt and is very much Vogt's boy . . . abrasive, I guess . . . fell out with the financial men, I heard, but Vogt stood by him. Quite a man old Vogt – sits on a Swiss mountain reading Nietzsche, and the Managing Board still jumps when he says to. Or maybe it's Novalis . . . that he reads. Sorry, Will, I must go: hot call from Frankfurt . . . marvellous that you rang . . . ciao, Will, ciao!'"

'Very useful,' said Klaus. 'Textile industrialists of the purple sage. But there is something a little louche about Vogt's Heidelberg-dyestuffs-Reich Office career, you know: it's all IG Farben territory. He must have known the Buna people and he must still know Fritz ter Meer: that one's out of prison now and Chairman of Bayer Chemicals. No doubt your Livingston is itching to get his money into Bayer too.'

'Yes', said Briggs, 'probably.'

'We do not know any of these Ravensburg people. Remember, we are not even of St Gallen. Folk like us from Basel hardly understand the dialect here. We live in a little enclave of academic outsiders, mainly.'

'No, Klaus,' Maria said. 'I know Mechtild Leinberger quite well. And even you have met her. It was she that spilt her drink over you at Ida Frischknecht's summer party.'

'Ah, the lunatic with the grin. She told me she could hear the universe breathing – not all the time, but quite often. Frantic.'

'No, Klaus. She had just drunk too much. I like her. Ida says she is unhappy in St Gallen, her husband busy and older than her. I don't know him. She goes around looking for company, I think. I've seen her in the bar at the Hotel Propp. No, Klaus, that grimace is most unattractive. Priggish! You know Klaus has Genèvois blood on his mother's side, Willi.'

'In any case,' said Klaus, 'what's needed is a local informant about the Ravensburger-Humpis business activity here, not their wives.'

'René Pfiffner,' said Maria.

'Hanspeter Hefti', said Klaus, 'knows all about textile machinery.'

'René Pfiffner,' she repeated. 'Hanspeter Hefti is not to be spoken to unless one wishes to discuss looms.'

'Looms have a role, both in life and in this problem. René also is a trial.'

'He's an old gossip but he really knows a lot about St Gallen people.'

Klaus looked at Briggs. 'Do you feel like playing chess? With an unspeakably bad player? René Pfiffner uses chess-men as an Arab uses beads.'

'René is retired now,' Maria explained. 'He used to be editor of the *St Galler Beobachter*, an awful little weekly newspaper that no longer exists. Nowadays he spends most evenings in the Café Schläfli. None of the proper chess-players there will play with him, they are so solemn, and if you sit with him you have to move pieces around – fidgeting as a background to chat, really. Anyone can do it.'

Klaus muttered 'move pieces around' with distaste.

'René does no harm, Klaus. He's just a little barren Balzac in a very small town. We'll go and drink coffee with René.'

They packed up and went out into the mist, thicker and wetter now, for the ten-minute walk to the Café Schläfli.

4

'Hah! *épée!*', René Pfiffner cried, and attended for a moment to the chess-board.

The Fleurys had left ten minutes ago. Maria would have been willing to stay and listen but Klaus had begun to behave badly and she had taken him off. Briggs had already lost a quick game to René Pfiffner, who was several classes better than him and did very well for a little barren Balzac. Pink and white in his blue velvet smoking-jacket, he looked more like a miniaturized Talleyrand.

The Café Schläfli was decorous – a large L-shaped, high-ceilinged, well-lit place with buff corduroy banquettes and booths and marble-topped tables. It was full but not animated: people sat and looked at chess-boards, or at newspapers on sticks, or just at the wall opposite. Every fifteen minutes or so the torpor was broken by the circuit of a severe-looking waitress with a large tray of cakes on a leather strap around her shoulders, when some people became quite vivacious for a time and made decisions and purchases. René had impressed Briggs by stylishly tickling the palm of this waitress as he handed over his money. She had not smiled.

'*Hinein die Hitlerjugend!*', said René, and made an eccentric pawn move. 'When he blockaded Napoleon, did your Robert Peel consider the consequences for the Swiss? No, he did not! Be that as it may, when you blockaded the continent in 1800 – let us say 1800 – you started something of greater consequence than you realized. You and I are historians: we know that the present has deep, deep roots in the past – *deep* roots. You look around the Canton of St Gallen today, and Appenzell and Glarus too, and you say: "How pastoral! How attractive these meadows, with their cows and cottages! This snug village here, that cataract there! Truly the land of Rousseau's Héloise, or at least of Salomon Gessner!" But let me tell you, Mr Briggs, you are wrong. You are looking at the Manchester of continental Europe. In 1800 this was the centre of the greatest textile industry outside England itself. The mills were small and they were widely dispersed, but there were very many of them. And most were powered by those streams and torrents of ours you find so picturesque.'

Briggs, who knew this, made an orthodox pawn movement and René Pfiffner instantly countered it.

'But, you then say, "What about the machines? The mules and the jennies?" And you are right: *Made in England*, as you would put it. But what, then, are the Swiss to do when Horatio Nelson sinks the boat that brings them? Exactly! They must learn to make their own – copies at first, but soon much better. We already had the fine mechanics. Clocks! Come, now, when the Switzerland of today is mentioned abroad, what does the world first think of, apart from its banks? No, no, not chocolates or ski instructors. *Clever machine-tools and clever chemicals!* Oerlikon and Geigy! And it all goes back to our need to equip our textile workers. Mules and dyestuffs! So, when you ask me what made a German weaver buy a small St.Gallen mill like Rapp & Schachtschabel AG, I answer you: "Horatio Nelson caused them to do so". That is the historical view. It is your move.'

'The Ravensburgers were after access to Swiss textile technology?' After thought, Briggs castled. René Pfiffner flicked a bishop slant-wise.

'Naturally. Rapp & Schachtschabel was a small firm, but very advanced in developing machine embroidery and lace. Walther Schachtschabel was a genius in his way and had close ties with avant-garde machine-makers in Winterthur.'

'And has this . . .?' Briggs shifted a pawn, defensively.

'Ah! Here we descend from the larger pattern of historical forces and encounter individuals,' said René Pfiffner without dismay.

'Check!' he said. 'Do you know Vogt at all? Kaspar Leinberger? No? It is true they keep to themselves. Well, now . . . Vogt, it may be, is a great man. A philosopher, almost. At least a thinker. I admire such a man, a man who with one hand directs a great organization, and with the other turns a leaf of his Plato . . . or his Jean Paul, perhaps. And he has felt the sharp edge of life! His only son killed on the Russian front, his wife dead of grief – that is not a man abstracted from life's pain. It is a Roman stoic on the old German pattern. It is Checkmate, I think.'

René Pfiffner started deftly setting the pieces for another game.

'I will tell you. Four or five years ago I went to interview him for the old *Beobachter* – one of a series of interviews with prominent men about the problems of north-eastern Switzerland. He had not long acquired his house near Arbon. It is not a businessman's house – it is the house of a cultivated gentleman, or perhaps of a retired professor with independent means. We talked in his study, full of fine books, the masters of German thought and letters. I remember there was a violincello and an old music stand in one corner and a medieval wooden figure of St Martin in another. He sat there and as we talked I was struck by the quality of his head. He has a wonderful head, a thinker's head with a tall straight brow. He was affability itself, and for an hour or more we discussed the Swiss experience, the meaning of the Swiss. I tell you, he knew as much about our history as I do. And he had an insight, a capacity for the large perspective, which the Swiss I was talking with at that time did not have. I felt I had been with a man who had thought long and deep about many things. And I came away with the best article in my series. "Weft and woof of the Alemannic Swiss: the historical-philosophical view of a German friend" – that was its title . . . you are White.'

'And with all this liberal ease he runs a business as big as Ravensburger-Humpis?' Briggs asked.

'He presides. He negotiates at a certain level. He has young men in Ravensburg who tend the shop. He does not mend looms or engage office-boys. He is the strategist: he thinks things out. This man has wisdom – you must not dismiss that. And he also knows many important people in Germany: his career has been of that kind. No doubt he reassures the Supervisory Board and the large investors with great ease. I agree, it is an old-fashioned type, a patrician type, but it is a fine type. It will be a bad day for Europe when all our great industrialists are Henry Fords. And yet . . . you are White, Mr Briggs.'

They drifted through the first moves of the Sicilian defence.

'And yet it is true that for such a man much depends on choosing the right subordinates. That is clear. On the whole Vogt must have succeeded in this: Ravensburger-Humpis prospers. But the one we see in St Gallen happens to be Kaspar Leinberger. It is a pity you have not seen him. To see him is almost to know him. Tall, raw, dark-haired, pale grey eyes, and stiff, stiff – above all, stiff. A grey man. He has not ingratiated himself with many here.'

'Then Vogt's judgement . . .', began Briggs, but René interrupted.

'Perhaps, perhaps – but perhaps not. Leinberger is by all accounts a sound engineer. I have not heard his technical competence questioned. There is a colleague of Klaus Fleury's who knows of such things, Hanspeter Hefti, and I am sure he would confirm that. And then, the man is safely under Vogt's eye here. And after all, though neither you nor I like such generalizations, there is some tendency for dedicated mechanics to lack that rounded polish which we ourselves value and Vogt so exemplifies. Walther Schachtschabel himself, though in some substantial respects not unlikeable, in his own way really quite human, was not a man of expansive culture or even particularly urbane address. And then again, Leinberger is the husband of Vogt's daughter.'

'She . . .?'

'Ach! The usual German girl of her class today. A coquette. You will have seen hundreds such in the cafés of Munich. Not interesting. But you cannot expect Eberhard Vogt to feel that. She is now his only child. That is beyond philosophy. And Kaspar Leinberger is her husband.'

'You know, you do draw him as a sort of basic Boche.'

'No,' René hesitated. 'Not really. He is . . . I would say he is too little at ease with himself for that. A man very capable of having bad dreams or high aspirations even, I would say. Unattractive but not insensible. Part of it perhaps comes from some inner unrest.'

'Bad dreams? One often wonders what such people did in the war. Could Swiss residence. . .?'

'No, no, no, you are quite wrong.' René was upset. 'In the first place, Vogt was no Nazi. He spoke of them to me with a genuine contempt: "lemurs", I remember he called them. And he would not harbour a son-in-law from that zoo. But more important, St Gallen is not the place for this.'

He sat back from the board and patted the table with a hand.

'Look, Mr Briggs, it is important you should understand these matters. We both know there were Swiss who would have made an arrangement with Germany in 1940. There were similar men in England, I believe. Of course, there are people in this town who spoke out for collaboration in 1940, who would have gone along with Pilet-Golaz, and perhaps further. One of them was drinking tea across this room a few minutes ago – a coarse and stupid man. But there were relatively few such here. We were too close to Germany, we knew too much about it, to *want* to join the madness over there. The strength of the Swiss fascists lay down in French Switzerland, not here in the north-east. Here the Right was not even of the National Front but of the Peasant Party. It still is. It is true those were bad days. It was hard to be sure of the proper course.'

'I was not suggesting . . .'

'Yes, it is easy now to see that Pilet-Golaz was wrong, morally and no doubt practically too, and that General Guisan was right. His was the truer Swiss way. But at the time Guisan and his alpine redoubt could seem irresponsible. You are too young to feel this. And that redoubt was some way from St Gallen. But you can see that there is a difference between an uncertainty of the spirit in 1940 – it does depress me to think of that time – and a liking for Hitler that would survive 1945. St Gallen would not provide a congenial ambience for people of the kind you are implying. No, there you are wrong, I assure you.'

René looked down at the chessmen but did not find his bearings. For a couple of minutes he had not been moving pieces. He suddenly seemed tired and rather old.

'This game looks like a draw to me,' Briggs said hesitantly. 'I hope I am not keeping you up longer than you would normally stay.'

'It is true: it is well past ten – late for me. If you could pass my coat, perhaps . . . but we must talk again. I am always here in the evening. It is a pleasure to talk to a younger man with a sense of the past.'

5

Briggs had wrapped René Pfiffner up in his coat and scarf and wide-brimmed black hat, walked him back to the door of a dark *fin-de-siècle* apartment block, shaken hands, and joined in vague noises about meeting again for historically-informed discussion. He turned up the collar of his own coat and set off back through the wet mist towards the Old Town.

He was in low spirits. Partly this would be the Café Schläfli and its hundred-and-five-proof essence of St Gallen, and partly too it was that René Pfiffner had turned out a little more complex than he had reckoned on.

But he was aware his low spirits also came from a feeling that he was more remote from Ravensburger-Humpis, further away from Eberhard Vogt and Kaspar Leinberger, than when the evening had begun. Then, he had seen them very fragmentarily as odd items of information in file or directory, a handful of pieces in a big jigsaw just started, but at least in relation to facts and even a few figures. Now any general pattern he might have been on the way to sensing had been compromised by passing through two successive distorting lenses.

The first distorting lens was what he had taken as René's rendering of the two men – the one as a farcically cultivated patrician of the old school, the other as an edgy Hun with gritty fingers. Prospero and Caliban, almost. These were not plausible types. But then, Briggs knew, these caricatures had been further distorted, not corrected, by his own resistance to them. He had reacted to René's images by almost idly imposing over them clichés from a puerile mythology of his own – a smooth smiling master-villain from a John Buchan adventure, and an SS officer on half-pay. Inane. But it would be hard now to dislodge these constructs entirely. That was the trouble with learning about people even from a single inform-ant: you saw them refracted not once but twice.

He came to the ring road round the Old Town and cut along it briefly toward the Fleurys' spoke of the wheel. And the ring road led him past the door of the Hotel Propp.

Briggs slowed. Hang around the bars, the better bars, and im-pend – Livingston had said, absurdly enough. When you came down to it, the bar at the Propp was the only high-burgess bar in town. Whisky would be good against the mist, and Maria and Klaus did not keep whisky. And then, too, apparently this was where Mechtild Leinberger-Vogt was sometimes to be seen, identifiable by a lunatic grin. It would be a small advance, a little step towards reality, if he set eyes on someone even tenuously connected with Ravensburger-Humpis. He walked across the road and into the Hotel Propp and then through towards the Bar Vadianus at the back of the lobby.

Outside the bar door was a nasty little easel with wrought-iron curls and on this the photograph of a snake-headed man smiling up from a piano, with the text: "At the keyboard: Heini Hufnagel". Inside, the room was not so much softly as dimly lit. It turned out that Heini Hufnagel was older and sadder than his picture, and really sitting at the bar talking with the barman. There were ten or a dozen people here and there, but Briggs saw no grinning girls or any good cheer at all. On the other hand, there were a couple of obvious Englishmen sitting up at the other end of the bar, in tweed jackets and cavalry twill trousers. He went and sat in a booth against the wall, ordered his whisky from the waiter in a firm north-German accent, and waited till he too became part of the furniture.

Those were dire Englishmen. One of them was tall and looked like a sheep, the other small and like a whippet. They

34

were bitching about colleagues somewhere, in cultured tones. Teachers from some school.

Well, how did one productively 'impend' in such a bar as this? Catch people's eyes and look knowing? He hadn't the personality for that. It would be neat if the heavy man reading business papers in the next booth accosted him and insisted on spilling beans, but at the present rate it would soon be a matter of consulting Hanspeter Hefti on looms.

Heini Hufnagel had returned to that keyboard and was tinkling proficiently away. 'How long has this been going on?' – a good tune. Mechtild Vogt must be in her middle twenties, about Briggs's own age, a good deal younger than Leinberger. Did she drink too much because she knew her husband was making an SS atom bomb disguised as a loom? No. Of course, boredom made some women drink, and St Gallen was boring. Inka had claimed that she drank because she was bored with Briggs.

'Bugger you and your *deuxième cristallisation*,' as she had said, 'I am not hanging around for you to work through your Doubts.' It had been a mistake to expound oneself as a Stendhalian lover. A cold fish, that Stendhal. There were episodes in love – 'Consuming Curiosity', for instance – the man just did not know. Next time, the natural Briggs . . .

Tomorrow. Well, tomorrow it might not be totally unreasonable to go and have a look at the Ravensburger-Humpis mill. Heaven knows what he could learn from it, but it was real. What could one possibly learn by looking at a factory? Klaus had an old monocular glass he used for mountain expeditions. He could borrow it and climb a tree . . . time to go.

Briggs got his coat and went through the lobby and out. The mist was no lighter. He set off across the street outside the Hotel Propp, working his way into his coat as he went.

Possibly the car approaching, a dark-toned Porsche, had been going too fast for the mist-slicked surface. It was also crossing the ring road at a sharply curving angle, apparently in order to halt outside the Hotel Propp, against the direction of the traffic that at this hour was not there. To avoid Briggs it braked. The back wheels broke away slightly and – very, very gently indeed – the car slid ten degrees off course and delicately nudged Briggs with its left rear wing as it stopped. Hindered by his half-on coat, he lost balance and toppled over. Grotesque! he thought, lying strait-jacketed in the gutter.

'My God! My God! You looked like a vampire. How are you?'

The girl's voice was German, not Swiss, and her hand was on his shoulder. He knew at once who it must be. He contrived to sit up and shrug on his coat at last, and looked at her. She was not grinning but she had the sort of under-fleshed mouth that looks strained when it is not. She was wearing a leather driving-jacket over a long brocade skirt.

'A vampire?' he asked stupidly and stood up.

'How are you?'

'Fine. You didn't really hit me: I slipped. But why a vampire?'

'All that flapping with your arms. I suppose you were just getting your coat on, but in the mist . . . wait here a moment.'

She pranced over to her car, manoeuvred it briskly to the kerb, and got back out at once.

'I drive rather well, in fact, but I was startled. You did look like some ghoul.'

'And walking out of the Hotel Propp, too.'

She laughed. 'Had you been having a drink in there? Do say you were just a little tight or anyway dreamy. It would be a comfort.'

'Not tight, but not very alert either.'

'Good! That's over and it could have been worse. But now you will be all sober and cold again, poor man. Look, I was dropping in here for a hot grog on my way home – from the most dismal evening you can imagine. Do come back in and have a drink, to restore you. You are not from St Gallen? I think you are neither Swiss nor German? Let's get out of this mist.'

Briggs was carried along. They went in and through to the Bar Vadianus, towards the table he had left three minutes before. The waiter greeted them rather ironically. The two Englishmen contrived to look both sour and shy. The heavy man with the business papers expressionlessly said: '*Grüss Sie, Frau Leinberger*'. And Heini Hufnagel went on playing.

6

Mechtild Leinberger and Briggs sat and looked at each other. In the dim light of the bar there was not that much to see of her. A blond young woman with a wholesome but frazzled air, like an athlete who has thoroughly broken training. They exchanged names, and their drinks arrived.

'Well,' she said, 'this is nice. I feel we already know each other quite well, after all that, outside. Now, what are you doing in St Gallen? May I ask that?'

'Staying with friends for a few days.'

'Oh? I wonder if I know your friends?'

'Their name is Fleury. Maria and Klaus Fleury. Old friends.'

'Oh, yes! Of course I know Maria. How good to be like her – pretty and clever. She is like one of those dolls in regional dress, isn't she? The same fair hair and clean pink face. Though their eyes are always blue, of course, not that strange hazel of Maria's. But you know those skirts and blouses Maria wears. Her husband seems rather fierce. Are they very old friends?'

'We were students together. Klaus isn't really fierce.'

'Perhaps not,' she said. 'Perhaps we got off on the wrong foot. He made me so nervous, glaring at me through his spectacles while I tried to make serious talk at a party, I spilled a glass of grenadine over him. Maria was so nice about it. It must have been a thing to get that syrupy stuff out of your friend's trousers. He certainly looked fierce then. They were fawn hopsack.'

She laughed and then quite suddenly slipped into gloomy silence.

'You live here in St Gallen?' Briggs asked.

'Much of the time. My husband works on textile machinery here – it's good for that. I also spend time in Germany. I would go mad if I were always in St Gallen.'

'So bad?'

'Even the other Swiss laugh at it. And people here disapprove of me because I behave badly, they think.'

'Surely you imagine that. They are reserved people.'

'Oh no, it is so,' she said. 'I do not stay at home and supervise the servants. I go out, and on my own. I would in Germany, so why not here?' She cheered up. 'And, of course, I drink in bars with men I have just picked up in the street. You don't *look* English, like those two over there. Your clothes are not the same, and your voice is different. No. You look more like a . . . well, like a Dutchman, perhaps. If a Dutchman had bought some of his clothes in Germany and some in London and perhaps some somewhere else, he could look rather like you.'

Her mood seemed to go through a recurrent short cycle. A few minutes of rather tense exuberance would suddenly end in a flash of unfocused exasperation; then there would be a moment of withdrawn glumness and then, it seemed almost by an effort of will, she would leap back into high spirits. Or perhaps it was simply that Briggs was being found inadequate.

'Look,' she said now, 'I hope you won't mind if I say that the one thing, almost the only thing, I notice about your German is that your R's are very bad. You should pronounce them more like this: *Rrrrr*. That's the thing I notice most. Try it now. *Rrrrr*.'

Briggs tried it.

'Oh, no! Your tongue is too loose, your mouth is too slack. Look, I'll put my finger where the tongue should be. So . . .now say, well . . . say "*Dreiruderer*". Please!'

'*Dreiruderer*.'

'No good!' She sat back. 'If I knew anything I'd make a good teacher. Infants, perhaps. Remember: arch the tongue!'

'My accent is perhaps more like a north German's – a Hamburger's, say – or so I have . . .'

'No, please don't let yourself be deceived. No one from Hamburg says *Dreiruderer* like that . . . but my God! Your jacket! It is torn, on the elbow. No! look, the seam has burst. That must have happened when you fell.'

'It doesn't matter.'

'Oh, but it does matter. I will *not* send you back to nice, neat Maria Fleury with a burst seam. We must mend it. But we cannot here: there's neither light nor needle.'

'Really . . .'

'I know what we must do. We must go to my house and mend it there. No, I insist. They will close up here soon anyway. It's the only thing to do, and it won't take long at all. We'll finish these drinks and go.'

So it turned out. Briggs still protested a little, but presently they were getting into her car.

Mechtild Leinberger took one of the roads that slanted up the north side of the valley.In valley towns it is the north slope that gets the winter sun, and there the well-to-do put up their first suburbs. This was a district of large houses in the inflated chalet style of pre-1914 central Europe, built by the embroidery barons of St Gallen and their stewards in the fat days of the town. It was a period piece. The embroidery industry and most of its barons had collapsed in the 1920s, and many of the houses had by now been turned into apartments or private schools or even discreet offices for doctors and the better sort of commercial agency, but it was still uncrowded and quiet. The girl drove fast up to the ridge-road at the top and then a short way along this to a rather smaller house that had the air of a moderately grand Wagnerian shooting-box – not quite Wotan's level, but Siegfried's perhaps.

When they got out the mist was a good deal thinner. They were almost above it up here.

'This way!', the girl said. She had not spoken in the three minutes they had been driving. 'Through here!'

They went through a high Teutonic hall with a broad stairway and a gallery-landing on two sides into a large living-room, already lit.

'Concetta and Carlo will have gone to bed, but I have one or two sewing things in my room. Stay here: I won't be a minute. Kaspar, my husband, is away. Take a drink from over there – I think there's some whisky. I hope so, anyway.'

She went out.

The room contrived to be both lush and bleak. The furniture was semi-antique dealer's stuff, the textile surfaces rich but deadly coloured; the woods polished to too high a gloss. Matters had not been shaped by interest, or by use. Other people's houses can register otherness more clearly than their persons.

Briggs walked over to a heavily carved walnut chest with bottles and glasses on its top and poured himself some soda water.

There were no books. There were some pictures on the walls. A slick nineteenth-century stag hunt in a snowy forest . . . a scene of an old man with a pipe, tending plants on a terrace, the varnish unpleasantly shiny . . . a Renaissance engraving of Penelope, presumably, weaving on a loom: signed HSB, whoever that was . . . but on the wall over the fireplace there was a big, slightly chunky view of a medieval Italian town with tall brick towers. The painter had left much of the detailed underwork showing through, and this seemed to be in some parallel-perspective convention, like a mechanical drawing. Over this he had sloshed about more freely, playing with effects of light and appearance. There was a signature in the bottom right corner: KL'44.

Briggs moved back to a large, hard chesterfield and sat and looked at the picture. Mechtild Leinberger was not finding her needle and thread very quickly. He sipped soda water.

'Now give me your jacket!', she said, coming in with some gear in a box. She walked with a tensed lope, like a high-jumper starting an approach. 'And could you pour me some cognac? It may steady my hand.'

She had changed out of her long evening skirt into a shorter tan cotton skirt and plain black blouse. Her feet were now in low-heeled mocasins and she had tied her hair back into a bunch behind. She looked business-like.

Briggs gave her his coat and got her drink. He took it over to the chesterfield, where she had settled, and sat beside her, holding the glass. She ripped lining in the sleeve.

'I was wondering if that painting over the fireplace was Pavia in Lombardy,' he said. 'Those towers look familiar.'

She frowned.

'Yes, Pavia. The house-spook.'

'I am sorry?'

'Nothing. A family joke. The picture is Kaspar's: he used to paint. This is quite good tweed.'

They were silent. Sewing was clearly not something she did with ease. She should have stuck her tongue out as she worked, but instead she shoved it into one cheek. The bulge of it moved as she concentrated on the sleeve. She looked up and caught Briggs's eye, grinned and made a sipping noise. He leaned over and held the glass for her. Then she went back to work.

Briggs watched her mend his coat. There was a nervous jerkiness, almost awkwardness, in many of her movements. The mouth was a little clown-like and there was a sort of instability about the light blue eyes, a hint of future haggardness somewhere under the fine fair skin over the high bony forehead. Briggs was enchanted.

'That should hold it.' She was finishing off. 'Better get it done by a proper person some time. But now Maria won't be shocked. There!'

She tossed the coat over the end of the chesterfield – her end, not Briggs's.

'I shall now have my cognac. I have earned it, don't you think?'

'Yes, indeed. Thank you very much.' Briggs passed her glass.

She laughed and leaned back with her arms along the back of the chesterfield, the brandy glass in her right hand, and looked at Briggs sideways.

'Not really Dutch, in full light,' she said.

'Not very German, for that matter. More Danish, I think. Yes, Danish.'

Badinage was a labour. Quite suddenly she stood up and went over to the window, drawing a curtain partly back to look out, and then using both hands to shade her eyes from the light in the room.

'Let's go out and look at the night: it's clear now and the moon is up. What do you think? I know a place not twenty minutes from here – you would not believe what it is like with a good moon. It's not twelve yet.'

Briggs walked across to the window too. It was mysteriously white outside.

'Yes,' he said, 'I would like to see that. I'd better warn Klaus I'll be late.'

'The phone's over there. But they'll be in bed.'

'Not Klaus.'

'Coats! And bring the cognac.'

7

They drove down and through the still murky town and then up out on the other side of the valley. Mechtild Leinberger did not talk. Doing something, she was a rather different person. She drove fast but well, as she had claimed, rather as if she could use driving a car as a means to organize herself toward an identifiable end.

The road went down into another valley and then southwards along it, but after ten miles or so they turned off left and up a stony track. It passed a large farm-house, quite dark, and presently a smaller one with one dimly lit window. They drove some way on up, more slowly as the track became rougher, through pasture, and at one stage there was a sense of trees off to the right below, but only as a dark impression and a resinous smell. Real vision was confined within the tunnel of light thrown ahead by the car.

By a small building, some sort of barn, the girl turned sharply off the track on to grass, braked, and turned off first the lights and then the engine.

'There!', she said.

Briggs sat for a moment, his eyes coming to terms with the dark, and then got out of the car to see what he had been brought to.

They were on a small grassy platform overlooking a broad valley. The valley wound away in the form of an elongated S towards a rough hill rather higher than their own stance. It was lit with the false white clarity of the three-quarter moon behind them. The hill was quite sharp and clear, but the valley was hazy. In the bottom one could make out the firm black splotches of woods and the white patches of ground mist. There were also a few lights. One of the lights was moving – a car. But it was oddly dim and slow.

Briggs's mind twitched and he realised he had quite mistaken the scale: the hill at the end of the valley was not just a couple of miles off, as he had thought, but more like twenty. Then it was more than just a hill: it must be the Säntis, the big mountain of north-east Switzerland. That meant the lights in the valley were not a few scattered farms but a number of villages and townlets. This was the great upland valley leading to Appenzell. He had never seen it from above. He had certainly never seen it as magical territory of this kind.

He turned to the girl. She was on the other side of the car, leaning against the front wing with her hands in the pockets of her coat.

'It's stunning,' he said.

'Appenzellerland,' she said abruptly. 'And for God's sake don't make jokes.'

It was not clear what was up with her, but something was. The Appenzellers – their dialect, their manners, their goats and cheeses, nunneries and unlicensed dentists – were a regular butt of Swiss jokes, but it was hard to see why she should be sensitive about it. He must not trample on her mood.

'I can see why you value this place,' he said.

'Can you? I am cold. I shall get back in the car.'

She did so. Briggs stayed out, puzzled and awkward. He looked out into the bleached valley, feeling an intruder. Perhaps the girl was used to coming here on her own; or perhaps with someone else. Or perhaps she was just irritated at his not having made a pass – if only, perhaps, to rebuff: it seemed to have been awaited for some time. He couldn't help that. Apart from anything else, he had an old problem: liking inhibited lust. He was now feeling in a false position. He liked her very much indeed.

He would give her a few minutes privacy.

The view held him – the great curved milky trough with its black and white and small scintillating accents, and the long jagged edge of the Säntis at the far end. And of course one knew the valley down there was full of folk sound asleep after a busy day of virtuoso cheese-making or intuitive tooth-drawing. But not quite all asleep: the light of that car was still slowly moving, miles off, as if making for the foot of the Säntis itself. Perhaps a vet. Perhaps an emergency call to a goat . . .

After a few minutes Briggs opened the car door and got in. Mechtild was slouched in her seat with the brandy bottle held on her lap. She took a nip and passed it to Briggs. He accepted this invitation to silence and took a nip himself.

There was an occasional click from the engine cooling behind them, and he could hear her breathing. He was very aware of her fine skin beside him, warm and enclosed in its leather coat. Even he could cope with making a pass in a parked car, but this was not a decent moment. He took another nip and passed the bottle. She took it back in her lap and did not drink. Indeed, she closed the bottle.

But something was happening with her. She had become stiff beside him, as if nervous, and her breathing had changed – not quicker, but sharper. Then, speaking rather more slowly than usual, but in a quite normal voice, she said:

'The moon shone bright and our friend the yarn-carrier insisted on making a further stage of our pilgrimage, since he must keep to his day and his hour, and arrive in each place at the right time. The footpaths would be good and clear, particularly by the light of such a flamboy as that moon. The journey through the night was full of grace and joy, and at last we came towards a gathering of huts which one might almost have called a village . . . we had come to a hamlet where, as well as spinning, people keenly practised weaving.'

She paused. Briggs willed himself not to hold his breath. He could feel her turning for an instant to look at him. Then after a while she went on in the same straightforward conversational tone:

'The first task, sizing the spun yarn, they had acquitted the day before. This morning the sized yarn was nearly dry and they were preparing to reel it: that is to say, to wind the yarn from the spinning wheel on to cylindrical spools. An old grandfather, sitting by the stove, saw to this light work; by him stood a small grandson, eager to operate that spooling-wheel himself. Meanwhile the father put the spools for the warp on a frame, set up with coarse and fine yarns in the order that the fabric's pattern, or more precisely stripe, demanded. The *Brittli*, an instrument shaped something like a *sistrum*, with holes on both sides for the weft threads, is held in the right hand of the weaver; with his left hand he gathers the threads together and lays them on the warp-frame, to and fro. Once from the top to the bottom of the warp-frame and then again from the bottom to the top is called a "go". The length amounts to either sixty-four or just thirty-two ells.'

She stopped again. After the silence had lasted some time, Briggs took a risk.

'Go on, please,' he said.

The stiffness was leaving her. She turned a little in her seat, now more towards him, and went on:

'Next day we set off early. With daybreak the rising sun now showed us a country more lived in and more tended. Up there, to cross streams we had met with stepping-stones, or sometimes a narrow plank bridge with a rail on one side; down here stone bridges spanned the ever-widening torrents. More and more, grace willed to couple with the wild, and we travellers felt the charming sense of it. And then, over the mountain, from another region, a lean black-locked man came striding . . .'

At this point she broke off.

'That's enough, I think,' she said. 'You didn't laugh.'

'But it was marvellous stuff. What is it?'

'Appenzell.'

'But who is it?'

'Goethe. Who else? Wilhelm Meister: the Wander-years. You should know that.'

She sighed and then yawned, and when they embraced it seemed less out of amorous purpose than a matter of animals seeking warmth. There was a dull thump as the brandy bottle slipped to the floor. Neither spoke for some time. But discomfort becomes a pander.

'Damn all gear-levers.'

'There are rugs behind and there will be hay in the barn.'

'Oh. There always is?'

'Don't be unpleasant. Hay is what barns are for.'

8

On the ridge road above St Gallen, the twilight before sunrise was as strange and destructive of hue as any moonlight – flattening, though, not ennobling. There was thick morning mist in the valleys, but the upper air was clear and the sky was without visible cloud. Looking at the Säntis now it would have been hard to be sure whether the suggestion of a cinnamon colour to it was actual, or known and assumed.

Briggs walked along the ridge. The roads from here into St Gallen all went down the valley side at a narrow angle, to ease the gradient. He did not take one of these. He was keeping to the ridge road until he was on a line with Maria and Klaus's, to take one of the long flights of steps that led straight down, every quarter-mile or so, into the town.

Off and on, he hummed the yearning motif used by Liszt to stand for the eternal feminine. *Das e-e-e-wig WEIB-liche* . . . Goethe again. The trouble with Liszt's phrase was that, having hummed it once, all one could do with it is hum it again a fifth higher. And then a fifth higher again . . . and again till the voice breaks. Nothing else could be done with it at all, not even by Liszt. The fragment of feeling will not develop. Romanticism has its problems.

Briggs came to the flight of steps he wanted and started down. The sun was now coming up with baroque fanfares somewhere over Austria and he paused for a moment. The Säntis was cinnamon to the eye, definitely. He went on down again. They were rough steps, old gravel revetted with planks held by big metal spikes, and there were several hundred of them. Quick descent took concentration.

Arrival in the mist down below was depressing. But from the foot of the steps it was only three minutes' walk, through grey streets and past a few self-absorbed people early to work. It was as if the town was dead.

He climbed the stairs to the penthouse slowly, paused for a moment outside the door, then knocked lightly and let himself in. Klaus was at a table in the window eating breakfast and reading a newspaper. Maria had been in the kitchen, but came out with a cup for Briggs.

'Hello, Willi. You will want coffee.' She was smiling but reserved.

'I hope you didn't think I had been knocked down or something,' Briggs said lamely. 'I got caught up in the whirl of your city.'

'You must tell us, but tonight: I have to go in a minute.'

Briggs sat down. Opposite him Klaus was watchful and amused. He put aside his newspaper and poured coffee into Briggs's cup. The smell of it was a thoughtful song well sung by an alto.

'I hadn't realised running-dogs ran quite so hard,' Klaus said.

'One thing somehow led on to another.'

'So it goes.' Klaus reached for another roll, cut it, and started meticulously buttering it.

'So what goes?' called Maria from the bedroom.

'Life and work,' said Klaus.

'Oh, those.' She appeared, dressed for outside. 'By the way, Willi, this evening there is a *vernissage* at Sybille Röösli's art gallery – some painter from Paris. Don't grimace, Klaus: nobody is suggesting you go. It will probably be terrible rubbish, at Sybille's it usually is, but if Willi wants to see Mechtild Leinberger, she's quite often there at Sybille's private views. Here's the card.

Let's eat at the Walliserkeller tonight at eight, say. If we happen to meet at the gallery we can go on together. Now I must go. Don't let Klaus keep you too long talking.'

Maria left, Briggs standing rather formally till she had gone. When Klaus had swallowed the last of his roll he got out his pipe and tobacco. Briggs drank coffee and looked out over the town, at the roofs and the emerging abbey and the changing light. The mist was beginning to glow above faintly, a sort of prologue to the great incandescence that would come when the sun began to work on the valley. It was good to be sitting quietly here.

'And now I must say a word about the basis of stable relationships of affection,' said Klaus, puffing.

'No, really, Klaus, there is no need for that at all.'

'Oh, but there is.' Klaus refilled both their cups. 'I recognise your look. I suspect infatuation. Again.'

'Nonsense.'

'I have been arranging my thoughts. I believe it will help us to think of the individual's range of feeling as something plotted along a curve that represents a changing balance of satisfaction between two goods. You may want to think of the curve as rather like the indifference curve in market analysis – but of course with no equivalent of a price-ratio line. The one good is, let us say, Excitement or Stimulation: we shall call this "E". The other is Repose or Tranquillity: "R". Our curve represents a boundary between them. And, if these are plotted on a graph, we will have the different proportions in which we can comfortably balance one against another at different times. One could see the goods as polarized, almost plus and minus, though that would take one dangerously close to Romantic metaphysics. You follow?'

Briggs gazed out of the window.

'Now,' Klaus went on, 'it goes without saying that we need both these goods. Without E, Excitement, we would fall into an entropy, and anyway it is enjoyable. Without R, Repose, we would go mad and get no work done besides. But mood and vitality vary from time to time, whether for intrinsic or extrinsic reasons, so that we move up and down our curves, varying the proportions best tolerable to us. It is rather like trying to plot on an indifference curve an individual with an irregular income. You see?'

'You are a Swiss monster, Klaus. It is good that I know your strange sense of tact.'

'Next, two very obvious points. The sort of vitality involved in relations of affection is partly a specialised vitality, you agree? Not just absolute vitality. And different people's curves come out differently placed on the graph. So, let us suppose my E/R range in these matters is sluggish – running from $2E/1R$ at enhanced moments to $1E/3R$ at low points. Let us just suppose those are the normal limits of my range. Well, then your curve might run from $3E/1R$ to $1E/2R$ – sharper, but moderate enough. On the same scale a thoroughly wild sort of woman might come out at $9E/1R$ to $1E/1R$.'

'I think you never did like Inka.'

'We are not talking about liking. "Liking" may be a factor within E as well as an expression of it, obviously, but it is *not* covered by this plot. What I am moving towards is a concept of constitutional compatibility of E/R curves.'

'I had realised that.'

'Yes, but let's follow it through. For two people to sustain a relation their curves need roughly, only roughly, to match: otherwise the strain will be too great. But – this is the problem – how does one know that at any one moment two people, oneself and another, are at the same relative end of their curves? In the first week, or month? No! One needs time and many observations. I can say it, since you brought the matter up: you and poor Inka – whom I *liked* very much, by the way – were swinging on wildly incongruous curves.'

He sketched with a finger two curves rather like a pair of slightly intersecting arched eyebrows.

'Now and then you met around . . . *3E/1R*, was it? Yes, around *3E/1R*. You were both thereabouts in the early days, you on a high and she at a low. Then she kept swinging off up towards *9E/1R*, and you off down towards *1E/2R* – or wanting to.'

'It did not just happen that I was up at *3E/1R* with Inka,' Briggs said. 'She took me up there. That's only one element your scheme leaves out: what uplifts. Also, I consider I usefully calmed her for a time. People do act on each other, you know.'

'Oh, I agree. Of course. A proper model would have the reciprocal effects built in. Lots of other things too. But I would still insist there are limits to the tolerance of extreme incongruity. Anyway, I have been making towards a limited point.'

'Very limited.'

'You will allow me, old friend, to say that you are immediately attracted by women on a much steeper *E/R* curve than yourself. For a time they stimulate you, and you depress them, but then later . . .'

'My God, Klaus, do you really think about people in this sort of way?'

'*E/R* curves and such?'

'Yes. It's bizarre.'

'No. I was just looking for a colourful analogy – my teaching instinct. And I am struck by the look on your face. I know it: like someone just off a *piste* several degrees too fast for them. But you are right to imply that I am not a tender of souls. Even so, do think about it . . . I must go.'

'Okay,' Briggs said, 'I'll keep my *E/R* quotient in mind. Klaus, do you happen to have *Wilhelm Meister's Wander-years* here?'

'I have indeed . . . a school prize, look: "For application and seriousness in Class S2a". But what has the Wise Man of Weimar got for you?'

'I have never read the description of the cottage weavers in Appenzell.'

'Those are the bits called "Lenardo's Diary". Here . . . it begins here. Every Swiss child reads it at school. Goethe worked it up from good technical notes made by a Swiss friend. Rather modern for you, but pretty enough. *Servus!*'

When Klaus had gone, Briggs sat in the window as the sun prepared to take a grip on the town and read through 'Lenardo's Diary': it was not long, but dense. Then he went to the kitchen and washed up the breakfast things, and then he went and lay down for a time.

9

The early mills of St Gallen had been built in small side-valleys above the town. The larger river below had been too violent, too quick in rising and too hard to regulate. It was the lesser, local streams that could be adapted to the water-wheels, often with fair-sized pounds some way above to even out the flow. When steam-power came, new works were built in the valley bottom too, but many of the smaller older mills of the side-valleys had remained, enlarged and converted to steam themselves, but still tight by their streams. Water was still needed, after all. Then there had been a sort of mediated return to the old prime mover: electricity made by the water of great torrents far away drove the mills nowadays. Yet some kept working in the semi-rural seclusion of their side-valleys. A well-made mill building lasts: land values had gone up in the main valley: trade was not booming. There was no reason to move.

The Ravensburgers' mill was one of these survivors, tucked away on its own at the top of a picturesque ravine a couple of miles from the Old Town. Briggs had approached it not by its own road in the ravine bottom but by a footpath along the ravine edge above.

It was a real ravine, steep-sided and wooded. The mill was splendidly set in a bowl at its head, just below the meeting of two watercourses which came together to form the larger stream that had once driven its wheel.

There were three buildings, set close to each other in an arc. The tips of the arc came near the stream, and the whole enclosed a metalled yard alongside the water.

Much the largest of the three was a long buff-rendered building on the right, at an angle to the stream. It had four storeys of white framed windows, rows of twenty or so along and four at the end. The roof was pitched and hipped, red-tiled, with large sky-lights set flush and louvred vents. At the visible end of this roof was a very wide but low dormer window, where a couple of men were at what looked like drawing-boards. Half-way along the crest was a neat onion-topped turret with louvres and round false-windows. It must have had some ventilating function, but its general effect was of a baroque clock-tower. In fact, the whole building had a neat and un-satanic air and was more like an abbey-school, say, than a factory. But it was clicking and humming and whining in a complex rhythm that rose above the sound of running water.

Next to this mill-building was a smaller and older-looking version of itself, rendered a fresh grey. Perhaps this had been an earlier mill, but now part of it was certainly offices and the rest looked like stores. Two cars stood before its door, and there was a neat aerial catwalk connecting it with the bigger building, spanning a gap of five yards or so at the level of the second storey. Every few minutes someone or other briskly crossed this bridge.

The third building was between this and the stream again, on the left end of the arc, an old engine-house of undressed stone with the stump of an inactive chimney. It looked as if it had a complicated history. Once, part of it would have held the water-wheel shaft and a few looms; later it would have been used for the steam-engine, fuel and stokers, but there was no sign of driving shaft now. It seemed to be used for something like artificers' workshops. Men with the look of fitters occasionally passed in or out, carrying bits and pieces.

Briggs sat on a fallen branch and looked down through larches at this compact and well-tended outfit. After a time the noise from the mill became simpler and softer, admitting more of the roar of the stream. He looked at his watch – just gone four. The sun had gone from the ravine and an evening mist was already beginning to mobilise itself. Work-people began to come out in twos and threes and move off down the road to town, walking or on bicycles: the descendants of the Appenzellers in "Lenardo's Diary".

A black car, a bulbous BMW, came up the road and drove in and around to the old engine-house. A car door slammed. Kaspar Leinberger back from his travels? Briggs could see nothing of him. Floor by floor lights were dimming in the big mill, and one or two had gone out in the office block, but some people here evidently worked later. A couple of the artificer-fitters were staying too, it seemed: they had come out of the engine-house and were looking at the BMW and talking. They had the air of people waiting for someone to come.

To get nearer Briggs only had to work his way down the side of the ravine, where there was plenty of cover. The only fence anywhere was on the lower side of the complex, where the road started down to the town, and even this was just a token wooden boundary, not a barrier.

He started down the slope, moving from tree to tree. It was steep but, with trees to hang on to, quite easy work. He took no special pains to be silent. The noise of the stream and some re-sidual sounds from the mill were a mask. In a couple of minutes he was at the bottom. The trees ended here and he stopped.

With the loss of height, in fact, he now saw much less than be-fore. The three buildings – engine-house, office-cum-store, mill – curved away, shielding from him the open paved area with the cars. He was now simply shut out. In particular, the grey office-building blocked him off from the car and the men. It was a mat-ter of angles-of-view. If he moved along a bit, he ought to see between the offices and the engine-house.

He moved along, keeping to the edge of the trees, until the gap between the two buildings opened out. It revealed nothing

interesting at all, just the opening, with nothing whatever showing up at the other side of it.

It was simply a gentle slope of mown grass between here
and the gap. No one happening to look out of a lighted window
would see a figure outside in the dusk . . . he trotted across.

But being in the gap turned out a disappointment too. It was
secure enough, blind walls on both sides with a sort of buttress or
minor chimney sticking out from the engine-house – for bolting
behind if necessary. The grey building opposite was some sort
of loading-platform on this face, with a big blank wooden door
on runners. But there was little to look at. The back of the BMW
was to be seen round the corner of the engine-house, leftwards,
but the fitters had gone.

Briggs decided it was time to leave. He had demonstrated
enough enterprise to prevent self-reproach for feebleness. And
he was becoming unsure of his motives. The sortie had gone
sour. He would go.

But not yet . . .

'Fritz! Bernhard! I'm ready now . . .'

The BMW man had evidently come from the offices on the
right and must be walking to his car. The engine started and the
car reversed neatly round into the gap. Behind the buttress, to
which he had retreated, Briggs was trapped. The car's engine
was switched off again. A second man, presumably one of the
fitters, arrived and there was the noise of the boot being opened.

'All right?'

'Yes, on the whole – though Cesare had absurd trouble with
that elliptical profile you wanted. These are the heddle-horses.
They seem to me a bit rough.'

'What about the cowl?'

'Here. Cesare said you could have bought a better one ready-
made in Zurich.'

'We don't want to go round Zurich asking for specialized gear
and leaving traces.'

'For heaven's sake! So you have a rougher one hand-wrought in Pavia? By the way, Cesare can't make those bobbins. He really can't handle manganese at all, you know. We'll have to make do with the old ones for the moment. In any case, I've been wondering whether it isn't the surface texture that's critical. We can try applying different finishes.'

'The stuff from Göschenen?'

'All here. This box. For God's sake don't drop it. I didn't like your friend at all. The electrodes are on top.'

'He's a surly devil, but he holds his tongue.'

'Where are you going to keep that stuff?'

'Locked up in the fine-metal store. You're not taking this seriously. We are: it *is* serious.'

'If you say so. I will think of it as a serious joke. Now, about the heddle-horses. Set them up tomorrow morning and I'll look in later. They are rough but we'll give them a short run . . . here's Bernhard.'

A third man was arriving. Briggs leaned out a little from his buttress to snatch a look while they were attending in the other direction, fractionally lost balance, came down heavily and – it seemed to him – noisily on his front foot, lost his nerve, and ran.

10

He ran the way he had come, up the grassy slope towards the trees. He heard a shout behind him – something about getting hold of that *Lauscher* quick – but by panicking so promptly he seemed to have caught them on the hop. As he got to the trees and glanced back, he could make out two figures just starting from the gap.

Knowing how he had let himself down into the ravine, from one tree to the next, he set himself to reverse the process – hauling himself up with great swinging pulls of his arms like an ape, pulling himself from larch to larch with a rhythmic swimming-like momentum that, even at the moment, gave him satisfaction. Not bad at all. By the time he had reached the top the two figures below were only starting up into the trees. To judge from the scrabbling of boots on the rock, they had not grasped the ape principle. He ran through to the path.

He would throw them off now. He was far enough ahead to take either direction along the path without them knowing which. They would expect him to go back the way he had come: he would go the other way, away from the town, right. He started running quietly along the path, then stopped. They did not *know* which way he had come. Anyway, they were two and could split. He turned and ran back again. It was the path to the town he knew, and it was the town he wanted to get to. Their scrabbling was near the top of the ravine now. He had lost much of his lead.

He ran fast along the path down the ridge, but it was hard to know how fast it was safe to run. A trip over a tree root or pothole could be a disaster. Behind him he could hear pursuit. It was both of them: he could hear words exchanged. After all, they had decided the path to the town was the one, as he should have known they would. Their feet pounded behind, whether gaining or not he was not sure. They sounded heavy men and Briggs felt fragile.

There was the noise of at least one of them falling and cursing. In fact, he did have a couple of advantages. He had been over this path an hour or so ago and still had a strong sense of its line and run. And he had been out in the dark longer and would be seeing better. Also, they sounded too heavily shod for this game, in work boots perhaps. The noise they were making, they could hardly hear him much. His light shoes let him run more lightly and sensitively. Briggs as gazelle.

But he was getting a stitch. He seemed to be gaining a little but could not keep up this pace for very long. It would be clever to disappear into a tree now, but the trees were not right. Conifers don't have the sort of big low boughs people swing on to in films and let pursuers pass beneath. He ran on.

A problem soon: in a minute the path would come out into the open at the end of the ridge, a long grassy hill side that in winter was a nursery ski slope. Once on it, the men would have a clear view of him right into town. He must get off the path, very soon . . . he tripped, not on a root or pothole, but a small fallen branch, which yielded a bit. Not too bad, except a bashed knee.

As he got up he saw a possible line off the path, to the right, and took it without pausing to ponder, and it started him down the other side of the ridge – not as steep or rocky as the ravine and not nearly as clean of undergrowth. He was now making more noise and – hell! – they had heard it from the path and were coming after. He put on speed, careless of noise. They were crashing after him through scrub now, with panzer-like weight. But the change in physical action had eased his stitch. Probably he was holding his own.

61

And then before he knew it he had run up against a low bar-fence. He swung over. He was in a lane, straight and semi-visible even now in both directions, so not for him. He ran to the fence on its other side, taller and paled, and swung over that too. Then it was difficult to know where he was.

He could make out a number of tiny houses in a row, none more than two metres high and varied, but all with pitched roofs and real little windows and porches and so on. He was in toy-town. He ran along the fairy street but the surface was uneven and soft like a cabbage-field or something . . . he realised he was in among allotments. The tiny houses were the whimsical Swiss versions of garden-sheds or summer-houses flat-dwellers bring their families to on fine weekends, picnicking and sunning them-selves on porches.

The men were arriving in the lane and barking to each other about which way. He would pick a doll's house and hide.

The first three he tried were firmly locked. The men had now opted for toy-town too and were starting to climb over. The fourth shed opened and he stooped and went in. But the door had no bolt: a key-hole but no key. He should prop it to with a fork or something but the shed was empty: that was why it was unlocked. It was no good just leaning against it. You can tell by the bouncy give when someone is holding a door against you. It must have the firmness of a lock. He lay down on his back and jammed his feet up against the cross-plank half way down the door. Then he reinforced his straight-locked legs by holding them and pushing.

He waited. It occurred to him that, if the men did push in, his attitude would be vulnerable and – almost worse really – igno-minious, but he was committed.

They were approaching and muttering and trying doors. One of them stepped heavily on the planks of the porch outside and stood there breathing noisily. Briggs braced himself and hoped he was not breathing like that. The shove did not come but the breathing went on. Briggs began to feel an impulse to shout 'Here!', as in a dream, but there was surely no way the man could know this door was the one. They could not be tracing footprints in the dark.

'This is no good,' the man said suddenly. It was the one called Fritz. The *Unteroffizier* rasp was unmistakeable.

'I'm not clear what we'd have done with him if we'd caught him,' the second man said, coming up from somewhere further away. It was a lighter, quieter voice Briggs had not heard before, and with an accent he could not place. Bernhard, presumably. 'Put your knife away, for God's sake. We can't hand out passports in St Gallen.'

'We needed to find out who it was, and we'd have frightened and thumped him quiet.'

'It takes more than a blue eye to keep a man quiet. I'm also not clear how much he heard from you two.'

'That depends on what he already knew. That's it – we needed to find out who it was.'

'Well, we've lost him. He's down into town by now. Let's get back.' The Bernhard voice was moving away.

Briggs was almost caught off guard as Fritz swore and gave an exasperated parting kick to the door, but it held. Fritz walked noisily away.

It was a minute or two before Briggs fully disassembled himself and got up. He opened the door a crack and looked out. No sign of Fritz and Bernhard. But he would give them a few minutes before himself leaving, just in case they were hanging around still. He peered at faint green dots and lines on his watch: not yet six. He leaned against a wall, rubbing a sore spine and a bruised knee. He felt cold and stiff and would have liked a drink. A thought came to him and he giggled quietly: he would be in perfect time for Sybille Röösli's *vernissage*.

11

'So candid and unafraid. And of course authentically constructive. Dégousse is from Paris, you know. He is the *other* Dégousse's
nephew.'

Sybille Röösli was tall and had entered on middle life. She
wore with great dignity an unwearable dress, involving among
other things much eau-de-nil net.

'Just look at this passage – the tension between the values and
the contours! Ravishing! I am so glad dear Maria persuaded you
to come: she needs cultivated companionship. And now I shall
leave you to enjoy the pictures. I gave my word I would show
people our new Picasso ceramic. You will love it: the vitality of
that little man!'

Maria was looking at Briggs and trying not to laugh. Briggs
tended to respect what he could not see the point of, but this
stuff here was transparent. Dégousse was a formula painter with
a marketable trick. The pictures were basically bland tourist
views of Paris, the kind of pastiche Utrillo you saw for sale on
the quays. But Dégousse superimposed a tasteful grid of blackish
lines which gave a chic and spurious air of analysis.

They looked round. There were thirty or so people comfortably populating the small gallery and tucking into this and that.
Maria caught Briggs's eye.

'You look a mess, Willi. What have you been rolling in?'

'I tripped.'

'Well, now is your chance to meet Hanspeter Hefti – he is old
Anton Röösli's nephew, you see. He is over there with Klaus's

colleague Lorenz. Lorenz is a sort of physicist, a viscosity man. I suppose he is here for the fun. Come!'

Standing together, Lorenz and Hefti made a sharply contrasting pair, like an old school-book illustration of two of the races of Europe. Hanspeter was a big blond teddy-bear in a loose tweed suit. His head was round and alpine, his hair cut *en brosse*, and he had a heavy moustache. He was smoking a cankered thin cigar with a straw in the middle. Lorenz, who turned out to be French-Swiss, looked more like a pre-war Hollywood Hungarian – a thin, pale man with noticeable cheek-bones and black hair swept straight back. He wore a double-breasted dark-blue suit and stood straight, feet together and hands clasped round an empty glass. His black eyes were super-alert and hyper-ironic, whereas Hanspeter's were pale blue and unfocussed, as if his mind was still on distant looms.

'I hope you are enjoying the art,' said Lorenz. 'I refer you to *Nocturne: Les Halles*. The painter himself has just told me he feels it best registers his perception of – as he put it – "how things are".'

'He's here?'

'That simpering little fellow with Ida Frischknecht over there,' shouted Hanspeter in a thick booming voice, and pointed. 'Sybille does pick duds, doesn't she? Poor Anton. He is long past controlling her, I am afraid.'

'Chut, Hanspeter!' Lorenz said encouragingly. 'It may be that your uncle withdraws more and more from the dimension we others must . . . but, no, I am wrong! Here indeed he comes. Even at his level of abstraction, art has a contribution to make. We must suppose.'

A malign-looking old man was tottering in on two sticks, flanked by the two acolyte ladies Sybille Röösli maintained to do the running of her gallery. Sybille, who was now holding a colourful spotted pot in the shape of a bird, supervised them while he was deposited in a chair – a reproduction Renaissance affair with padded arms and big acorn-knobs at the top. Once he was stowed away, she resumed her progress with the ceramic, held like a chalice before her.

Hanspeter Hefti was staring at Briggs – not at his face but, it seemed, at his heart. Suddenly he put out his hand and grabbed the lapel of Briggs's jacket. He rubbed it between fingers and thumb. Lorenz was watching and hugging himself with pleasure.

'Too much soda in the scouring, you know,' said Hanspeter. 'Brittle, and over-brushed.'

He lost interest and let go. Briggs was irritated.

'I should like to ask you something,' he said abruptly to Hanspeter. 'Why would a heddle-horse need an elliptical profile?'

'An elliptical heddle-horse? Is that some joke?'

'No. It is something I heard referred to recently and did not understand.'

'It's rubbish! Elliptical pirns – yes! An elliptical profile for bobbins too would make sense, within clear limits. Hugi & Nef of Gossau were trying to market a semi-elliptical tenterhook at one time, though it was not a success. But an elliptical heddle-horse . . . *Danke vielmals*, Sybille' – the preoccupied Hanspeter tapped ash from his diseased cigar into the Picasso ceramic being held out for admiration – '*Danke*! An elliptical profile on a heddle-horse is nonsense.'

There were muttered exclamations of discreet outrage – '*Mein Gott!*', '*Incroyable!*' and the like – from Sybille's entourage, but Sybille herself seemed frozen for the moment. Lorenz was now hugging himself so tight that his empty wine-glass perched on his left shoulder like a pet bird. Hanspeter observed none of this.

'All a heddle-horse does is to carry heddle-sticks,' he chided Briggs. 'It is the heddle-sticks that sustain the doups.'

He became aware that Sybille had not left. '*Danke!*', he said to her again, nodding dismissal.

Briggs decided it was time to disengage. He mumbled that he must have been mistaken, pretended to see a particularly striking picture on a distant wall, and fled to it. Not a polished performance.

'You and woolly bear seem the life and soul of this party', said a young woman in a severe tweed suit standing nearby.

'Mechtild! I hadn't seen you.'

'I've only just got here. What was it all about?'

'I said the wrong thing and then Hanspeter Hefti did the wrong thing – in an intellectual passion, no doubt.'

Lorenz was arriving and Maria was on the way. Hefti was still booming in the middle of the room.

'Good evening, Lorenz.'

'Good evening, Mechtild. You look as beautiful as ever, and more than usually happy. Do I intrude?'

'You don't, Lorenz. But I shall go and get myself something to drink.'

'Oh! allow me . . .', said Lorenz and Briggs together.

'No, no. I must greet Sybille too. Hello, Maria.'

She loped off. Lorenz took Briggs by the arm. 'Tell me . . . '

There was an uncouth noise behind them. Anton Röösli in his cardinal's chair was mouthing away and pointing peremptorily with one of his sticks.

'Mister Universum wants something, it seems,' said Lorenz with a flash of impatience. 'Ah, yes!'

He trotted over to a table, picked up a platter, and took it deferentially over to the wreck in the chair. Anton Röösli put it on his knees and started pushing goodies into his mouth with the palm of his hand.

'Not quite immaterial yet, one is happy to see,' said Lorenz when he had got back. They watched for a moment.

'Can that be good for him?', Maria asked.

'He will thrive on it. Just avert your eyes. It is unpleasant, but there is a sort of elemental strength – we must both have come to know – about St Gallen folk.' Lorenz turned back to Briggs. 'Now, may I ask . . .'

But there was another disturbance from the cardinal's chair. Anton Röösli was already having some sort of choking seizure and beating on the padded arms with his fists. Sybille arrived, tight-lipped, and extracted a pill box from his waistcoat pocket. She put a pill in the old man's mouth and flushed it down with water from a glass provided by one of the handmaidens.

'Vitus! and perhaps Herr Bösiger? Be so good as to carry Anton – in the chair, please – into my office! No one need worry. In twenty minutes he will be quite himself.'

Two short but stocky and well-matched men came forward and began to carry the chair and its contents across the gallery to a door, staggering and weaving and barking their shins as they went. Hanspeter Hefti, who had taken possession of his uncle's sticks, shambled after with a stick in each hand, giving the men little guiding taps – now Vitus with the left stick, now Herr Bösiger with the right – like a shepherd directing sheep into a pen. Once Anton Röösli had been got into the office he was left, the door part open, and the company became newly animated. The two chair-bearers in particular enjoyed their aura: they eased their arms and shoulders in a stylized manner and leaned forward to sip intently at fresh glasses of Sybille's Chateau Couthey, with exclamations of craving satisfied.

Briggs had escaped from Lorenz in the excitement and was talking with Mechtild. Maria walked over to them and quite uncharacteristically put her arm round Briggs.

'Mechthild! I'm glad you've met Willi.'

'Yes, we bumped into each other last night.'

'Ah! Nice!'

'Yes. But, Maria, you should use your clever needle – I do love that dirndl: Willi! Isn't Maria's dirndl clever? On his trousers. I am surprised you let him out so.'

'He *has* become a bit ragged since last night. Who can have torn his trousers?'

'I tripped,' said Briggs, glumly. He realised that he was not an object of flattering contention but just a wall, as in squash or fives, off which these two were bouncing their ball in a more or less established private game.

'Trousers . . . Oh! My Good Lord!'

Briggs and Maria looked round. Hanspeter Hefti was proceeding very slowly across the room in the direction of the entrance. He still had Anton Röösli's sticks and was bent like an old man, supporting himself with them as he went and shuffling his feet in short steps. He might have seemed to be offering a satirical version of his uncle's entry twenty minutes before, but was quite self-absorbed, so that the responses of the audience – '*Ungläublich*!', '*Pas possible*!' and such – were not reaching him.

'Now what has Hanspeter in mind?' Lorenz had joined them again. 'Perhaps a narrative tableau of the kind dear to Goethe? If so, of whom? Or can this be a mimed art criticism – an acting-out, as it were, of the mood brought on by exposure to the sensibility of Dégousse? One would like to know.'

'Do be quiet, Lorenz,' Maria said.

Hanspeter stood upright and turned, brandishing the sticks.

'Sybille,' he boomed to his kinswoman, 'I insist the sticks are too short. No wonder Anton slouches about . . .'

Sybille, who had meanwhile swept across, wrested the sticks from him and said something sharp and quiet. Hanspeter lumbered sulkily off to the office to check on his uncle.

'It was empathy,' whispered Lorenz. 'Moving!'

'What an extraordinary display!', said someone behind them in French. 'Will you allow me to introduce myself? I have been anxious to do so for some time. I am the painter, Dégousse.'

He crinkled his eyes and cocked his head, first at Maria and then, a little more particularly, at Mechtild. Possibly he had been a charmer in his day.

'Herr Hefti is our old and good friend, M. Dégousse,' said Maria.

'How unfortunate that at just this moment I must leave,' said Mechtild. 'Goodbye, Maria! Lorenz! And Willi – *à bientôt*!'

'We too must leave M. Dégousse to discuss personalities with Lorenz,' said Maria as Mechtild went off. 'Good night, Lorenz! M'sieu!'

They left Lorenz assuring the painter he was desolated to be already late for an appointment in another part of the town. He was closing ranks too, or perhaps just reckoned the fun was over for the evening.

'Not much reverence for the artist, in St Gallen,' Briggs said to Maria. 'You were rather rough, weren't you?'

'Dreadful little fraud!', she said. 'Patronising the Swiss peasants. He must not think, just because he takes in Sybille, the rest of us are deceived by his rubbish. Hanspeter is at least *good* at looms and, in any case, his mother was some sort of cousin of Klaus's Aunt Friederike.'

'If Hanspeter says elliptical profiles for heddle-horses don't exist, they don't?'

'I don't think so. Why, anyway?'

'Nothing much really.'

'Sybille!', said Maria, as they came up to their hostess. 'Such an interesting evening, though I am not sure Dégousse is quite my sort of painter, I must confess.'

'Yes, indeed,' added Briggs meaninglessly.

Sybille had kept her dignity through all.

'My dears,' she said, 'there are a thousand mansions in the palace of art. And one must peep into many before one finds one's . . . one's . . .'

' . . . room?' Briggs blurted out at last.

'Precisely. Maria, I am so glad you have found an authentically perceptive companion. Bless you both! Adieu!'

They went for their coats.

'Does Sybille not like Klaus?', Briggs asked.

'Klaus has a view on Sybille. He is quite incapable of concealing it from her.'

They came out into the cool street and both took deep breaths. Maria laughed.

'Of course', she said, 'you are not used to the pace of our cultural life here. We are meeting Klaus at the Walliserkeller. This way.'

Twenty yards ahead of them Lorenz was walking along the otherwise deserted street. Suddenly he looked up at the sky, punched the air with a fist, and gave a little skip. Then he turned off down an alley and disappeared.

'That is a strange man,' said Maria, slipping her arm through Briggs's. 'He shares jokes with God.'

For a dozen steps they were silent.

'It was Mechtild Leinberger you were with last night,' she said then.

'Well, yes. But it was all more diversified than that makes it sound. We talked about Goethe and things.'

'You're seeing her again?'

'Lunch tomorrow.'

'But surely you are not going to use her to find out things about her husband? That won't do, you know. In fact, I won't have it. To use her loneliness to find out money things for that American would be foul.'

'Maria, love, simmer down! I called Charlie Livingston early this afternoon and told him I wanted out of it. I *am* out of it now.'

'Oh. Was he upset?'

'Not extraordinarily. I suspect he has other ways of getting at the Ravensburgers. That isn't the problem.'

Maria slowed down their pace for a moment.

'In some ways gender is a nuisance,' she said.

'Yes.'

'No. What I mean is that, but for gender, you and Klaus would make a marvellous couple – and I and Mechtild too. Wouldn't

71

you and Klaus be a nice couple? But you would have to do the shopping.'

They had arrived at the door of the Walliserkeller, and Maria broke away to lead in. They found a table and sat to wait for Klaus.

'So would you,' said Briggs.

'So would I what?'

'Have to do the shopping.'

'You think so? Here *is* Klaus.'

12

The Gasthaus zur Linde above Urnäsch was a small and isolated inn in the Appenzeller style: log-faced front, shingle side-walls, pale grey-green window-frames. It stood on a by-road above the village of Urnäsch some way up the east slope of a fair-sized hill, looking over minor ridges and valleys to the long ridge – grey now on a grimly grey day – of the Säntis. No lime-tree was anywhere near, to justify the inn's name.

It was not yet midday. Briggs was early and sat in his car on the gravel parking-place a little below the inn. There were no other cars: it was not the season. He should have been trying to work out a way to tell Mechtild what had to be told, but his mind evasively drifted off: Säntis – Lenardo   René Pfiffner's historical view – Appenzell – 'Abbot's Cell' – Abbots and their officers – Bailiff=Vogt. Mechtild's father was still, effectively, a quite unknown quantity . . .

Mechtild drove up, early too, and parked alongside. She smiled toothily across and gestured an invitation to the seat beside her. Briggs went round and got in.

'Welcome back!', she said. She wore the same leather coat and was in high spirits. 'Let's get together, honey, before we join the crowd,' she intoned in a mock-sultry voice.

Briggs saw them slipping already into a situation in which he would be unable to say his say. He shrank from breaking into her mood but was driven to unload: not to do so was corroding every moment.

'Mechtild,' he said elaborately, 'I have something rather complicated to tell you, a sort of confession.'

'Come on then! I enjoy confidences. Two wives and seven children? No. On the run from the seminary, then?'

'You won't understand till you have heard all of it. Wait till I have finished before you get angry.'

'I'm terribly easy-going.'

'Please.'

Briggs knew he had muffed it already, with his portentous prologue, but he launched himself into his tale anyway.

He told her about Livingston and about Livingston's worry, and how he himself had come to St Gallen with a view to finding out about the Ravensburgers there. He explained how, the day after their encounter, he had called it off with Livingston and gone for a walk to the Ravensburgers' mill to think things over. He tried to convey the almost accidental way he had come to hear the conversation by the BMW. It sounded implausible, as it came out; he began to wonder if it was true. Rather hopelessly, he went on to say that he did feel there was something strange about it. He then went on too long about the puzzling tone of the conversation and Fritz's unfitter-like abruptness, and also about the disproportionate intensity of the pursuit through the wood to toy-town. He sensed he had failed to make his point here. He realised he had said nothing explicitly about his feeling for her, and made a clumsy declaration of this. He finished by asking her what she wanted him to do, offering his services in a *cavaliere servente* way that seemed grotesque even to him.

At the end, he was unclear why he had felt the need to say all this. There was no sense of having got things into the open, only of having put his boot through something.

Mechtild had drawn away. Briggs had been talking at the windscreen. He turned to look at her, and put a hand formally on hers, which was on her knee. She shook it off quite gently without looking at him. Her face was set, her mouth in an odd rictus, like some sly child caught out. Briggs was very aware of the bone of her head, the temples and occiput and cheekbones. Under the fine brown skin the skull was close to her surface. The set of the eyes had a hint of the steppes. He was enthralled.

'Just when did you get to St Gallen?' she asked at last.

'Late afternoon, day before yesterday. We met that evening.'

'Just when did you call it off with this man in Munich?'

'Yesterday, early afternoon. I slept a bit in the morning.'

'And then you went for this walk?'

'Yes.'

'I don't understand why you spied on Kaspar then.'

'It just happened. I hadn't set out to.'

'Why did you tell me all this now?'

'God knows! I think I wish I hadn't. Half-an-hour ago it seemed necessary. It was spoiling things that I hadn't told you.'

'It's not to wheedle information out of me?'

'No, it's not,' Briggs said without emphasis.

Mechtild opened her door and got out, and Briggs did the same and walked round to her. She suddenly swung her arm and struck him in the face with the back of her half-clenched hand: it was her knuckles that hit but not with full force.

'You gave me a surprise just now,' she said in a friendly enough way. 'There's one for you. Now we'll have lunch. I'm hungry.'

She started walking towards the inn and after a moment Briggs started too, rubbing his cheek. She led the way in and went to a table by a window. The inn was empty, but a waitress appeared and, without consulting either a menu or Briggs, Mechthild ordered food for both of them. Then she took a roll from the basket on the table and started to eat it, staring out of the window. She ate hungrily. Briggs, who had never seen her eat before, watched. She caught his eye.

'My exercise out there has given me an appetite,' she said. 'You are going to have a bruise on your cheek. Does it hurt?'

'Yes.'

'Good. Or perhaps you like being hit by ladies?'

'Not as a regular thing. I am feeling ill-used.'

'Poor fellow! Feel free to massage your hurt. You need not act stoical with me.' She went back to her roll.

They ate their meal in silence, less hostile than remote. There was no need for them to meet each others' eyes much, over the table. The window they were sitting by gave on to an open world of undemanding pastoral features and the occasional special stimulus of a moving cow.

'Lenardo's country, out there,' Briggs said eventually, as the waitress brought coffee.

'Not quite. Too tame.'

'I read "Lenardo's Diary".'

'Oh, yes.'

'How did you come to learn it by heart?'

'I didn't learn it by heart. I just know it.'

'But so well?'

She fiddled with her coffee, rotating the saucer with little twitches.

'I suppose you don't have any cigarettes?' she said.

'I'll get some.' Briggs went to find the waitress and got some Murattis and matches.

Mechtild smoked quite clumsily. 'All right,' she said, looking out of the window again, 'though it is an impertinence of you to ask. I like thinking of it, so I'll tell you.'

'It was my mother. In 1944 we were living in Berlin, out in Grunewald, in a rented house. Father was at the Ministry, really all the time. I was ill with pleurisy and Mother used to read to me. There weren't children's books in that house and anyway I didn't much like them by then – I was thirteen. Mother found a *Wilhelm Meister* and read me the tales that are inserted into it – you know, the separate short stories he put in – "The Nut-Brown Maid", "The New Melusine" . . . but the one I liked best was "Lenardo's Diary", even though it's hardly a story. She must have read it to me half-a-dozen times. Did you ever have pleurisy?'

'No.'

'With pleurisy you have a fever and you lie and day-dream a lot. I used to lie and think about those spinners and weavers after Mother had gone out. It was mixed up with Father being a spinner and weaver too. But Appenzell seemed a warmer world than what I gathered of his. I made stories about myself in it. That's what it was: a world I liked to imagine myself in. Sometimes I entranced Lenardo, sometimes I was just wife or daughter of the lean black-locked man who came over the hill . . .'

'The loom-builder.'

'Yes, but have the kindness not to make a thing of that. Anyway, Mother died soon after, soon after news came from Russia that my brother Peter was dead. A bad time. I was sent away to people in the south, in Baden. These people just had that big collected works of Goethe, thirty shiny black volumes of it in a glass-fronted case – not the separate *Wilhelm Meister* we had in Berlin. That had had a rough red-brown cover of dry-spun linen, some natural lichen-dye. Warm. But I found it in the big set and read the parts I liked again, over and over. I don't know how many times I read "Lenardo's Diary" in those days. It was Mother now, you understand: her voice was in the words. I can't hear it any more, to be open with you, though I still like the book.'

She stubbed out her cigarette. 'That's all. A touching story, you'll agree. Let's go now.'

When they got outside neither of them seemed clear about where they were going.

'I am really sick of talking with you in that car,' said Mechtild. 'Let's walk up the hill for a bit, up that track.'

She set off fast up a track that started just above the inn and Briggs tagged on behind. The track went up through pasture and around and above small woods, climbing all the time. It was a real track, at first, wide enough for a cart and covered with loose small stones, but presently it became narrower and rougher and firmer. Mechtild kept up a punishing pace. Her pouncing gait covered ground quickly, but even so this was clearly flat out. It was not clear which of them she was punishing. Every now and then she glanced round to see how Briggs was managing. He had set himself to keep about five yards behind and not show much exertion. After twenty minutes they were above any woods and off any track, on a steeper line now, over coarse dry grass and rock outcrops. It was not a race, nor a hunt, but some odd kind of reciprocal coursing that was going on. But it came to an end after another ten minutes, since they came abruptly to the top of the hill and there was nowhere further to go. Mechtild stopped.

Briggs picked a flat grassy spot a few yards beyond, and half lay, half sat there, and panted, mostly because he needed to, but also because he was willing for her to have her due now. He let her recover, behind, without witness. In any case, he felt nauseous.

On a good day the view would have been spectacular. Today was not a good day. The light was dead, and the Säntis a flat thing cut out of dirty felt.

After a time he heard Mechtild walk over, and she sat up against him, back to back, so that they were like a pair of re-dundant book-ends. It was uncomfortable. Perhaps – more than facing across a table or side-by-side in a car – it registered a sense of peculiar relation.

'You've got the cigarettes,' she said.

He dug them out of his pocket and passed them. There was little breeze, but he heard and felt three matches being struck be-fore a cigarette was lit.

'How can you want to walk so fast up a hill, straight after eat-ing as much as you ate?', he said. She did not reply.

Back-to-back was too awkward to sustain for very long and, by the time Mechtild had put out her cigarette, the arrangement had become more irregular, but not familiar.

'Well', she said at last, 'I suppose I have a couple of things to say to you. One is that you are wrong about Kaspar. I will not pretend we have a complete marriage: you are evidence we do not. I do not quite know why not. You realise Kaspar was my brother Peter's friend? Well, he was. They were engineering students together until the war, and for a short time they were together on the Russian front too. In some way that has something to do with it. Anyway, that's none of your business . . .'

She paused. Briggs said nothing.

'You don't know the sort of thing that happened to quite good men of that age in the war – neither you nor I can know. It froze him, or part of him, in some way. I knew him before, as Peter's friend: he was different. But he is – Oh, God! – well, he is a *virtuous* man. A serious man. It's mad to think of him doing something criminal. If you knew him, you would realise it is mad. You can tell your man in Munich he is on a wrong track.'

'I am no longer reporting to him,' Briggs said. 'He had nothing criminal in mind. I don't even know what your husband was in the war.'

'An engineer, like my brother. But Kaspar just looked after transport, trucks. He was running a small repair unit for trucks in Italy towards the end of the war. You've seen that picture. He insists on keeping it there, almost penitentially.'

'Pavia, 1944?'

'You *were* spying a bit, you know.'

'No, not then. But there it was. I liked that painting.'

'Kaspar no longer paints. He draws but goes no further.'

'I am sorry, Mechtild. I am not saying your husband is involved in anything criminal. How could I? I don't know him, I've never even seen him. But there was something odd about the conversation I heard and about the way Fritz behaved. There is something secret there.'

'Oh, Fritz! I know Fritz quite well. Kaspar has a small workshop at the house where Fritz sometimes does things. I talk to Fritz. He was Kaspar's sergeant in the war and he's a good mechanic – a Pomeranian tough, unable to go home, but all right. Anyway, new machines can be a kind of secret, you know: you shouldn't have been eavesdropping on them.'

'There was something worrying about it all. I don't want you involved in some awkwardness.'

Mechtild lost patience.

'You see yourself as St George. An odd St George you are! You rode into St Gallen to save Princess Dollar from wicked Kaspar, didn't you? And now, because I recite a bit of Goethe, you've shifted from her to me. You say. Such have been my charms. Fickle! Well, Kaspar isn't *my* dragon, so clear off!'

'I . . .'

'And that's the second thing I have to say to you. It is no good you hanging round St Gallen because of me. I am a married woman. I had a fling with you one night. I've had flings before. Don't romanticize! You happened to be there.'

'Chance conjunction,' Briggs said ironically.

'Not entirely. You looked fairly clean.'

Briggs stood up. Mechtild looked up at him almost shyly.

'I am sorry, that was a foul thing to say,' she said. 'It wasn't really like that. But I don't pretend to feelings I did not have. I liked you. You were a friend of Maria's, and I trust Maria. I still like you. But you were only staying a few days in St Gallen and would soon be gone. I am sorry.'

She got up, and they started back down the hill, on a line with each other and at a certain distance. Mechtild was in one of her glum patches. Briggs swung between self-pitying chagrin and a newly sharp recognition of being in thrall. No one said a word.

When they got to the cars, Briggs went to his and unlocked it. Mechtild leaned against the front wing of hers, hands in coat pockets – as he had seen her once before – and looked at her shoe. Briggs decided she was manoeuvring him into driving off first, in a huff, and was suddenly very angry. He would not be manipulated.

'I shall be away from St Gallen for a couple of days,' he said in an elaborately normal, even voice but improvising wildly as

80

he went. 'I am going to visit a friend in Pavia. I shall be back quite soon, I think, but will try not to get under your feet. I have no idea whether I shall be getting under your husband's. Maria will know where I am, if you have urgent need of someone clean. You had better go first now: your car is the faster and I do not want to slow you down.'

He got half in and started his car, but clumsily, and there was a farouche grinding noise as he pressed the starter button too long.

Mechtild came over and Briggs childishly simulated preoccupation with warming up his aged engine, prodding pedal and adjusting choke.

'You're going back to spying for that man in Munich?' she shouted above the noise.

'No: private research. The textile industry is my subject.'

'What?'

'No!'

She leaned forward and turned off the Volkswagen's engine.

'Spite or blackmail – which?'

'That's simply insulting. You've made your point "clear off!". But, if I do, I shall have to work my way away, and that means settling my mind. Don't worry – I really won't rock your menfolk's boat. But I want to know a little more. They interest me.'

'You bore me.'

'Sorry. Better appraise your pick-ups better.'

'The light was very bad in the Vadianus.'

'Try the Bahnhof Bar: it's brighter lit.'

'At least they are on their way, the fellows there.'

'You can even check their tickets, first.'

'I'll just be hoping they have a bit more . . .'

Briggs pressed his starter button again, slammed his door, and drove off in a fury. His mind was a mucky soup of red anger, panicky dolour and fragments of wounding retorts. When he got to the crossroads at the bottom of the by-lane he could not think which road was his.

A horn blared behind and the Porsche cut fast round him, making for the road to the right. Briggs stalled. As she passed, Mechtild made a derisory gesture with two fingers and then sped off in a spray of gravel. Briggs swore. The woman had been smirking again.

II

October 17–18, 1956

13

Pavia is only a hundred and fifty miles from St Gallen but the Alps lie between. One way to go is by the St Gotthard, but Briggs disliked the St Gotthard as a forced and parvenu pass. He favoured the Splügen, which had been a going concern since Roman times.

Passes, he believed, stand for the accessibility of success in the pursuit of knowledge and many other human endeavours. The last sharp climb to the summit is rarely the problem of a pass: and the immediate terrain of the summit itself tends to be much like that of any other pass, whatever the differences in the outlook. What sets the problem and the character of a pass is the lower approach. It had been the long sullen gorge of the Reuss on the northern side that had kept people from the St Gotthard for so many years, not the St Gotthard itself. Whereas they had been led early to the Splügen by the easy valley of the Upper Rhine on one side and the sparkling availability of Lake Como on the other. It was the natural line, the benign line, from St Gallen to Pavia, as he had told Maria and Klaus at breakfast.

'Give our love to Pasquale', Maria had said. 'We haven't seen him since that Spoleto conference, last year. I still laugh when I think of Pasquale's paper and how angry it made people. "Toeplitz, the Textile Barons and the Financing of Fascism." Do you remember how that old man walked out in the middle shouting "Giacomo Toeplitz was my friend"? Klaus thinks Pasquale should stick to demand theory and not play politics. That is your third roll, Klaus. You two . . . half of the time Willi is travelling in a medieval dreamworld and you, Klaus, exist on a level where what any actual person may actually do or think or desire is inadmissible in principle. My God! Pasquale likes looking in on real things here and now. Anyway, has it occurred to you two that you are on the edge of a sort of league? In nearly every part of Europe we have a friend like Pasquale, someone we were students with somewhere and share a general view of things with and see occasionally. Then they have other friends and those friends have friends. Except for you two, it's like a government in waiting. I ask you now: are you preparing yourselves to be the guides of Europe in ten years' time? Pasquale is. So are Dieter and Maurice and Wieslaw and the rest. Why aren't you? It worries me. And what can I say in your defence to Ewa and Jeanette and that strange little person who was with Dieter last time? Shouldn't you think about this?'

'We do', said Klaus. He was incongruously dressed as a sergeant in the Swiss army. Autumn manoeuvres began today, and he was off to military service in the Vaud. 'But not at breakfast.'

St Gallen – Chur – Splügen – Chiavenna. Maria's indictment came back to Briggs, stuck behind a petrol-tanker on the road that winds along the steep shores of Lake Como. The good thing about Lake Como, till a hundred years before, had been the easy water passage from Chiavenna to the city of Como itself. This no longer held: the stretch was tiresome.

At Como, at last, the Autostrada began, but so did the Po valley fog and as he drove into Milan it was already dusk – making the town a great theatrical set for a grim realist opera. Here must be corrupt officials and inefficient revolutionaries and strong but victimized women. Briggs blundered around in the centre until he found the Pavia road and then joined a file of vehicles bowling south along a straight poplar-lined avenue for the last twenty miles. It was half-past-six when he arrived in Pavia.

Pasquale Cefis had an apartment near the University, in a dark and narrow street of timeless brick houses that looked more decrepit than they really were. Briggs parked his car close up to an ancient wall covered with a tattered mixture of cinema and obituary posters, got his bag, and climbed a single flight of dimly lit stone stairs. 'Key with Bragagnolo opposite', said a note pinned on Pasquale's door. Briggs crossed the landing and rang a bell marked 'Bragagnolo'. A tall woman and two small children opened the door.

'Good evening, Signora! My name is . . .'

'Briggs, of course, and you need the key. A moment! Riccardo, run and get Pasquale's key off its hook. You won't mind waiting a short moment, Signor Briggs? It is good for the child to do small tasks.'

'Of course, Signora.'

She was handsome in the grand equine Lombard way and was looking at him curiously with clever dark eyes, eyes set high in relation to a bold beak of a nose so Greek it almost looked broken. Briggs searched in pockets for the remains of a tube of fruit lozenges bought that morning at a petrol station. She could have been Pasquale's sister, by her looks.

'Mama! Where is the hook?'

'Where Pasquale's key hangs.' Signora Bragagnolo turned to Briggs. 'He said he would be back by eight at the latest, but that if you like to go and meet him he will be at the PCI in the Piazza della Vittoria. He does a discussion group for the Young Communists. His Gramsci group.'

Both of them smiled, and then both stopped smiling quickly, as if catching themselves in an act of disloyalty.

'The key is not on the hook, Mama!'

'A moment, Signor Briggs', said Signora Bragagnolo and went inside.

Briggs squatted and winked cheerily at the tot remaining. It scuttled away and did not come back till its mother returned, preceded by Riccardo holding a key.

'Riccardo was right: it was on the dresser.'

'May I . . . ?' Briggs asked, giving her a glimpse of the tube of sweets.

'Very kind.'

As Briggs went across to open Pasquale's door they stood and watched, the children sucking cautiously. The little group was troubling. Where was Mr Bragagnolo? Was he satisfactory? How did Mrs Bragagnolo pass her life in that apartment with the children? Briggs swung his bag just inside the door and closed it again.

'The Piazza della Vittoria is the big market square?' he asked.

'Yes. The PCI is on the south side.'

After thanks and goodnights Briggs ran down the stairs with an odd guilty feeling.

He set off along the cobbled alleys in the direction of the market square. Lombard fog was subtler than the fat mists of St Gallen, not misplaced cloud but an expiration of the plain. Where it had made Milan a nineteenth-century city, it turned these old brick houses and towers into something purely medieval. In an occasional small shop there was a bleak weak light and a stooping figure or two.

A wood-slat blind rattled sharply and a shaft of stronger light fell from a high window on to a skeletal threadbare black cat in the street. The creature turned its head awkwardly upwards for a moment to face the light and then made off with a taut, uneasy gait somewhere between walking and running. From a larger building there was a noise of children: 'Orfanotrofio Municipale A. Majocchi', said a sign by the door. Shrill voices came from an open window but only a ceiling and an unshaded low-watt electric bulb could be seen. Further on again was a noisy wineshop and a woman in a shawl outside trying to look through its window. Briggs sighed. In low spirits he was a glutton for glum vignettes.

He came to the Strada Nuova, the main shopping street that

had been cut through the old town. It was lit strongly enough to penetrate and so, seemingly, disperse much of the mist and there were pavements and people, at this hour mainly adolescent youths with elaborate coiffures; when there were no girls to whistle at, these hung around singing snatches of songs and combing their hair, jostling the older passers-by.

Briggs crossed the Strada Nuova and cut down a side street back into the dark old world. And here was the Cathedral, with its oddly unfinished look. A great cupola, the ugliest cupola in all Italy, went up into the mist. One could not make out at what point, quite, it disappeared. The dark brick of the church faded imperceptibly into the lesser darkness of the night. He stood and worked on this allegory until two old men in the winter garb of the elderly – short black cloak wrapped several times about, round-crowned black hat – came along the street and looked at him too curiously. He walked on, thinking he might buy such a cloak but not such a hat while he was in Pavia, and came out into the Piazza della Vittoria.

It was a long oblong square with tall arcaded buildings on three sides, and was now quite empty: no stalls, few cars, no people. In one corner was a newspaper kiosk with its small window shut and a faint, dirty yellow light within. The light was so weak it would have been brown, if that were possible. Perhaps it was brown anyway.

The Communists hung out in a squat romantic building at the far end of the square. Briggs made for it across the cobbles. The battered door was ajar and he walked in. No one was about but there were voices from a back-room, and he went towards these and listened for a moment. This was it.

14

He opened the door and tiptoed in, raising his eyebrows and holding his arms stiff in a mime of apology and self-effacement. Pasquale Cefis, standing in a bare room crammed with a score of young
people, raised an arm in greeting and went on talking. There were
not enough chairs and several Young Communists were sitting
against the wall, on the floor. Briggs joined these and listened. His
grasp of the Lombard idiom was not of a kind to let him follow the
discussion fully. It seemed to be about Gramsci's analysis of 'common sense' but also about Mussolini's 1938 prohibition of shaking
hands in salutation, and presumably about some relation between
these. He let the voices flow over him and just looked around and
enjoyed the atmosphere. It was cheering.

Poised in restrained *contrapposto* behind a table with a book
in his hand, Pasquale made a glamorous figure. He was tall and
fine-featured and had a neat naval sort of beard. His head was
held very high, and proud. He wore an elegant but severe dark
grey suit, and beneath it a thick white sweater with a polo neck:
the effect of this last was rather like a ruff. In fact, he had the
look of a Venetian patrician in some elongated late-Renaissance
portrait, and Briggs had known him long enough to be certain
he would be aware of this. He spoke fluently but precisely, quite
without gestures. And his Young Communists were an attractive
lot too – of an age with but remote from the corner-boys in the
Strada Nuova. Were they of the same social class? Here at the
PCI it was not indecent to ask oneself that. The tone was that of
some sports team, but the game was the serious game of Italian

socialism played with dash and – that much Briggs could follow – independence. Pasquale clearly had to extend himself here.

He was winding things up now and setting the readings for next week, and he also pointed to Briggs:

'This is Mister Briggs, by the way, a strange type of anarcho-syndicalist from the north, but my friend. If ever the Party needs help with the fifteenth-century fustian industry, we may persuade him to have a role.'

Strained, but the Young Communists laughed politely and got up with a clatter of chairs and feet. They began to drift out. Pasquale came over and shook hands.

'William! How are you? We'll go straight and eat once I've packed up here.'

He collected books and papers from his table, shouted good-night to a caretaker somewhere in the building and got a shout back, and they left. The Young Communists were crossing the square in a group, making for the Strada Nuova.

'Impressive squad, your children.'

'Not so bad.' Pasquale kept his poise. 'But I have no illusions. In ten years three-quarters of them will have reverted. But they'll still be that much more open, I think. I do think that. We'll go and eat at Zi' Elena's, no? It's rugged, but just round the corner.'

'Fine. Klaus and Maria send their love. Also a cheese, which is still in my car.'

'Bless Maria! It will be Appenzeller. A song from the hills. This way.'

Zi' Elena's was in a back street off the Strada Nuova. From outside it looked a modest grocer's. One edged through an obstacle course of hanging sausages, sacks of beans and rices, antique-looking cans of vegetable and bottles of oil, into a small back-room with a few tables covered by white oil-cloth. There you ate what was brought by the cook's niece. Tonight it was to be *risotto alla sbirraglia*, a *spezzatino* of something that did not quite look veal, quasi-mushy peas, fontina, a pear.

'So what brings you to Pavia?' Pasquale delicately forked Parmesan into his risotto. 'Fustian again? I thought you had cleaned that up.'

'Almost. There are two or three transcriptions I'd still like to make in the *Archivio* here, a day-book and a letter of recommendation from a man in Ulm who interests me. They won't send microfilm. I'll be doing that, though the reason I came just now is too absurd to speak of.'

'Speak of it, do! You know at least two absurd things about me.'

'Do I? Well . . . I lost my temper. I rather pointlessly told someone in St Gallen I would be going away, here. So I came.'

'A woman. I hope not Maria.'

'No, no, not Maria. Pasquale, suppose I wanted to find out about a German who was here in Pavia during the war – is there an obvious way of doing it? If not, I won't bother.'

'Who, when, what was he?'

'A man called Leinberger, an engineer lieutenant in the army. He ran a unit repairing trucks here in 1944 and early 1945. I think there may have been some incident he was involved in, I don't know what.'

'Some "incident"? William, have you any idea what it was like here then? There were a thousand incidents and they won't be recorded in the Archivio. I am from Mantua, not Pavia, but I know they were busy here.'

'Well, no matter. I doubt if it was anything spectacular. He still comes back here on business now and then.'

'What business?'

'He is a textile man, a machinery specialist. He seems to have odd bits made by a mechanic here whose name I don't know, except that it is Cesare something.'

'Now *that* one might be able to discover.' Pasquale finished his risotto and sat back. 'Some of Laura Bragagnolo's family are of that ambience, fine metal-workers. It interests me, and ought to interest you, that Pavia should have developed from a textile town, in your period, into a textile machinery town. Not just the big firm, Necchi and its pretty sewing-machines, but a whole lot of little satellite specialist workshops. There are three or four streets on the north side that are full of them, some with a couple of men, some with a dozen – like Laura's uncle. It's rather how one imagines Milan in your time.'

Briggs knew this.

'Tell me about Laura Bragagnolo', he said.

Pasquale looked speculatively at Briggs.

'No, you tell *me* about Laura.'

Briggs put his fork down and considered.

'The predicament of the Italian woman . . .', he said. 'Very intelligent, I would guess, but I imagine her family would not have reckoned on a girl having a proper education. Then trapped by marriage. I wondered if perhaps the husband might be no good. He wasn't there. Perhaps he works abroad, perhaps even in Switzerland – something like a coffee-jerk or chauffeur, may be, rather than a labourer. He would send money, but not enough. Feckless. Her family tops it up and disapproves of him. She looks a really interesting person. I don't like to think of the constraints of her life in that apartment. What a waste! Riccardo looks rather like you, you know.'

He picked up his fork again and chased a last fragment of risotto.

'Yes', said Pasquale after a moment.

'I am right?'

'No, you are wrong. I meant: Yes, still the sentimental stereotypes. It is a sort of contempt, William, and an evasion. You must stop it.'

'Well, you tell *me* about her.'

'Laura is an assistant in the Department of Engineering in the University – part-time while the children are so young. Her doctorate is in hydraulic engineering, irrigation in particular.

Piermario, the husband, teaches at the University too: medieval philosophy. Like many of us here he teaches a couple of days a week in Milan – by the way, I shall be away in Milan myself tomorrow – but I do not know where he was today. You'll meet him: he's fine. As for your curious last point, Riccardo and Laura and I are all Lombards. To the ignorant all Chinese look the same.'

'There are more of my type of Laura Bragagnolo than there are of yours.'

'Of course. Agreed. But you put the cart before the oxen. You let the type be the origin, and individuality be fallings-away from some first mould. Whereas I, with a livelier sense of life and altogether more generous view, see people as unique in origin. Sure, they later converge into types, but that is because of shared . . . *Dio mio!* this is stupid!'

'Yes.'

'We have framed the issue stupidly. Let's talk of something else.'

'Yes.'

'OK . . . about your German: we will go on after this and ask Zanzi – you don't know Zanzi – if he knows anything about a truck repair unit in 1944. Tell me more about it. *Caspita!* I hate to think what kind of beast this *spezzatino* came from.'

15

Later they left Zi' Elena's and walked down to the narrow roofed bridge across the river. Zanzi, whom they were going to see, had a wine-shop in the Borgo Ticino, over on the south bank.

Over the water the Borgo Ticino, lying low, showed up as a line of dim lights in the mist like a coast seen from the sea. It was another country. Once across the bridge it still looked different — out-of-town, but not rural. The buildings were lower and smaller here, the shops fewer and poorer, the gaps left by wartime bombing of the river-crossings unfilled. There were a few poky bars. It was a haggard Bohemia.

Zanzi's, when they got to it, was a hole-in-the-wall with no sign. Inside there was a counter on the left, patchy varnished wood and chipped marble top, and on the right were half a dozen hard chairs and two small tin tables. Two middle-aged men were leaning behind the counter and three old ones were sitting on the chairs. If anyone had been talking, they stopped when Pasquale and Briggs came in. There were no more than a dozen bottles on and around the counter, and the functional ones were unlabelled. At the far end of the counter an iron stove jutted half across the room with a zig-zag chimney going up into the ceiling. A small cauldron of some sort of broth simmered on the stove top. Beyond the stove was a back-room with one large wooden table and nine or ten more chairs. No one was sitting there.

Pasquale greeted one of the men behind the counter, made some introduction of Briggs, took one of the unlabelled bottles by the neck and smelt it. He was speaking now in thick Lombard and Briggs got no more than the gist of what was being said. The man seemed to be Zanzi, and the talk seemed to be about this year's pressings of Nebbiolo and what was best to be drunk now. Some decision was made and they went on through to the back and sat down at the big table.

'Zanzi's stuff is fierce', said Pasquale. 'You have to be careful what you drink here. He's one of those who didn't make a good thing out of the resistance.'

'He was in it?'

Pasquale did not reply at once. He leaned back on his chair and fingered his beard, looking at Briggs.

'"In it?"', he repeated. 'Foreigners laugh – don't they? Because so many Italians say they were of the resistance. In a sense, though, it was so: it happens in tyrannies, you see. You make a point, say, of greeting Signora Chierichetti in the street the day after the police have been to see her about where her son is, poor woman. You know her; you like her. You are resisting, in a certain sense. Or you keep quiet about a late caller at the Rolandis' next-door: it could just have been the doctor, and in any case they are decent enough folk. Why make trouble for them and, perhaps, for yourself also? You are amused by a joke about that frightening buffoon Farinacci of Cremona. You buy black-market meat, of course, because by the last winter there was no other; by the last winter all you could buy easily and legally was wine. Well, it all adds up. Life was full of little resistant acts and this is what you remember of yourself. They were the active rather than the passive things you did, you understand. It is a natural illusion . . .'

He paused for a moment, almost at a loss.

'I am thinking of my parents, you understand. Anyway, Zanzi was much much more than this, first-degree resistance, and not off in the hills but here. "In it", as you say. For over two years this wine-shop was a post-office for the ORI. Pavia was likely to be a crux because of its location: confluence of Po and Ticino.

Hitler had sworn he would hold out along the Po. As it turned out, the Germans gave up and moved out of here two days before the Allies arrived. But Zanzi was the man on the spot. Party member since the 'thirties . . .'

He broke off as Zanzi arrived with three thick tumblers and an open bottle, poured wine and sat down. At first sight he looked an unlikely hero, slight and dapper, a bullet-headed little man in a blue apron: but he had a striking air of total self-control, both in how he held himself and in how he looked at people. There was some elusive, austere authority about Zanzi.

They drank wine. It was a thick black grapey stuff with a fermenting tingle. Zanzi refilled their glasses. The three old men in the front had started a spasmodic shouted conversation about something Briggs could not make out.

'*Pan al color e vin al saor*', said Pasquale.

Zanzi nodded with a routine air.

'Proverbial saying', Pasquale explained to Briggs. 'The wine tastes better than it looks.'

For twenty minutes Pasquale and Zanzi discussed mixed topics – vintage, Archbishop Montini of Milan and what he might really be up to, a local scandal about building licences, the Party's plight in Pavia – and Briggs listened. Much of the time Zanzi, with dry courtesy to the stranger, spoke in slow school-Italian. They emptied the bottle and he went for another.

'The second bottle is the time', said Pasquale. And when they had full glasses again he put his hand on Briggs's arm and spoke to Zanzi.

'My friend here has an interest – an almost historical interest, one might say – in a German officer who was in Pavia during 1944, 1945.'

Zanzi nodded and looked politely towards Briggs.

'Was there a German engineer unit in the town, repairing trucks?' Pasquale asked.

Zanzi's eyes went remote as he considered.

'In the town itself there was a small unit in the Collegio Praga', he said slowly, 'principally for trucks running through. Otherwise there was a much larger depot twenty kilometres east, towards Lodi.'

'I thought the Collegio Praga was used as a hospital?'

'Only the second courtyard. They opened up the main gate and used the front court and some of the *pian terreno* rooms for repairing their trucks. But I was never inside and know nothing of the personnel.'

'You know the Collegio Praga?' Pasquale said to Briggs.

Briggs nodded. The Collegio Praga was a large and ornate eighteenth-century building near the University, a grand hostel for students, one of several such old foundations here. He had the impression that it had been founded for German-speaking students from the Empire and Italianized only after Independence. He could see its merits as a first-aid post for military vehicles en route. It was no more than a hundred yards off the main road south. Four massive wings enclosed a great cobbled courtyard with just the one great portal giving on to the street. It would have been well placed and very secure. Leinberger's strange painting of Pavia could well have been done from its upper floor.

Zanzi and Pasquale had drifted off into a mild argument about the relation between something called the CVL and something else called the CLNAI. Briggs drank wine and thought about Mechtild.

'Signor Briggs.' Zanzi was suddenly addressing him directly. 'There is a man, a man who would know more than I about the Collegio Praga. His name is Aldo Guardamagna, a type of dealer. He is not a particular friend of mine, I do not know him well, but he was much concerned with trucks. I remember hearing of an encounter between him and the Germans at the Collegio Praga. Nowadays one sees him around the Caffé Moschen in the Strada Nuova. I think he does business from there.'

'"Il Popolo" Brigade', he added, to Pasquale.

Pasquale raised his eyebrows and shrugged.

'*Be!*', he said. 'We will finish this bottle, and then I and my friend will seek out this Guardamagna.'

Half an hour later Pasquale and Briggs left the wine-shop. They were warm but could still walk quite well. But before they came to the bridge Pasquale was groaning.

'*Quel ch'a fa mal l'è l'ültim bicer*', he said.

'A proverbial saying?'

'Almost. I need a panino and a glass of grappa to settle my stomach. That stuff of Zanzi's tastes like fruit juice at the time but kills you after.'

'What did Zanzi mean by saying this man was much concerned with trucks, do you think?'

'Probably that he blew them up.'

Half-way across the bridge they stopped and leaned on the balustrade to contemplate the river. It was almost soundless. Two miles downstream these waters of the Ticino would combine with the Piedmontese waters of the upper Po to form the greater Po, the spine of northern Italy. It would run on eastwards in the mist of the plain, past more old red-brick cities Piacenza, Cremona, Pasquale's Mantua, Ferrara – brimming and dark and large, till it ran up against the silts and muds of its own delta and, parcelled, strained through them into the Gulf of Venice. Briggs stood moved by poetical resonances.

But Pasquale's mind was upstream.

'Like you', he said, 'these waters have come from Switzerland. In the spring, when the Swiss snows melt, the river floods and makes a mess down here. And sometimes – every four years, they say – a disastrous mess. Ask Zanzi. My God, how that mess smells! Many things come to us from Switzerland. You know that Mussolini was one of Switzerland's gifts to us? But yes! Don't laugh it off! He was nothing when he went up there, an emigrant bricklayer from a village, but seeing the wealth up there made him political: union work, Swiss jails, self-education. Imagine Benito sitting learning German in Lausanne, with his feet in a box of saw-dust against the cold! So . . . after three springs he came back here, an accredited politician. What a mess *that* was! But when he wanted to run back to Switzerland in 1945 they wouldn't take him.'

Pasquale brooded and then laughed.

'I agree there is rather more to it than that', he said.

'Pasquale', Briggs said, 'would you speak some German with a Lombard accent?'

'Benito was not Lombard. He was Emilian.'

'I know, but do it anyway. I have a reason.'

Pasquale shrugged and thickly addressed the dark waters below:

> 'The girl grieved on the twilit shore -
> Bereft; forlorn; undone:
> She was hurt *and* saddened *very* much by
> The going down of the sun . . .'

'Thank you.' Briggs said. 'And now just say: "I am not sure what we would have done with him if we had caught him."'

Pasquale did so. 'What is this about?' he asked.

'One of Leinberger's men in St Gallen – I had wondered about his accent. It was Lombard, I think.'

'Likely enough. I'm cold, almost sober. Let's move on.'

They re-entered Pavia and made their way along the Strada Nuova, now even emptier, to the north end. The Caffé Moschen was on a corner, a bright brash place with a juke-box and pin-ball machines and a television set above the brassy bar. It seemed a small-time sort of Rialto, with flash characters at every other table making deals behind the din.

'First, grappa', said Pasquale. 'Then enquiries. I cannot say this is my ambience.'

When the harassed elderly waiter brought the glasses Pasquale asked him directly if Guardamagna was there. The man glanced round, shook his head and moved painfully on.

'That poor devil hasn't many years of this left in him', Pasquale said. 'Well! There's Manlio!'

A youth in an apron was moving round the tables and emptying ash-trays into a small bin. When he got to their table he grinned.

'Manlio!', said Pasquale. 'You work here?' Briggs recognized one of the Gramsci group.

'*Buona sera, Signori*. Yes, a couple of hours three times a week. A little cleaning up, a little circulating like this, a crate or two to shift. Not so bad. And here one can study economic individualism at first hand. The real thing', he added slyly.

'I imagine. Do you know an individual called Aldo Guardamagna? We were told he comes here.'

'Sure. He's a man as should be, Aldo. Not here now – he deals in truck parts and tyres, and moves about. You want his number?'

'You have it?'

'I can get it. *Aspet un minüt!*'

He put his bin on a spare chair, went behind the bar and conferred with a barman. The two of them consulted an area of wall that served as a directory, the barman pointing something out. The boy came back.

'27037', he said.

'Thanks. Are the panini good here?'

'No. But you are meant to be too busy to notice. *Buona sera, Signori!*' He picked up his bin and moved off.

'"A man as should be"', Pasquale repeated ironically. 'A nice boy, but cynical. I think he comes to my class because of a girl called Margherita Heilmann. But, then, why not? Order more grappa while I try that number.'

He made for the wall-phone before one of the dealers could

annex it again. By the time Briggs had signalled successfully to the old waiter, he was back.

'Not at home', he reported. 'A woman said he should be back some time in the next hour, but one could never be sure. That seemed to anger her. We needn't wait here till then. Drink up, and we can go somewhere else.'

They left the Caffè Moschen and the Strada Nuova, and Pasquale led the way to a nearby place that looked like a run-down Austrian coffee-house, which no doubt it had once been. They drank better wine than Zanzi's, Pasquale ate a panino, and they discussed Marxian consciousness and the making of salame di Felino. It took two more calls before Aldo Guardamagna was at home.

'Got him!', said Pasquale, sitting down again. 'He will be at the Caffè Due Fiumi tomorrow from about noon till three. It's a truck-drivers' place three miles east of here, on the road to Piacenza. You are to ask for him at the bar. He was a little suspicious of it all: God knows what shifty games he's involved in. I mentioned Zanzi and he got more friendly. One more glass and then we shall go, no?'

They drank more wine and talked about Pasquale's work on demand theory until they finally pulled themselves together and left. But half-way to Pasquale's they realised he had left his Gramsci books behind and turned round and went back for them. A thin young man with a priestly look about him was sitting at the table and reading one of the books, and he made a dismissive remark about Gramsci as he handed it over: how, he tediously asked, could the man claim to transcend his own moment? They sat down and got this more or less straight for him and two law students at the next table, leaving again three-quarters of an hour later. But on the way they stopped for a while to study a carved capital on a romanesque church they were passing. Briggs was struck by the fact that the ornament, rendered in stone, was based on patterns derived from interwoven threads. This could be seen as standing for a cultural centrality of weaving – the 'textile moment' might be a good term – in any human making above the level of opportunistically picking up sharp flints: he thought a German had gone into this in some depth. Pasquale spoke up for the potter and mud and hands, but someone opened a window and shouted, and they moved on, discussing wattles: whether wattles were to be classed as textiles, and what the best material was for making wattles, hazel or willow.

'That's my car', Briggs said. 'We must be there.'

'Yes. We are.'

'We must not forget Maria's cheese.'

The catch of the boot was stiff. They had just got it open when a small Fiat drove up and a large man with bushy black hair and metal-rimmed spectacles got out.

'Piermario!', Pasquale cried. 'This is Briggs, of whom you have heard me speak. William, I mentioned Piermario. Piermario Bragagnolo: William Briggs. Look at this cheese. Straight from Appenzell, the last refuge of direct democracy. Hold it with care – it is transmontane – while we close the car.'

In time they started up the stairs, Pasquale first, Piermario last.

16

Laura Bragagnolo was on the landing.

'Two exalted economists with a Swiss cheese', Piermario said to his wife. 'Coffee for them, perhaps? If we treat them kindly they might let us try their cheese.'

She hustled the three of them through the living-room to the kitchen, as furthest from where the children were sleeping. It was a big, white, untidy room with a red-tiled floor and a scrubbed table in the middle. No one wanted coffee. All judged the cheese prime: a little could do no harm even at this hour. Laura produced knives, glasses, a bottle and a loaf. They settled round the table.

'*Pan coi büs, formai sensa büs, e vin saltam in dal müs*', said Pasquale after a while.

'No dancing', said Laura.

'Briggs has led me round and round the town on a quest: my feet hurt. No dancing, I agree. Just the soft pavane of . . .four? yes, *four* dialectical intelligences.'

The quest was sketched, mainly by Pasquale.

'Have you thought about Don Ivo?' Piermario asked him.

'But this was 1944.'

'He was there. You are from Mantua and do not know these things. He stayed in his lodging and acted as chaplain to the hospital.' Piermario turned to Briggs. 'Don Ivo Pavan is Rector of the Collegio Praga and a big piece in this University. He was there. He's been there for the greater part of the century.'

'But would he be disposed to talk of that time?' Briggs asked. 'To a stranger?'

That was discussed but not decided. Laura was consulted about a metal-founder called Cesare: she knew none, but thought her Uncle Leonida the person to ask. One could walk over in the morning, before Briggs went to meet Guardamagna.

'This Guardamagna was in an "Il Popolo" formation', Pasquale started grumbling.

But Briggs protested: 'Look, all these brigades and initials . . .'

Piermario laughed. He reached out and took half-a-dozen toothpicks from a maiolica holder and laid them on the table in a little bunch.

'CLN: Committee of National Liberation', he said. 'An alliance of six political parties, directed from Milan: Liberals, Demo-Christians, Republicans, Actionists, Socialists and Pasquale's Communists. Various specialised offshoots – ORI for intelligence, CVL as overall military authority, that sort of thing. But the fighting brigades were party-based – Communist "Garibaldi" formation, Socialist "Matteotti" formation, and so on. What Pasquale is moaning about is simply that the "Il Popolo" people were Demo-Christian. That's all.'

But Laura took another tooth-pick and put it near the six.

'Green Flames', she said. Pasquale snorted.

'No, she is right', said Piermario. He turned to Briggs again. 'The Green Flames were separate and quite strong at this end of Lombardy. They were based on old army units after the armistice in 1943. Very conservative and on bad terms with the CLN. They had a tendency to sulk. Monarchists, you understand.'

They looked at the seven tooth-picks.

'Some Green Flames had style', said Laura.

'They had time to: the "Garibaldi" brigades were doing the fighting', said Pasquale.

'More than their share', Piermario agreed. 'Worse armed than the rest – the Allies saw to that – but well led. Let's bring on the bad men.'

He set his knife and glass formally opposite the tooth-picks.

'Black Brigades – the Fascist Party squads – and, above all, Tenth Torpedo-Boat Flotilla. They had turned into the one big anti-partisan force round here, fifty thousand men based on Brescia. Some of those were appalling. Then there were variables like the different police forces: they hadn't been disarmed by the Germans, unlike the army. The Civil Guards – well, that depended on the local Prefect and their officers. The Finance Guards actually came in strong with the CLN, towards the end. But things were always changing.'

Pasquale was asleep. Laura was years away. Piermario brooded over his battlefield, slowly rolling neat bread pellets for police forces. He made a clucking noise.

'We have left out the Germans. Pass me the salt and pepper? The German army and the German SS. They did not work well together. There was something odd about the SS towards the end, particularly at the top. Some of them decided the war was lost and blocked anti-partisan measures. They were making little trips to Switzerland and talking to Americans. Strange. One didn't know all that at the time.'

Briggs sat quiet and thought about these three in their adolescence, eagerly on the edge of the brigades and committees. Pasquale, he knew, had run minor errands for the partisans in Mantua. It was less mediated than his own experience of the war: he, personally, had fought a toy war mainly with model aeroplane kits – manufactured, now he thought about it, by a firm called Frog. It made a difference.

Piermario had twisted round on his chair and from a clutter of toys on the sideboard behind him picked out a small celluloid doll, a sexless object that had lost its clothes and hair. He carefully stood this naked thing up on its feet in the middle of the battlefield.

'So', he said. 'Your lieutenant would have found himself in a complex field. A dangerous field, too, because people made choices without fully realising it, often without knowing a choice was being made, often by not doing anything. For people involved in all this, there was a sort of systematic short-circuit round the moment of intellectual choice.'

'Shouldn't he be with the army, then – by the salt?'

'No, I think not. Not if we take all this as a diagram of the moral dynamics. With your breeches off, like that one there, you are the middle. The colour of your breeches is accidental, not proper: contingency, that's what breeches are.'

Piermario blew softly: the doll fell over. Laura looked up.

'Homiletic at midnight, Piermario?' she said. Piermario made a gesture of apology.

'Well', said Briggs, starting up, 'I must get Pasquale to bed.'

Laura put out a hand.

'Wait a moment and I'll tell you a story first. Piermario has heard it – though not in this context – and Pasquale would scoff. You know where the Milan canal runs into the river and there are those strange slow whirls as the waters meet? Well, there are. I used to go there – in 1944, I suppose – to make drawings of eddies. I think I thought I was Leonardo da Vinci. That place was one of the things that made me interested in water. I was drawing eddies, on a Sunday afternoon, I expect. And a German officer came up and looked and talked. I was shy. German soldiers tried to pick you up if you were tall for your age because they didn't recognize what class you belonged to. . .'

'*Ahime!*'

'Accommodate realities, Piermario. Soldiers trying to pick up girls in foreign countries don't recognize which are for picking up and which are not because they don't know such *class* signs as gait and so on. You may not be aware of this: I am.'

'OK, Laura.'

'Well, I was shy, and one didn't like the Germans in any case. He was quite shy too. He was not so young – twenty-five or even thirty? Nearly that. He began talking, in quite correct Italian really, about the water. He told me how the persistence of the eddies was due to the water from the canal being a different temperature from the river, warmer, so it would not mix. I knew that already, in a way, because of all the fishing the people do down-stream from there. But he told me, very clearly indeed, about *how* it would not mix. One of the reasons I remember all this is that that was the first time I really understood the word 'molecule'. He explained it very clearly. And we talked about my drawing a bit. He knew about drawing, and about Leonardo. He was a decent man.'

'And?'

'And nothing. End of story. After twenty minutes or so he said goodbye and went on and I never saw him again, to know it. He had one of those anonymous German faces.'

'Do you think it was my man, the engineer lieutenant?'

'I have no idea. I just thought it a moment to tell the story.'

'Homily, second part', muttered Piermario. Laura shrugged and smiled. Briggs got up and they set about getting Pasquale to his bed.

17

It was another morning of hazy sun. Briggs manoeuvred the push-chair with the youngest Bragagnolo – Lanfranco Bragagnolo – across a narrow street into a safe patch of sunlight to wait for Laura. Lanfranco's appetite for knowledge centred on a desire for names: it tested Briggs's Italian. Now he was pointing to a drain-pipe.

'Huh? Briggs! Huh?'

'*Tubo di scolo*, I think. Yes, *tu-bo di sco-lo*.'

The child was unconvinced and turned away. Briggs was feeling only so-so this morning, though in better shape than Pasquale, who had left very late for his Milan lecturing in Briggs's car. The Leinberger business was getting out of hand. He had really come to Pavia to cool off: the Archivio would have been just right today, with perhaps a quick walk this afternoon, if the sun kept up. But as it was, he was committed to Uncle Leonida first and then this Aldo Guardamagna. He did not feel like meeting new people and having awkward conversations in a language he did not know well enough. But the thing seemed to be developing its own momentum.

'You look wan', said Laura, coming back from the school where she had been leaving Riccardo. 'We'll go by way of the Castle gardens, for the sun. It's little more than ten minutes away.'

This was so. They soon came to a quarter of small workshops, many of them open to the street. As Pasquale had said, Milan with its swordsmiths and needle-makers must have been slightly like this five hundred years ago. These little men were partly secondary suppliers to the big Necchi plant, but they were also specialist metal-workers for a range of users. They had lore and low expenses. If you wanted not too many of a piece, well made and quick, this was a rational place to come, even from up in St Gallen.

Uncle Leonida – a manganese and tungsten-steel man, Laura said – had a relatively large shop, a resonantly clangorous barn with a small glass-fronted office at the back. They worked their way through an evidently productive clutter smelling of hot oil: whining turret lathes, pitiless grinders, a milling machine and old-fashioned buffer with a big emery band, trolley-trucks with steel bar. Overalled machinists waved or nodded to Laura and Lanfranco as they passed. Uncle Leonida was in the office with an elderly clerk.

He was a stocky man in late middle age with short white hair and sharp blue eyes, and he looked as if he might be less comfortable as a business rival than as an uncle. Briggs was made known as a visiting friend. The clerk sent a boy out for coffee and orangeade. Relatives were asked after and Lanfranco received attentions.

Eventually Laura mentioned Briggs's curiosity about a man called Cesare he had heard of in Switzerland as having a workshop in Pavia.

'Cesare? Cesare . . . It would have to be Cesare Pappalardo. There is no other Cesare working here, is there?' The clerk agreed. 'Pappalardo has a shop on the corner of the Via Mantegazza, not large, just a couple of men. Smaller castings in copper alloys. We do not do much with him, we are not close, are we?' – the clerk confirmed – 'but we do a little because Pappalardo works copper well enough and we don't like it here: brass and bronze get in the way. So sometimes we have put such jobs out to Pappalardo. He is glad of the work. An unsympathetic type, to tell the truth, properly a Fascist in his day and no regrets, and his son ran out in 1945 – he had to: he had been a *sott' ufficiale* with the Brescia boys. At the time people were saying he'd got a passport to Switzerland . . .'

'That is a knife in the ribs: a passport to Switzerland was what the partisans called a knife in the ribs', the clerk explained to Briggs.

'Right! . . .people said he had got a passport to Switzerland, but he had not, he had run out while he could. I have not seen him about, myself, but others have so now and then, in Milan and a couple of times in Pavia, I think. People don't forget and some don't forgive, but they get used to bigger swine than Cesare Pappalardo's son flourishing, you see, and now they shrug and leave it, just that. It might be different if he lived here. Then there would be a few people who would want to settle up, this way or another.'

'The younger Pappalardo, was he called Bernardo?' Briggs asked.

Leonida looked at the clerk. The clerk shrugged:

'I am not sure, after this time, but he might be, yes.'

'You know him?' Leonida asked Briggs.

'No. But I may have got under his feet in Switzerland, I think.'

Leonida laughed.

'Watch your back if you meet him again. Properly a swine was that young Pappalardo. Anyway, Cesare has no kin around his business' – Leonida winked at Lanfranco – 'and it can take the courage out of a man, that. A sour man is Pappalardo, *tipo bisbetico*. But he knows copper.'

A machinist holding what looked like a half-made die arrived at the office door with a problem and Leonida got up to deal with it on the spot. It was a moment to go. They worked their way out through the shop, the elderly clerk going before signalling to them as if they were a reversing truck. As Leonida's deputy, he stood briefly and waved as they went down the street.

'Let's pass by Pappalardo's shop on the way back', said Laura. 'I am curious.'

It was only two minutes away, an open affair hardly larger than a double garage, a small foundry with three men bent over a bench and another in a greenish overcoat leaning against the wall with his arms folded and watching.

'Huh? Huh?' Lanfranco asked, pointing in. Laura paused with the push-chair for a moment.

'*Fonderia*', she said. '*Fond-er-i-a.*'

The three men at the bench glanced up and then turned back to their work. The fourth man had not moved by the time they passed on round the corner.

'That man against the wall was not Italian', said Laura. 'Overcoat, haircut, stance. But I don't know what he was.'

She was now taking Lanfranco to his minder and then going on to the University for a couple of hours to catch up with engineering. Briggs would set off for the Caffè Due Fiumi. His way went with hers at first. They both were thoughtful and did not discuss the meeting with Leonida but, just before they reached the University, Laura said:

'I wonder if the son of Pappalardo was original Tenth Torpedo-Boat Flotilla, from the start. It began as a true naval unit, you know, an elite one, but grew into this huge anti-partisan thing, much more disciplined than the Black Brigades. Valerio Borghese, the chief, was close to the SS. And he is still very much with us. It's disgusting, really, isn't it? Either way, of course, Pappalardo would have been a tough, but one asks oneself about his training. Have a good walk! And remember to look at the eddies.'

'Surely!', Briggs said. They shook hands, and she went in.

Briggs had decided to make a walk out of his tryst with Guardamagna, since Pasquale had his car, and with some advice from Laura he had chosen a route that would be better than following the road. He would walk along the Ticino some way towards its meeting with the Po and then cut across to the Due Fiumi from the river. Three or four miles perhaps: little more than an hour.

Pavia did not sprawl on its eastern side. Once out of the University quarter there were only a couple of modest residential streets before one passed through the remains of a city gate to the canal that runs from Milan into the Ticino, and a hundred yards beyond that was country.

It was still an active canal and the little lift-bridge for foot-travellers was raised to let two motor-barges pass through the lock that leads into the river. Briggs stood on the quay to wait. The lock was something of a resort and there were other idlers in the sun. From a wine-shop on the quayside there came the curiously cold smell of lees and the clacking and shouting of a bowling alley behind.

The bargees were elderly and elaborately dignified men and took their time, leaning elegantly on their tillers as the vessels eased into the lock along with a flotsam of leaves and a few dead birds. Briggs thought of where they were coming from – the shabby little dock in Milan with its squatters' shanties and faded PCI posters – and where they were going – down the river to one or another small half-medieval city: time-travellers. The barges settled into the lock. The lift-bridge came down and Briggs crossed.

He first went along the lock to the riverside to find Laura's eddies. They were there, a large intricate zone of shifting but recurring vortices trailing from the canal, and so were the fishermen below. He studied the whirls conscientiously but got little from them except, after a time, a slight light-headedness. They demanded some analytic mapping energy he lacked. So he sought out the path down the river and started walking.

18

The path took a line between a waste of thin scrub next the river and, on the left, cultivated land above the flood-line. Across the river was a great plantation of larches set in a quincunx so rigorous that there always seemed some avenue receding over there; as he walked, Briggs was aware of it as something like a regular slow flashing in the corner of his right eye. But this side of the river it seemed that the wasteland was quarried for sand and gravel.

There were rutted tracks running down into it and, near one stagnant backwater, a bent old man in a waistcoat and black hat was filling potholes with what looked for a moment to be bleached children's bodies. In fact, his material was from a large dump of broken plaster casts of cherubs and saints and so on. He had made himself a primitive hut no bigger than a telephone box, basically a sloping roof of brushwood supported by four poles. He had also hung a couple of plaster heads from the branches of bushes, a ghastly touch, and set two of the less broken figures, an adolescent angel and a bearded saint, who were not of the same scale, one on each side of the track. An ironic old man, perhaps, with a resonant activity: Briggs greeted him but was ignored entirely. If the old man had thoughts about it all, he was keeping them for himself.

The path presently angled a little away from the river, up and along a raised dyke protecting the country to the north. This country was a monstrous pale chessboard with its squares marked out by leafless poplar wind-breaks and deep muttering ditches. Men had laboured and schemed for hundreds of years to achieve this – draining, dunging, planting, watering – but the present quadratic pattern would be rather more recent: a creation of Enlightenment. It looked simple but was not.

After the river had bent away to the right, he came to the meeting of four great fields and the dyke became briefly a bridge over water. He stopped to look down. Eight straight leats, two from each quarter, met here in a sort of sump. They were all of a size but each was of a different impulse, coming or going at varying rates of speed and volume. This traffic was determined by almost imperceptible differences of level and by black plank barriers variously adjusted in the entrances as baffles, or as brakes, or as weirs. A watery ratiocination . . .

Briggs, after a time, moved on. From within, one apprehended this plain as endless. Only on rare days were there glimpses of the Alps to the north or the Appennines to the south, and certainly not today. Psychically the flat was infinite. Men had brought form to this world by digging ditches and dykes and by planting poplar and larch and birch in lines: compare Switzerland, a culture of clearings in an up-and-down wilderness. And then, of course, these Lombards cubed, baked and collocated some of the earth they dug up, to shape into shelters.

But how far was this Lombard environment a projection of Lombard minds, and how far was the peculiarly Lombard mind a response to the promptings of this specific environment? No telling. Bad question. Still, such form as this world had was the deposit of minds addressing a few ground rules of nature: earth, sun, water, gravity, and the talent of some organisms to live and grow by transpiring. This landscape was Mind itself and he, Briggs, was walking along in it. One should talk more with farmers . . .

To the right there was now a glimpse of the Ticino bending yet more south and conjoining with the Po. Two rivers. It was time to strike north. He turned off on a subsidiary path along a lesser cross-dyke bordered by bare young birches. He could see the hamlet he was making for half a mile ahead, a line of pale bistre-washed houses not that much different in colour from the faded yellow grass in some of the fields.

And it was high time to think about how to handle the meeting with Aldo Guardamagna. It might be awkward: Pasquale had said the man seemed wary. He must somehow justify his curiosity, but what did one say? That Leinberger was the relative of a friend, and causing anxiety? That, yes, one was a busybody, Signor, but it would be a kindness to indulge one? That Life was Question, and Question, indeed, Life? Well, if the man did not want to talk, he would not press. He would buy another hero of the resistance a drink and let it lie.

The path ran into the Piacenza road on the Pavia side of the village, and the Caffè Due Fiumi turned out to be no more than a hundred yards along on the right. It looked an ordinary country wine-house except that it was well set back from the road with a broad gravelly space in front. Two cars, two vans and three trucks with trailers were parked here, and a couple of men stood talking.

Inside it was dim, after the sun, but the place was half familiar. It was a much larger and rather more modern replica of Zanzi's – long zinc-covered bar to the left, a handful of customers eating or drinking at four-chaired tables to the right, a great black stove and a back-room beyond. Briggs asked after Guardamagna at the bar. He was outside with a driver but would be back. Briggs asked for a *bianco secco*.

After a couple of minutes there was the roar of an engine starting outside and a thickset man in a suit came in, repossessed himself of a glass standing on the zinc, and looked at Briggs.

'The gentleman who is interested in the past?'

'Yes. It is kind of you to meet me.'

'It is nothing. I am here often.' Hands were shaken; names were confirmed. He looked at Briggs's glass. 'You do not want to drink that in this weather. We will have a more suitable bottle and sit – no? And you will tell me what you want to know.'

Guardamagna spoke to the man behind the bar, took Briggs by the arm and led him past the stove to the empty back-room and one of two large tables, here covered with green baize.

They sat facing each other across the table. Guardamagna did not speak at once. In a practised and open but somehow inoffensive way he was sizing Briggs up. He himself was a physically powerful man in his thirties with a shrewd and fluid eye. He was not yet gross, but he was sanguine and the veins in his neck were marked. He was the townsman, hair cut carefully, sharply cut pale grey suit, a silvery Milanese striped tie. He might have been the owner of a small cinema or garage. He was almost as out-of-place in this rural pull-in as Briggs himself.

The wine turned out to be much like Zanzi's.

'That is a little better, no?' Guardamagna lit a cigarette. He was speaking a careful Italian. 'Well, Signor . . . Briggs? Briggs. Good. You are a friend of a friend of Giorgio Zanzi. A good little man, that, though with inconvenient politics. I know only that you are interested in the German engineer unit at the Collegio Praga. But what, more precisely, do you want to know?'

'I am interested', Briggs said flatly, 'in a Lieutenant Leinberger, who I think was one of those in command there.'

Guardamagna looked down at the green baize and smiled. He flicked his glass lightly with a finger nail, making it ping dully, and then stretched in his chair, as if in embarrassment.

'You are a friend of this Lieutenant Leinberger?' he asked.

'No. I have never met him.'

'Then – you will permit me to ask – why do you want to know of him?'

Briggs sighed. This was hopeless.

'It is difficult to explain', he said. 'I have heard something of him. I have met one or two people who know him. I became interested in him. Since I am in Pavia . . .' He trailed off.

Guardamagna looked at him with good-humoured disbelief.

'And, tell me, what is Lieutenant Leinberger doing nowadays?' he asked.

'He is an engineer still, and a member of the managing board of a textile company in which I am interested.'

Guardamagna pondered this. He opened his mouth in a soundless stylized 'Ah!' and smiled again. He had his bearing now on the kind of battle-ground for which Briggs was seeking a weapon. He knew where he was. Briggs was nettled.

'Naturally', he began, 'if you prefer not to discuss those times, I would not wish . . .'

'No, no.' Guardamagna had made his decision. 'I will happily tell you of my only meeting with this Lieutenant. I will do more.' He looked at his watch and smiled to himself. 'It is an hour before I need leave for Piacenza. One short meeting like that would be a poor thing to describe – so shall I not give you some particulars of what led to it? The tale of my earlier life, my childhood and early youth, is a simple one but will perhaps help you see why that one unimportant meeting had importance, for me. No?'

He laughed and filled their glasses.

19

'I was born', said Aldo Guardamagna, 'in a village beyond Voghera, fifty kilometres or more from here in the foothills of the Appennines. A very ordinary hill village, not twenty poor houses, a poor school-room and a small neglected church – no resident *parrocco* – all built on a ridge below a rock on which there were some slight remains of a castle. Not many remains: the castle had long been our quarry.'

'My father was a small tenant farmer, as were most of the men in that village. My mother was the daughter of a farmer, my father the son of a farmer. My father knew that his sons – I had two younger brothers – would be farmers too. But my mother . . . of course, they say Italian mothers wish their eldest sons to be priests, but my mother came from an anti-clerical village – not impious, you understand, but not friends to priests. In fact my mother thought at one time that I might be a postman. A good occupation: to bear words from one person to another, to travel with regularity from here to there and on again – that was something! I must work hard at school so that I would pass the examination. And indeed, since the age of nine or ten, writing and figuring have been easy for me, something to enjoy.'

'Have you ever lived in a village? Yes? Then you will know that villages are malign. Only a man bred in the town could like the thought of living in a village. The people are not specially bad by nature: it is the village, the living together as in a big loveless family. All know all: old errors are never forgotten. You are watched, always, and you watch, always. None of the virtues of a real family – villagers are not loyal to each other because they are rivals and also because they are cowards. They become cowards because they are at the mercy of landowners, who can take the land away, and of officials, who know rules. If you have something the others do not – a small orchard, an influential cousin, some paltry legacy from your wife's family – you are envied; if you do not, you are despised. But you have lived in a village and know all this . . .'

'I was six years old when I first remember visiting a town – Voghera, twenty kilometres away, where I was to see a physician. You know Voghera? It is a small town – perhaps three, four thousand hearths – and dim. But to me, then, it was . . .I would say it was Revelation! Two particular things I saw. First, there were many people in Voghera who did not know each other: they often walked past each other and ignored each other – knew nothing, nothing about each other. What amenity! I still believe this to be a condition of civility. Second, there were many fine trucks. Yes, of course I had often seen trucks before. Trucks came even to my village: to carry away crops, to bring goods. But I had never seen so many trucks, so fine, so varied. The colours, the wheels – four, six, ten – the special purposes, the deep rich coughs and snarls. They were so varied in Voghera. A banal experience – all children are enchanted by something of the sort, I know it – but I must tell you that for me the enchantment has lasted. There are moments of boredom, fallings-out even, sometimes an interest in another quarter, but I have loved the truck, and she has responded . . . but this is to anticipate, Signor Briggs, and we do not want that!'

'Now, in my village there was a smith, Andrea, who also worked on the primitive machines in that valley. Andrea could mend a plough or fit a wrought axle on a cart and he knew a little, a very little, of petrol engines too. I attached myself to him. He was an isolated man, not quite of the farmers' world, and he did not mind my spending my time at his forge. And I – it is absurd! – I believed that by learning his skills I would make my-self a mechanic. As long as I was out of school and not required in the fields I was at the forge. My father said I was wasting my time and would be better watching the goats. My mother was more indulgent: she respected a passion, I think. Yet when I was fourteen, it was to the fields I went. It occurred to no one – not as a real question even to me – that I should not.'

'My God! How I hated the fields! Our village is some way above the land we worked in the flat of the valley. At dawn one went down the hill with the tools, the ox-cart, the cattle from the byre, and the neighbours. All day one harrassed a soil too feeble even to stick to boots in wet weather. At dusk one dragged oneself and the tools and the cattle and the ox-cart, perhaps with a burden of some poor produce, back up the hill. One stowed the tools and the cart and stalled the cattle, and often fetched the goats from up the hill too. Eventually one ate and then one slept till an hour before the next dawn. Some days one might speak no more than a hundred words, not counting to animals. But for one blessed event I should have been trapped for the rest of my life.'

'The war! For village boys military service is the key to the world, though not all use it: my brothers are farmers yet. I knew that armies have trucks, and trucks need to be maintained, and that some soldiers must do this. In the army I might learn enough to become a mechanic afterwards. So when the time came to reg-ister – it was the winter of 1941–2 – what I wrote for "Occupa-tion" was "Mechanic (Trucks)". Effrontery! But I half-believed that what I had learned in the forge had equipped me. I could hammer and I could file, I could judge temper and I could braze. I had used calipers and raddle to achieve a fit. Andrea had ex-plained to me such things as how a carburettor mixes petrol with air. My father was angry: he believed I would be punished for the lie. But I persisted.'

'So in 1942 down from the valley I went, into the army and some months of general training in Modena. There was much that was new and fine then – city girls and shop windows to look at, of course, but also the division of days into time of work and time free, the order and companionship of the barrack-room, even the strange pleasure of having drilled well. This was a clean world. When the day came for me to go to the mechanics' course in Genoa I think I had forgotten my goal enough to be a little sorry, as well as afraid.'

'A day of reckoning, you may well suppose. Well, Signor Briggs, enjoy the irony of what I now tell you. It is true that I was unmasked: the instructors saw my ignorance within days, and I survived at first mainly because I was willing and robust. There are many tasks in workshops: floors must be cleaned, heavy objects shifted, stubborn nuts neatly split with chisel and hammer. But what soon emerged was that there is a place in war for a man who knows something of the simple forge in a quite practical way. There were trained men there who knew how to identify faults, order replacement parts, and then fit and adjust them. But the primitive skills of the smith, the feel for temper, the patient filing-and-trying and filing-and-trying so that you do not file too much, the experience of working metal without resources – I had these as others did not; and when you cannot order replacement parts they are needed. I was all right. Carburettors! One can learn about them. I learned fast and passed the tests.'

'So, in July, not long before Benito was arrested by the King, I was one of a group sent off to join a transport company in the south. We worked at repair points rather behind the front and at the end of September we were at a camp on the outskirts of Naples. The Allies were not far away.'

'You have heard of the Four Days? Yes, the Naples uprising. We found ourselves in the middle of it and it was a turning-point for me as for others. To tell the truth, I had not thought much about sides, or about rights and wrongs. Benito had been Italy since I was born. For me the war had been good; and in armies one need not think about the reasons for war. But Benito's arrest, the armistice, Benito's escape – these things were unsettling, you understand. And now here, during the Four Days, here were the Germans starting to kill the Italians – Neapolitans whose language I scarcely understood, you will say, but still Italians. There had been a change. Remember too: this was my first sight of real killing. Many men were deserting, if that is the word for it. The Germans had already disarmed most of the Italian fighting units: very soon they would come to us in the support. With a friend I too left and set out for the north.'

'It was a strange time and a strange journey – it stays in my mind like a dream. I saw more places in that five weeks than I had seen in my life. A pity there is no time for that story . . . but the country we passed through – sometimes walking, sometimes begging rides, once rashly taking a train – was full of men like ourselves, and we talked. Some wanted no more fighting, others wanted to fight the Germans. Myself, I had no great stomach for fighting, but there was a problem about where I should go. I did not want to return to the village: it might be dangerous for my family, I told myself, and besides it would be a retreat back to the fields. My friend, Adriano, who came from Pavia, was more angry about the Germans – he was altogether a man of greater spirit than I, I must say – and had decided to join the resistance there. I went along too. It was, to speak frankly, the easiest thing for me to do.'

'By the time we reached Pavia it was well into November, and our arrival was well-timed: Brigades were forming. Adriano made contact through his family – his father was a notary – and we were in. He went to a fighting unit but I, yes, I went to the trucks. It was the village blacksmith's skill again, you see – the ability to work with little else but hammer and fire. This was needed: to avoid betrayal we moved base often – farm buildings, a bakery, on one occasion a cemetery.'

'A revolutionary movement – that is what we were – has need for specific kinds of vehicle. Principally one uses modest commercial vehicles, closed not open, to move men – the whole-saler's van or telephone repair truck, the more ordinary the better. We had a shifting set of these: they were relatively easy to procure and also to maintain. But very occasionally one may need a military vehicle, the military vehicle of the enemy. They are difficult to procure and dangerous to keep but, as the Allies approached and the day of final uprising appeared to come closer, it was decided we must have some. How else to move men – as for at least one planned purpose would be necessary – through a war-zone in enemy hands? So one night a German convoy was attacked between Piacenza and Cremona, fifteen kilometres from here. It was a bloody engagement, bloodier than had been expected. We acquired two trucks of a kind – just two. If you wish to understand my story you must know that my friend Adriano was one of those killed in the attack.'

'Well, the two trucks were taken to a hiding-place of their own: it was in part of a fertiliser warehouse near Casalpuster-lengo, behind a wall of sacks, and I slept there alone with them in this secret cavity for five weeks. It was too dangerous to move them before the moment. I was to put them straight, since they had been shot up, and prepare them thoroughly, since they must run without fail when the time came. It was the most important task I had yet been given.'

'Kfz 234/3! These trucks – it will mean nothing to you but it came to mean everything to me – these trucks were of a type called Kraftfahrzeug 234/3. They had fine diesel engines made by the Czech factory Tatra. I had had almost no experience of diesel engines. I wish to pass over this part of my story quickly, Signor Briggs, and not only because I must soon leave for Piacenza . . . the fact is that, within ten days, I had tinkered with them to a point where neither of them would run any more. They would not go. I did not know how to make them go. I did not know what I had done to stop them going. The trouble – this much I was clear about – lay in the electrical system. There I was lost.'

'Even now, to tell you of this makes my skin creep with horror and shame. Figure to yourself – it was not just that I was failing the Brigade. Adriano, my sponsor as well as my friend, had died painfully to win those trucks: with my coarse fingers I had promptly disabled them. And the future mechanic? What the clever northerners had made so well, this Italian peasant could not understand, only destroy. I was a clown playing with clockwork. Night after night I lay sleepless in my blankets next to the trucks, unable to cease revolving how to work it out; then I would get up to try something and make the tangle worse and return to my blankets weeping. By now I had been on my own in the fertiliser warehouse for three weeks or more. In truth, I became a little mad.'

'In particular I began to develop a vision, an image of the manual, a maintenance handbook with wiring diagrams, which would solve my problems. The book of knowledge. It was the sort of image you can feel with the fingers, which you can smell. It was this high, this wide, this thick: dark-blue shiny cover, thick glossy paper. In one part of my mind I must have realized that it would be written in German, but my image was somehow as accessible as a children's book in Italian. With this good book I would be on a footing with the northerners and the trucks would run like Swiss watches again.'

'One evening what was left of my good sense snapped. Where were there such manuals? German maintenance centres. The big depot at Lodi? Impossible and anyway too far. The small one in Pavia? There was no alternative. I must go to the Collegio Praga and filch the book of the Kfz 234/3. I consulted no one but took a chisel as a prise and went.'

20

'You know the Collegio Praga. The front courtyard was used by the transport unit, the rear courtyard was a transit hospital and had its own entrance at the back. There was no possibility of my entering the front court directly: except for letting vehicles in and out, the main gate was closed by great wooden doors, and to enter on foot one had to go through a small door to the right through the porters' lodge which served as a guard-room. But since the Collegio is normally one whole it seemed to me there must be a way from the rear court to the front court. And in the hospital we had a friend, a college servant now acting as a civilian orderly, through whom we had previously got drugs.'

'I will be brief, since in a few minutes I must leave and we still have not met your German colleague . . . I found Giuseppe the orderly before he went on night duty, I questioned him about the arrangement of the building, I insisted he smuggle me into the hospital that night. For a time it was as if my having made no proper plan, having given no thought to complexity and detail, made all simple. Soon after midnight I was in the rear court with Giuseppe. The archway giving on to the main court, the cortile, was sealed with concrete blocks, but Giuseppe showed me a line through the Rector's lodging at one end of the cross-wing – in through the kitchen, out through the *salone* – and I was soon there.'

'So there I was, I say. The cortile is cobbled and paved, with a fountain basin at the centre, and it is surrounded by arcades on two storeys, with doors on the inner sides of the arcades. On the ground floor there are perhaps ten, perhaps twelve doors: the rooms are large down there. On the upper storeys are very many more, for these had been the students' rooms. All was quiet and empty, but for five or six parked vehicles, and with these and the columns of the arcades there was good cover. I stood there surrounded by a hundred doors, and I woke up.'

'Now imagine to yourself: for weeks I had been living alone with machines and emotions. I had sleep-walked here and now I had woken up. It was a bad moment, that – suddenly to see things as they are. What had I had in mind – a door labelled "Books of knowledge"? I had no idea what to do, I was terrified to find myself here. But I realized that, having come, I must make an attempt to do something.'

'I got out my prise and set to work on one of the ground-floor doors. It gave after a couple of minutes and I found a fuel store: I decided not to start a fire in it – not yet, at least. I set to on another; after several minutes it had not moved and I left it. I began on a third and then something, someone hit my head from behind. Or so I suppose: I do not remember the blow.'

'When I came to I was on a chair in an office. It was very hot. There were three others there. A heavy-built sergeant of a kind to deliver such a blow was standing over me. Now and then he shook me. Behind a desk were two German officers, both lieutenants, one sitting, the other on his feet. They were discussing something quite stiffly with each other, almost arguing, and though they were aware that I was no longer unconscious they continued to do so for some minutes. But then the one who was standing left abruptly, and without looking at me.'

'By this time I was shitting myself. I am not speaking in figures: I was shitting myself and was ashamed. I knew the chances. I might be shot at once or I might be passed to Italians for questioning – one knew what that meant – and shot afterwards. If I was very lucky indeed I might end up in a forced labour company, but for this I must persuade them I was a common thief – a thin hope.'

'We have three minutes before I must leave . . . the lieutenant at the desk – yes, I was later told it was Leinberger, your friend – began to question me, in slow but good enough Italian. It was a strange interrogation. I tried to play the part of the petty thief in search of petty pickings. He ignored that. He made a show of interest in my needs. What spare parts was I in need of? Was it not difficult to procure replacement magnetos? Did I not find there was a tendency for the new artificial rubber tyres to crack, particularly in the walls? They themselves had problems with them. And so on. His manner was of one making conversation with an opposite number in another firm. It was strange, but I found myself beginning to see him as that. After twenty minutes of it I was unable to keep up my role as petty thief. I went dumb. The big sergeant shook me a little but I was quite unable to speak.'

'When he got no response from me the lieutenant picked up a small piece of paper from his desk and looked at it. I knew what it was. It was a note I had had in my pocket of some component numbers on the Tatra engines: there were different versions or marks, you understand, and I had wanted to be sure of not mistaking marks. He must recognize the numbers: he did recognize them. He read them aloud – I could tell the sergeant knew them too, as he snorted and shook me again – and then asked me what these numbers could be. When I was still silent he said, simply: "Kfz 234/3, Mark 2 engine. Yes, we are missing a couple of those."'

'Well, that was it – no? The sergeant and the lieutenant started speaking to each other in German. Again I sensed an argument, but less stiff, more familiar than with the other officer. The sergeant seemed to be urging against some course. Finally the lieutenant spoke to me again in Italian, no longer playing the sympathetic colleague but with a sort of suppressed, violent irritation.'

'"We cannot supply you with the components you seek. You are going to be thrown out of here by the sergeant. Our security seems at fault: it will be looked to. We may owe you a very little for alerting us to this, but not much, so do not come back. If you come back, I shall hand you over to men who are not engineers. They have skills and tools we really prefer not to have here. Do not come back."'

'The sergeant kicked me out of the front entrance into the cold air and I was sane again. The trucks . . . they were set straight by another man, a Milanese I asked for who knew diesels. They were never used for the plan – the Germans left suddenly two weeks later without fighting.'

'I cannot feel great warmth towards your Lieutenant: he treated me with a certain disdain as well as mercy. But I acknowledge a debt, and I have no knife for anyone to put in him. No knife at all.'

21

By the time Briggs was once more on the dyke leading back to Pavia, the light was fading. It had become a different country from before. Fog was the autumn crop here now; mist was ripening low on the ground. The dyke was a causeway above great enclosures of a dense milky stuff. The water in the ditches was only heard and smelt.

But also he was seeing differently. In this twilight he saw more dimly but more widely than two or three hours before. Then he had seen sharp and narrow: now the field of vision was becoming soft, but broad and even. Rods and cones — they are differently distributed in the eye: the widespread dim-light rods were beginning to take over from the focussed bright-light cones. Things out on the edge, in the corner of the eye, were present as they had not been then.

For instance: that movement of two human figures coming off the side-dyke from the village of the Caffè Due Fiumi behind him – he would not have noticed it earlier. If there had been two such figures over there then, he might not even have seen them, in the full sense.

Briggs turned back to the dull puce glow, west, behind the towers and monstrous dome of Pavia and walked on. He felt a little cold. It might be a good idea to cover this path and get to the canal before the light quite went: the last part by the riverside was rough. He would trot a little.

It turned out to be pleasant running along above the mist fields. Among other things, it more or less excluded thought. He felt the last wisps of hangover dispersing and the first hints of a great hunger for dinner. It felt so good that he kept up the trot for a mile or so, slowing only when he was coming near the end of the dyke, towards the rougher section by the waste land and gravel pits. Before going down to this he looked back for a last time at the strange country where he had been.

The two figures were still there. He would not have made them out if they had not been moving, but they were, bobbing up and down as if in a trot of their own. Odd. They were closer than before.

He walked down off the dyke towards the scrubby waste and presently passed one of the tracks that ran down to the pits. The old man with the plaster casts, further along, would be off home by now, but no doubt the whiteness of the casts would make them visible when one came to them.

A thought: suppose one had wanted to elude and also inspect the two people behind – an elegant ruse would have been to lurk in the scrub by the old man's track. Then, if one's face showed up in the dusk, it would be just one more angel's head on a branch. But somehow it felt the sort of trick that tells more cleverly than it lives. Besides, there really was no reason to interest himself in them. When he came to the plaster casts, which did indeed show up, he walked on without pausing and a few hundred yards brought him to buildings and the lock.

The footbridge over the canal was raised again. A single barge, this time on a voyage north from the middle ages to the nineteenth century, was only just starting to enter the lock from the Ticino. It would be three or four minutes yet, though a couple of people were already waiting on the other side: the next bridge was nearly half a mile away. Briggs leaned against the rail to wait. The quay was weakly lit by lamps on the walls of buildings on both sides.

Much sooner than he expected – it seemed almost at once – two men came in from his path at a run, slowed, and walked over to stand by the lock ten yards away, their backs to Briggs. They were large, tidily overcoated men, but he got no very clear impression of them. One of them rather reminded him of the watcher at Pappalardo's foundry; but he was not sure. He wondered whether to manoeuvre for a better look: he could ask them the time. But he decided he would instead hold his position by the bridge. The men were discussing something with what looked like some urgency.

Slowly the barge passed through. While the lock-keeper was still finishing the stately process of winding the footbridge down, Briggs ran and jumped across at the first opportunity, snatching priority over half-a-dozen indignant people now accumulated on the other side, and then ran along the quay to the street he had come by.

At the corner he glanced back. The overcoats were only just coming off the bridge, but fast, and no longer concealing pursuit. It looked very much as if the game had changed. His own style of departure must have shown he was aware of being followed.

Briggs ran along the nobbly little cobbles of the empty street. He was moving towards the University. He knew the layout better there and its courts and arcades and corridors might offer opportunities. But first, as soon as he could, he turned down an alley right and then he turned left, to take a line parallel with the first street and just possibly get loose. There were a few people about here and one or two looked at him curiously as he ran by.

He glanced backwards again. One overcoat was still with him, but a good hundred yards behind. The other would be covering the first line. Two more blocks and he was passing what he recognized as the Chemistry Department – quite close to Pasquale's, in fact, but he certainly had no business taking these people there.

He ran another block, took a street to the right and one to the left again, bore left again across a square with trees in the middle, then through a heavily baroque archway and a court with a lot of bicycles and vespas, into an unexpectedly floodlit small *piazza*.

He was near trapping himself in a pincer. The only other line out of this *piazzetta* was southwards, and this would probably be where the second overcoat would be coming from.

Briggs's self-esteem was insisting that he make one last attempt at being clever. And he was out of breath. The building with the floodlights fixed on it was a four-storey structure with a rusticated basement, elaborate *pian terreno* windows flanked by colonnettes, and a short flight of steps leading to one big locked-looking door. He ran over to one end of this building, used the rough keystone over a basement window for footing, stretched for a handhold on the wrought-iron grill of the window above and hauled himself up on to the window ledge. He crooked an arm through the grill and snuggled up to the *colonnette* to one side. Just beyond the *colonnette* was one of the floodlights.

He was no more than eight feet above the ground and within the line of sight of almost anyone in the *piazzetta*. But several things, he reckoned, should be working for him. First, they would expect him at ground level. Second, in the lee of the *colonnette* he was in the deep shadow made by the floodlight behind it. Third, the abrupt brightness of the *piazzetta* was generally disorganising of perception. Rods recoiled, cones were caught unawares: the sensorium was thoroughly put out. He had felt it himself.

It would be interesting to see what happened. He waited.

It was much like a stage-set down below. The floor of the *piazzetta* was paved in two contrasting shades of grey, patterned in a cross with a circle in the middle. Opposite, a Corinthian portico dignified what looked like a sort of grand lecture hall. Something was going on in there: probably that was why it was floodlit. The wings of the stage were filled by two yellow-washed structures, dark-windowed and doorless, and these abutted on Briggs's building with the lights. The wing on the left had a dribbling wall-fountain in the form of a large scallop but the other, prompt-side, did not. Entrance to the *piazzetta* was on each side of the porticoed building, and nowhere else.

The overcoats arrived on cue – first a green loden on the left, then a double-breasted brown on the right. Briggs waited for dialogue.

Instead there was a mime show. Green put up a hand like a policeman halting traffic. Both stood for a moment at some distance from each other, as if to seal the two entrances, and looked briefly around with their eyes screwed up. Green stroked his ribs three times with his hands, quickly. Brown nodded, pointed first at himself, then at the door in Briggs's building. He ran up to the door, tried it, and went back to his station, making a circle with thumb and index finger as he did so. Green now put out a hand, flat, wagged it up and down, and then pointed to the portico. Brown nodded and pointed at Green with one finger. All this took less time than it does to tell.

At that moment two middle-aged professorial people came out of the door in the centre of the portico. One was shaking his head, the other limply flapping a hand; both were tittering. They left the *piazzetta* without taking notice of the overcoated men.

Green went over into the portico, glancing right and left behind its columns, and went in through the door, closing it after him. Brown stood alert, his back to Briggs, covering the three points that interested him. But Green soon came out of the door again, shielding his eyes from the floodlights with a hand, and walked over to him.

'Not there', he said in German. 'It is some kind of sermon, inside. But he is not there.'

'This way, then', said Brown. They left by the way Briggs had come.

Briggs stayed on his ledge for a moment and pondered. Green had certainly spoken with the voice of Fritz, Brown nearly certainly with the voice of Bernhard. He was not entirely surprised, but how had they got on to him? He felt a little like Guardamagna waking up to reality in the courtyard of the Collegio Praga. There had been something formidable about that practised silent performance. He had dodged them twice now but only by luck. He was getting cramped up on the ledge . . .

Green, or Fritz, quickly and quietly passed through the *piazzetta* on a bicycle much too small for him, entering from the left – where he would have stolen it – and leaving by the right . . .

The best place to wait till they had cleared out of the area would be the one they had eliminated, the auditorium opposite. Briggs swung himself down from the window ledge, ran across to the portico and went in.

There was a lobby inside. Light and a plummy voice came from through a doorway ahead, up a dozen steps. He brushed himself with a sleeve and looked around. A printed notice was tacked to a board on a stand. Professor Pecorari of the University of Padua was well into a special lecture for the Faculty of Letters: 'Jacopo d'Abbiategrasso (1402(?)-1457) – A Man of Science and the Science of Man'. That would be nice. He went up the steps and found himself at the back of a neo-classical theatre, not very large nor very full. The thirty or forty auditors were mostly down at the front of the half-circle of steeply graded seats. Briggs discreetly took a place up in the empty back row.

The lecturer down below was a plump bald man with thick-rimmed spectacles and a scrubby moustache. He seemed to go straight back from his eyebrows: he had so little forehead, it was disturbing, but what there was was importantly puckered. He accompanied the cadences of his oration with one rhythmic hand, as if conducting a chamber orchestra.

'. . .and so it is with a pang', he was saying, 'it is with a certain lively sense of loss, that we contemplate today such a figure as this son of Abbiategrasso, a human being who, in the bleak and fragmented wretchedness of our own cultural plight, may appear to us, yes, polyhedral, but who yet was not, *not* polyhedral, in so far as, while it was out of those – as we would now call them – those *different* "branches" of science and those *different* "branches" of art that he brought forth the generous and glistening fruits which it is here my purpose to sketch or (better) adumbrate, yet was he one single, one singular man, as too, for those great men of those great days, were one single, singular activity – such was their good fortune! Both science and art: singular the activity in that all human knowledge has, surely, its roots deep, deep in one – I say "*one*" – humanity, in "human-ism" indeed, if only we will understand that noble word in its higher sense, and then singular the activity too in that, just as science was one thing together with art, so too was art one thing together with . . .'

Briggs switched off. He was hungry. He thought about Fritz and Bernhard, and about whether he had learned anything worth knowing about Kaspar Leinberger. Then he thought about Mechtild, and then about what he should do. Probably nothing at all. Tomorrow he would polish off the *Archivio*, and then he would decide.

It seemed from the lecturer's tempo that he was moving into his coda. An old man with a stick and a hobble chose the moment to get up and leave noisily from the middle of the front row. A younger man a few rows in front of Briggs was thrashing about in impatience, twisting on the bench as if in the first stages of convulsions. He caught sight of Briggs behind him, and Briggs saw that it was Piermario Bragagnolo. They raised eyebrows at each other and Piermario drew a finger quickly across his throat. But the lecturer was now really finishing – with a slowly spoken period so vacuously ornate Briggs cringed – and it was over.

Applause was brief. Briggs stood at the back waiting for Piermario, but Piermario beckoned urgently and he went forward.

'William! What in heaven's name did you come to this disaster for? For me it is duty. But it is good you are here. You can meet Don Ivo Pavan – you remember, the Rector of the Collegio Praga. He is here: the very tall priest trying to get away over there. Come!'

He was off, and Briggs unenthusiastically followed. Don Ivo, a gaunt man with a mane of white hair, looked in no mood for conversation but had good manners. He was delighted to meet a foreign friend of Piermario's; had long had a strong but (he must say) under-realised curiosity about the late-medieval textile trades; hoped Briggs was finding his visit to Pavia productive.

'Signor Briggs was asking only yesterday about the Collegio Praga', said Piermario, more directly than Briggs quite liked, 'though in a special connection. He has an interest in a German business-man who, it seems, spent time there during the war.'

For the first time Don Ivo's attention became more than just courtesy. He looked at Briggs sharply.

'A German business-man? I ask myself who that would be.'

'He is called Kaspar Leinberger', Briggs said clumsily. 'I have never met him, in fact, though I have met his wife, but I recently had a certain professional interest in a textile company for which he supervises the machinery.'

Don Ivo ran a hand over his white hair, a somehow secular gesture, and studied Briggs coolly.

'*Bene, bene*, Signor Briggs', he said slowly, leaning on the trochees. Then he turned crisply to Piermario. 'Signor Briggs has not seen us at our best here, Piermario. I allow myself to insist on his coming with me now to the Collegio Praga. We shall drink a small glass to cleanse our palates and I will persuade him Italian scholarship is not quite what our poor Paduan colleague may have conveyed to him. This will not disrupt any arrangements you may have made for the evening.'

It was an assertion, not a question, and Piermario was rather promptly submissive, Briggs thought.

'Excellent!', Piermario said. 'We are not dining until eight. At the Ristorante Foscolo', he reminded Briggs, bowed to Don Ivo and left.

'The Collegio is no more than two minutes away.' Don Ivo took Briggs firmly by the arm and steered him out of the lecture theatre.

22

Once away from the lights of the *piazzetta*, the streets were thickening again with fog.

'All Saints', St Martin's, St Catherine's, St Andrew's', said Don Ivo as he walked briskly along. 'Festivals of the mists before the snows. A riddle: *Pü ch'agh n'è, manch as ved* – the more there is of it, the less you see. Answer: mist. A false paradox; just a verbal trick – you are induced to *supply* the error in order to complete a symmetry. I would not blame the child who failed to solve such a riddle: on the contrary . . . but the real paradox – what do you think? – is that popular wisdom should be so shaped by its hunger for verbal trickery and pattern, by a sort of instinct to evade experience through art. Nothing, nothing as sophistical as the folk. That is why so much of true education must be a struggle to de-sophisticate and de-aestheticize, indeed to spoil children's games. And that, Signor Briggs, is one reason why a person like Pecorari of Padua – I am sorry you were exposed to him, you should have been warned – is so altogether disreputable. His mind is regressive. His place is not in a university but in a wine-house, offering peasants or labourers occasional moments of retreat from their hard reality. Language is the opium of the masses . . . this way! We go through the porter's lodge here – good evening, Giuseppe! – into our great court. Yes, we are quite proud of it – designed by a disowned but enterprising pupil of the great Pozzo. And Pozzo, when he saw what had been done with those triglyphs there, is said to have fallen over in a syncope. Heh, heh! It is here, by the way, that Kaspar Leinberger tended his motors. My lodging is on the far side. Come! Signor Briggs, come!'

Don Ivo's rooms were still eighteenth-century apartments, softly lit, crimson and gilt faded and rubbed to the point of comfort. In his soutane he himself took on the colour of an eighteenth-century figure here, some enlightened *abbé* with a past in diplomacy, perhaps, and now with a microscope as well as a breviary in his study. His tall man's stoop and old man's careful step became a type of courtliness. He had fetched a decanter and two parcel-gilt glasses from a wall-cupboard, and passed Briggs some sort of bitter herby cordial. He carried his own to a chair and sat and looked at Briggs with pale grey eyes, down one more Lombard beak.

'*Bene, bene*, Signor Briggs. And now, pray, tell me how things stand with Lieutenant Leinberger. I have not heard of him since April of 1945.'

Briggs had little enough to tell. He did not mention Leinberger's visits to the other Pavia of the metal-workers: it was uncalled for. The rest was soon told.

Don Ivo's eyes were moving about the red-brown and cream marble flags of the floor, as if playing some mental board-game on them.

'And you, Signor Briggs', he said, 'when you have never met him, why are you interested in the man?'

'It is no more than casual . . .'

'Kaspar Leinberger would be older than his wife?'

'Yes. I do not think . . .'

'No, you are not my charge. And in any case, I would hazard, you are interested in Germany? In the German? Yes? Yes, the German *is* interesting. I find that too. I shall tell you something of this one German, if you will. Hearing his name from you just now brought back that time in a way that I find curiously disturbing, and I should discover why. Though he was only one German.'

He gave up his board-game on the flags and sat back, looking past Briggs.

'There were others. They came suddenly in September of 1943 and left even more suddenly in April of 1945 towards the end of winter, before the beginning of summer. We have just three seasons in Lombardy: no spring. There were two young Lieutenants and about thirty men. Lieutenant Leinberger was the technician, the engineer officer. The other, a Lieutenant Schulte, was in charge of administration and answered to the big base at Lodi. His given name? Florian, as I remember, a Catholic name.'

'But Kaspar Leinberger was of the Lutheran culture, not a practising Lutheran but yet of Lutheran formation. The Lutheran religion – I hope I do not give offence? – can be harsh for those who lose faith. It can leave them quite . . . quite naked in important respects. The other man, Lieutenant Schulte was also a man without faith but of a Catholic formation. He still kept remnants of its armour, a nostalgia for its morale, perhaps, some sense of spiritual regime. Lieutenant Leinberger was naked, and so one felt for him.'

'I know, I know! For two hundred years stripped Lutherans have been forging their own new armour. Plato the anvil, Kant the hammer; and the outcome a metaphysics with more answers than I would ever expect to have questions. But this is available only to minds of a certain temper and Kaspar Leinberger's mind was not such. He was an engineer: physics was his New Testament, mathematics his Old – so he claimed. But you and I know that the practical man must feed larger feeling too and without guidance may drift towards dubious tables.'

'I should say clearly that he was no National Socialist, neither formally nor by any sympathy. In this respect he was perhaps purer than Lieutenant Schulte – also no National Socialist, but yet a man with a talent for accommodation. But remember! Both these men were convenient men. Outside the gate of the Collegio there were quite different kinds of man, not by any means all German: casual murderers, collected torturers, wild-fowlers in the deluge.'

'Come! I will show you something . . . Kaspar Leinberger lacked armour against the times but he had one spiritual exercise. Indeed both our Lieutenants were accomplished amateurs of an art – Lieutenant Schulte was a musician, but Lieutenant Leinberger was a painter. This is his – a view along the river before the bombing: the Ticino, the Borgo, the city, the covered bridge. Strange, no? In one aspect it is an engineer's diagram, a Euclidean reduction of complex things to some scheme of a reality beneath. In another aspect it is a child-like exclamation of raw colours. Prudent with lines: vehement, exasperated, I would almost say blustering, with hues. And we see the two aspects clearly because these two artists are clearly not on intimate terms with each other. And, then, do we not see this even rather *too* clearly? Perhaps they are knowingly enacting, personating conflict? Kaspar gave me this picture, I think, as a declaration '

'I should explain my own position a little. I had stayed on here in this Collegio, a kind of caretaker, while the young men were away at the war. Simply because I was here, I began to act as chaplain to the hospital installed in the second court, where there were at first Italian, later Italian and German, finally almost only German soldiers. It was a small affair, hardly more than a casualty station, a staging-point for men often on their way to larger hospitals or occasionally the Campo Santo beyond the canal. But I was the pastoral priest as I have rarely been in my life, and it was in this guise – the ministering priest rather than the academic person in orders – that I first appeared to the Germans.'

'To Lieutenant Schulte I was one more *Pfaffe* and an Italian one at that: our relation was reciprocally sceptical. To Lieutenant Leinberger I was more interesting, almost an exotic, an adept in some unpenetrated ancient lore or mystery. He had expectations and came to me for conversation. He was working at his Italian: I have some German.'

'Yes, the peculiar perils of language again! After the first meetings we usually conversed in two tongues, he speaking mainly in German, I in Italian. Both of us understood the other's tongue more easily than we spoke it. It seemed natural to do this. But where did it lead? Each spoke with the real voice of the mind, yes, but at some point contact was thwarted. Concept never quite kissed concept, not on the lips. And the consequence went further. I spoke in Italian, a softened Latin – the language of Cicero and Augustine, one of the most precisely diversified vehicles the human mind has evolved. He spoke in German, a quite recently regularized and elaborated Gothic – the tongue of warriors and hunters and other forest-dwellers communicating about . . .well, woodland matters. From our tongues we took roles – you see? – his an improving youth, mine a type not of maturity but of post-maturity.'

'You understand? I found I had become his casuist.'

Don Ivo got up and filled Briggs's glass and then stood and looked at him, still holding the decanter.

'You know what casuistry is, Signor Briggs? No call for casuists in the church of Enrico VIII? Good, good! It is no more than the analysis of complex cases of conscience, the resolution of compounded and apparently conflicting obligations. Such conflicts were of those times: we discussed them. I will not recount the detail of those discussions, though there was nothing formal about my status. But it is proper enough to alert an Anglo-Lutheran – forgive me! – to two characteristics of the casuistic process.'

He half-filled his own glass and sat down.

'Special cases: general principles', he said. 'One plots a position and proposes a course from bearings on fixed points in ethical doctrine and in natural law. But, you see, Kaspar was not of my Church. My fixed points were not his fixed points, not quite. And so, for his benefit – so I thought – I brought out older charts. That first winter we sat in this room, I in this chair and he in yours, and I introduced him to Cicero's *Offices* and such, but also to special texts like the forty-eighth book of the *Pandects*, in which Justinian deals with duty to the state. To you it may seem bizarre. Yet it was the wisdom of ancient books he craved, and these were wise books from which my own law had learned.'

'But, yes, I will admit to you that I am uneasy about this episode. Not because I was laying out heterodox positions – that is legitimate in the process of enquiry – but because there was an element of playfulness in what I was doing. It was rather amusing, really, to play at St Ambrose educating the pagan. I do not know if it led him to erroneous courses, but I do think I have basis to reproach myself.'

'And just this leads me to the second characteristic of casuistic method. It lays weight on motive, on the actor's intention. Yes, famously slippery ground, all too easily an emergency exit from principle. But half the casuist's art is to avoid just this snare. I asked myself more than once how things went awry here. Partly, I have no doubt, it was my lack of real pastoral experience: a more practised priest would have recognized dangers in better time. More grounds for self-reproach, though not quite as severe. But partly it was a false resonance between casuistic attention to motive and some sub-philosophy of the north about which I knew nothing – some Germanic myth of the strong man justified by persistence in his course, the hero who gains meaning from even self-destructive striving. A sort of stoic nihilism. Lieutenant Leinberger had not met these ideas at their source, whatever that is. He was not a philosopher. He had met them in dilution – in the feuilleton and in the mouths of characters in stories: such half-thinking is a problem of our time . . .'

'But we will not speak of that. Instead we might try, not to think – Pecorari of Padua really has unmanned thought for the day – but to feel our way a little into the generic plight? We are an engineer. To make or mend an engine can seem first a neutral matter, technical not moral. No moral dimension in metallurgy.

But of course Kaspar had long moved beyond this. Engines function. A bomb is instrument to an end with a moral dimension. To make or mend it is to participate as an enabling agent towards that end. But one is not mending bombs; one mends trucks – placid growlers carrying food and clothing to people who need them. Yet sometimes these do even carry bombs too. Enlarge the canvas a little. Because one reads feuilletons and stories, one is a man of lax allegorising habit – why do you start, Signor Briggs? – and so trucks and roads can be, say, the blood and arteries of war. Or interpret the grim symmetry of the Collegio Praga here: in this court trucks, in the next court broken bodies, these sometimes beyond mending.'

'And so the questions multiply and ravel. Is the state's cause good? What is the standing of an individual's view on this? What *is* "the state"? Adolfo? If my view differs, what do I do? More particularly, what do I not do? And what, then, of obligations to friends or kin? The questions become peremptory, banal only because epidemic – so very many good men had been working their way through this agony – and singly they were not intractable. But in complex they made up a tangle not always easy to unsnarl into one clear line of decision. Small wonder that so many lacked confidence to arrive at a singular conclusion firm enough to act from! Understandable that some – not Kaspar Leinberger, to his credit – should retreat into a technique and lock the door. Or take a stand on sworn loyalty – the plinth on which Lieutenant Schulte thought to keep his feet clean, and dry. Or generalise local bestialities into some universal winding-up of things, the full point of some irresistible cosmic process. It was to this particular evasion Kaspar was inclining when his crisis came.'

23

'That critical day was an unusually limpid Sunday between July and August of 1944. Lieutenant Schulte had been playing the organ, quite well, in our chapel here: the sublimely armoured Bach. Lieutenant Leinberger had been painting one of his strange pictures from the top floor of the Collegio – as I remember, a prospect of the city and its towers. I was in my rooms, reading – Lucretius, I think: he suited the times. But we were cultivated people at the Collegio Praga in those days, Signor Briggs!'

'In the early evening, as was usual, came the motor-cycle with dispatches from headquarters at Lodi. After a time I began to hear shouting in the main court, angry shouting, uncontrolled shouting. When it continued and when I thought to recognize the voices as those of the two Lieutenants I went into the court. It was truly a quarrel. Lieutenant Schulte was leaning against a column with his arms folded. Kaspar stood facing him, shaking himself with fury. His canvas and satchel were set on the ground, against the next column behind him.'

'When I appeared they ceased their bawling. The one, Schulte, kept his position and looked away. The other muttered some Germanic ejaculation, and then violently tore open the first of several envelopes he held in his hand.'

'I have never seen anything like what followed. Shock following on anger – perhaps it involves some freakish reversal of the system? Once Kaspar had read a line or two of the paper from within that envelope it was as if he had been struck by some spell. Or indeed as if I had myself: for a moment I thought it was my perception that was charmed, rather than his behaviour. In an instant his movements, after being so emphatic and so sharp, had become extraordinarily, preternaturally slow. With his eyes on the paper he stepped slowly, slowly backwards, perhaps three, perhaps four interminable steps to the column behind him, and then moved a hand inch-by-inch towards it, like a child reaching for its mother. Then Lieutenant Schulte tripped forward and asked what was amiss, calling him by his name: Kaspar.'

'He did not reply. But after, I suppose, a few moments he dragged his eyes from the paper and saw us and looked around him. His eyes fell on the canvas set against the column and in a neutral but quite good-humoured tone, like a man instructing students, he spoke.'

'"It is mostly flax, you know", he said. "When painting, one is playing with flax. Heterogeneous but mainly mineral dye-stuffs are suspended in the oil of flax seeds: linseed. That is what the paints are. And the fibre of flax stalks is spun single-warp – single-warp – then bleached and plain-woven. That is the canvas. One smears the first on the second."'

'He nodded to each of us, picked up his picture and satchel, and walked with a strange rigour, an embarrassing rigour, away to his room. Schulte looked at me. He seemed on the point of saying something but turned away and went off in the other direction. And I went back to my lodging.'

'I was never told directly what was the cause of the quarrel, nor who wrote that daunting letter. But in the weeks that followed I learned of two events and attached them, one to the quarrel, the other to the letter.'

'The first was close to the Collegio. Some time before, a young man and a young girl, local people, had been caught by one of Kaspar's men attempting to take objects from the back of a truck outside the gate. Kaspar had passed them to Lieutenant Schulte, as responsible for the security of the trucks. Lieutenant Schulte passed them, as his standing orders urged, to the Security

Service, the SD. The SD passed them, as Italians, to Alessandro Pavolini's Black Brigade. The Black Brigade interrogated them, doubtless with torture, and then killed them. In time word of this was passed back. Kaspar was of the opinion that both he and Lieutenant Schulte were actors in an outrage against children. Indeed, that such happenings were almost commonplace at the time made this one no less horrifying, no less disgraceful.'

'The second event had taken place far away. Kaspar had one close friend, an engineer like himself, of whom he had spoken to me several times. They had been students together and later had invaded Russia together. But the friend had become a junior staff officer, a thinking man, on the staff of an army group in Russia that was, one later came to know, a centre of the conspiracy to kill Hitler, the attempt of that July. The friend had spoken to Kaspar – though only rather obliquely, I gathered – about this project and Kaspar had spoken to him against such slyness. Four days after the attempt on Hitler's life the friend had been killed, killed in battle, it was reported. Kaspar did not believe that was the way of it. He believed his friend had been executed, like so many others at that time.'

'It was ten days before he came to see me again. We did not resume our readings. He was now following paths remote from me. In retrospect I am aware of three stages – overlapping stages, yes, but sequential.'

'The first stage was an episode of apocalyptic dreams. One dreamed of slave-ships and in conjunction, of course, of shipwrecks; of plague and of maelstrom, though separately; of – a pictorial moment – lewd gibbons inhabiting a ruined cathedral, in the snow; on one occasion of an autobus station that was also a labyrinth. Many more. One was perhaps a little proud of such dreams? They were not entirely closed to one's shaping impulse? But let us agree that they were an exasperated extension of the previous stance, seeking reassurance that one was a mite in a general cataclysm. I became weary of the dreams.'

'The second was the episode of aphorisms – dropped a little coquettishly, it may be, during the winter. "Guilt is oxidized principle". "Meaning is the fourth dimension of doing". "Strong men behave like hieroglyphs". "Deeds may speak clearer than words: all the more, then, watch their grammar!". "A motor is a metal argument . . .". No! "An argument is a verbal motor . . .", and then something about spark and vapour. I forget. Do project it yourself, Signor Briggs! Is this a northern error? To take such *frottole* as distilled wisdom? They were just beads of sweat from the brow of someone fleeing real reflection. Yet I will say they were briefer than the dreams. And the theme was becoming significant action.'

'The third stage – it began with the snows in late January – was not taken, not quite taken, to its conclusion. Indeed the evolution from January to April was like that of some long German sentence, sowing potentialities and laying foundations, diverging into pending clauses and participles as yet dormant, all leading towards the one raw final word that will instantiate the whole – the word "is". Kaspar never quite reached "being", but the sentence was unrolling. You understand, this was really the least verbal of the episodes. There was a little talk of "actual adherence to the idea" and other such nonsense, but it was primarily a phase in which he was feeling his way to an act that would be richly emblematic of a complex attitude. Dangerous! I urged him to read Epictetus, but he was unreachable. Yet, absurdly, it was me Lieutenant Schulte blamed for matters that were now causing him trouble. I cannot entirely hold this against him. He was harassed and it is only just to say he protected his colleague, and at some risk to himself. A less well-disposed man might have informed his superiors of what was happening.'

'What was happening? Very little. Almost nothing at all. This was a preparatory phase of significant *non*-activity. Vehicles with gun-mountings were not repaired with the usual priority. The best mechanic was sent away with irregular compassionate leave, unapproved by Lodi. The men sat around a great deal. On one occasion a partisan intruder was caught, but simply sent home. On another occasion one of Kaspar's own men was caught giving stolen stores to a woman in the town, and no more than admonished. Twice trucks were lent or sent on humanitarian errands for the local population – admirable, but not what they were here for. All this Lieutenant Schulte had to fail to report to Lodi. It was an accelerating series of small acts or non-acts demonstrative of piecemeal principle. What one awaited was some culminating gesture that Lieutenant Schulte would not be able to conceal, some comprehensive symbolical bellow that would be heard as far off as Lodi.'

'It never came. The pace of the war was quickening and early in April the two Lieutenants were unexpectedly ordered to horse. More precisely, they were ordered to take trucks to Milan. The German SS came with some overriding authority, and the men and serviceable vehicles were sent to carry urgent cargo away to the north, leaving all else behind. There were stories afterwards of gold being transported at that time from Milan to Switzerland, but there were many such stories, few true: the cargo would doubtless have been filing-cabinets for Berlin. Farewells were distrait. We all had much to think about that April.'

'An unsatisfactory story? You are too young to find bathos consoling. If the last act of Lieutenant Leinberger's comedy had been played out, it could not have been amusing, least of all to someone who might feel some involvement. My role had not been admirable. I have wondered – not constantly, I admit, but occasionally – what became of him. You will understand I am happy to hear he survived. Back in his northern forests, spinning and weaving! Wholesome!'

'And now we shall drink one more glass before you go, and you will want to tell me a little – only a little, I fear, since time has passed quickly – about your work . . .'

24

An hour or more later Briggs was eating. For the last five minutes Pasquale and Piermario had been developing competitive accounts of the frame of mind to be expected in a Kaspar Leinberger, after the experiences suggested by Briggs's summary of Don Ivo's narrative of the last year of the war at the Collegio Praga. Pasquale argued for a meticulously planned process towards an aggressive act of something called constructive retribution, probably never to be consummated. Piermario preferred a disabling repression potentially, but not inevitably, issuing in some impulsive act of aggressive atonement. Briggs ate and said nothing.

He had arrived at the Ristorante Foscolo so late, the others had long started their meal. By the time he had sketched the various events of his afternoon for them, they had long finished. Now he was at last eating, at the moment eating cheese, and no more than half-listening to them. He had listened a lot today.

The monologues of the afternoon had been accumulatively oppressive. He felt he had spent hours, days, with unhappy people in the enclosed cortile of the Collegio Praga. For that matter, he was feeling something near a mild claustrophobia about Pavia more generally. Narrow streets in the dark, towers in the mist, pursuers cruising around somewhere, and analytical talkers behind every glass of heavy red wine or whatever else it might be.

Briggs shook water off black grapes. Tomorrow he would clean up his transcriptions, and the day after that he would go back north. What to do about Mechtild, he had no idea: there had not been time to feel it through. But he was clear that the poking about in Kaspar Leinberger's affairs should stop before something got out of hand. He had not intended to push this far. What he had intended, he was not at all sure.

Pasquale and Piermario were now disagreeing about Justinian's precise position on treason . . .

'William!' It was Laura addressing him. She had been silent while the other two elaborated their interpretations of the case. 'William, tell me again about the gestures or signs those two men made when they were looking for you outside the Aula.'

Briggs did so.

'And tell me again what the things were that were being got in Pavia and the rest, the things you heard mentioned when you were eavesdropping in St Gallen.'

'I think it was heddle-horses and a cowl. Bobbins had gone off the menu. Something was elliptical in profile – I thought heddle-horses. Then there was a box of stuff from Göschenen – a quarrying place, by the way – not to be dropped. Electrodes on top. Do you make anything of all that?'

'Probably not. But it all somehow keeps pointing to water, for me. It would, I suppose – professional deformation.'

'I don't understand', Briggs said.

'Those signs the men chasing you used – they make me think of diver's code. I can't remember all of them. I've only done a little aqualung diving, and that not for years. But Piermario and I took some lessons at Santa Margherita, and wagging the hand up and down with the thumb sticking out, and then pointing somewhere – that is the sign you are taught for someone warning people of things. It means there is something of concern, over there. I've forgotten what rubbing your ribs three times means, but that certainly means something too.'

'Short of breath', said Piermario. He had broken off the argument with Pasquale.

'Yes. And "cowl" – in the context of "electrodes", "cowl" makes me think of the cowl you have to use on an oxy-hydrogen torch, to make a pocket of air in the water for the flame. You can't cut metals under water with ordinary oxy-acetylene gear. Even for repairing locks and sluice-gates under water they usually use oxy-hydrogen. Either way, it's the electrode that ignites the oxygen. And, of course, there is always a cowl for under water. I suppose the profile of the cowl *is* more or less elliptical.'

No one spoke for a time. The noise of the restaurant around them grew in their minds and eventually they leaned forward almost simultaneously, as if to reconstitute some sense of group.

'Leinberger bought a house down towards Glarus last year', Briggs said. 'For the skiing, but there are mountain lakes down there. I don't think I've mentioned that.'

'Leonida mentioned that the Pappalardo son was one of the Brescia people, Laura told me', said Piermario. 'Didn't he?'

'We are all thinking roughly the same thing', said Pasquale, 'but somebody had better lay the pieces out. I volunteer.'

'We have a man', he began, 'one's guess is a decent but prevaricating man. He is generally troubled by his part in those years and perhaps particularly by his own lack of action. One who knew him well at the time has suggested that he might be liable to take violent symbolic action on some moral base. We really don't know enough about him to say how far the impulse in this might be retributive or penitential or what. But at present he seems involved in something covert. And in this the character of his gear and his associates points, as Laura put it, to water – and more specifically *under* water. A couple of things about the associates – whose motives might well be much simpler than his – suggest experience of some sort of diving. One of these men may even have been trained in it by the Italian navy, the Torpedo-Boat Flotilla. The gear suggests metal-cutting under water.'

'Then', he went on, 'it seems possible that when he left Pavia his mission was to transport SS loot to Switzerland. We all know the story of the SS gold bullion – symbolically resonant stuff. As we also all know, the Swiss government some time ago started to keep some of its huge and – one must say – discreditably gotten bullion reserves in underwater vaults in mountain lakes, out of the way of possible invaders. That is a totally open secret: I've even had one of the lakes pointed out to me by a stranger on a Swiss train. It is an incitement, a positively Wagnerian invitation to an aggressive – ah – hieroglyphic act. For myself, I'm inclined to wish an intending taker luck. But everyone knows too that those vaults will be secured with alarm mechanisms so elaborate that anyone tampering with them must surely be caught. Certainly three ageing *duri* like these would be caught. Oh! and our friend William is marginally involved with this mess in what we gather, vaguely, is an inelegant way. Does that cover it?'

Nobody bothered to nod. Again, for some time no one spoke.

'I think we should stop', Laura said at last. 'We really know very little about these people. We are arranging a few random fragments of information into a fantastic pattern, mainly to entertain ourselves. It's frivolous. That would not matter if it did not matter to William, but it does matter to him. Let's stop.'

'William wants to know about this man', said Pasquale, 'or at least he wanted to. We may not know much, but one does the best with what one does know. What I described covers what we know – and coherently.'

'Some of what we know. There are bits left over. You can't want him to act on the basis of this story. William, do you believe the bullion-in-the-lake story?'

'No. Do you?'

'No. Piermario?' Piermario shook his head. Laura looked at Pasquale and raised her eyebrows.

'Nor me', he said. 'Obviously it's fantasy. Still, one rational way to act on it would be just to try to learn more.'

Laura stood up and the others followed suit.

'I am not sure I want to do that', Briggs said.

'Let's go home and release the *bambinaia*', said Laura.

Coats were fetched, the bill was paid, and they straggled out into the town. As they walked slowly and rather separately through the empty streets nobody said much, and even what little they said was casual and unrelated to the case.

The telephone was ringing in Pasquale's apartment when they started up the stairs and he ran on ahead. Laura and Pier-mario waited silently on the landing with Briggs till – as all three seemed somehow to expect – Pasquale came to fetch him.

'For you, William. The German woman, I think. Intense, but not out of control.'

III

October 19–21, 1956

25

Unlike the main chain of the Swiss Pennine Alps, which runs on eastwards in a diminished form through much of Austria, the satellite northern range of the Bernese Alps peters out to the east quite soon. It does so in an obscure tract of high moor, bounded on two sides by an east-south dogleg of the Upper Rhine.

To the east and south of this tract of moorland, on the other side of the Rhine, is the sprawling highland Canton of the Grisons, which is where some people speak Romansch. To the west is Canton Glarus, where cotton is both spun and woven, and green cheese is made by adding a kind of clover; and then Schwyz and the original Forest Cantons. But – in complex historical circumstances that are not at all to the point here – this territory had centuries before become a sort of south-eastern tail or appendage of Canton St Gallen itself, to the north.

It is more to the point that the region is also a physical anomaly. Here the monstrous pressures that elsewhere pushed mountains up, pushed down. The outcome was a huge double-fold of the geological layers, a sandwich fifty miles long in which two layers of the usual strata held a third layer that is inverted. But with time the top layer was eroded or abraded away so that now the surface is the inverted middle layer – sandy, pebbly Palaeozoic stuff on top and strata beneath reversed to go downwards through to the nearly modern Eocene. Time is upside-down or inside-out. It is a dizzying window back through the more recent Alpine mountains all round, if it is known about, but the form the region now takes is undramatic: a fairly steep-sided table of rolling moorland and tarns and high shallow valleys, nowhere rising very much above eight thousand feet except at the southern rim. Here there are rather higher rock peaks ten thousand feet or so high, the absolute end of the Bernese range. To the north again is the sombre trench of the Walensee, a lake ten miles long and a mile across, with the craggier limestone mountains of Appenzell and St Gallen beyond.

It is sour land no one has found much use for, except strenuous cross-country skiing in the season. Mainly for this purpose, Kaspar Leinberger owned a hut or small house on the eastern edge.

Briggs knew none of the geology but, after re-crossing the Splügen pass by night, was driving north down the valley of the Upper Rhine very early next morning and looking up at a little of the east slope of the anomaly. There was a dirty grey cloud ceiling no more than three hundred feet above, and every couple of minutes he put on his wipers to clear mist drops from the windscreen. His headlights were still on. Coming to Bad Ragaz he sought out the railway station and parked in its forecourt. Within five minutes he was asleep.

Half an hour later he was shaken awake by Mechtild.

'You were asleep', she said. 'We are going on the Walensee road. We drive along it as far as Flums, where we will leave your car. Then we will go on in mine to Unterterzen, and turn up through Quarten to Oberterzen. From there we will walk.'

Without waiting, she went back to her car and drove off, and once Briggs had coaxed his car to life again, they drove in ill-matched convoy for twenty minutes to the railway station at Flums. Briggs got out and tottered stiffly over to the Porsche.

'It's proper you tell me more – why I am here', he said.

'Yes, but I'll tell you as we are walking', she said. 'It needs time. Lock up.'

She drove them with her odd intense concentration along to the Walensee, even more than usually a dreary stretch of water today, and presently bore left up into cloud and left again up to

Oberterzen, a village perhaps a quarter of the way up the north slope of the table. A little beyond the village they turned into the empty car-park of a small and inoperative ski-lift base station, where the road ended. There was nothing to be seen but the dead cables of the ski-lift disappearing up into the cloud in an ugly cutting through the trees. It was a desolate spot.

Mechtild, who was wearing a dark green windcheater and skiing pants and walking-boots, started manoeuvring from behind their seats a large object that turned out to be a fully stuffed rucksack on a frame.

'I think you had better carry this.'

'What's in it? I'm really not dressed for a mountain expedition.'

'Just things we'll need. Let's get going.'

She set off down the road, map in hand, and after loosening his necktie Briggs followed, easing his arms into the straps of the rucksack as he went. It was as heavy as it looked. A hundred yards along Mechtild waited at the start of an established foot path going up into the trees.

It was a graded, zig-zagging, well-made path. But the air was extraordinarily still and oppressive among the trees, and both Briggs and many vicious small black flies soon found he was sweating. He had been panting almost from the start.

'Well?' he managed to ask after ten terrible minutes. 'Tell!'

She slowed a little and began to talk about why they were there. What she told him over the next hour or two was disjointed and punctuated by periods of silent walking, and what it all amounted to was still a quite unresolved state of affairs.

The first element in it could be reduced to a sort of calendar of the last few days. Kaspar had been on edge. Asked on his return from Lombardy on Friday how his trip had been, he had quoted two lines from what he said was Hölderlin, about a man stumbling around in a mist. The day after his return, Saturday, he had gone to the mill in the morning and stayed on for much of the afternoon to catch up with things. On Sunday he had stayed home, pottering in his workshop during the morning and sitting idly with a drawing pad on his knee during the afternoon. They had had to eat out with people in the evening.

Yesterday, Monday, he had gone to the mill at his usual time but in the afternoon had driven, she learned only later, to Arbon to see her father. This was not unusual: there was often business to discuss. But it would certainly also have been usual to tell her he was going. She might have had messages. In the evening he received and made several quite long telephone calls, in his study, so that she had not overheard. But this was not unusual either. At one point he had asked to borrow her key to the skiing hut, since he couldn't put his hand on his, and a friend might want to go there for a few days, for the walking. Mechtild wondered which friend: asked who it was, he had said it was someone she did not know, an engineer in Winterthur, Gademann by name.

Finally, he had reminded her that for the next three days, Tuesday to Thursday, he had to be in Ravensburg for the periodic forward-planning session of the Managing Board and would, as he sometimes did, stay there for two nights so as to put in a long middle day on head-office paperwork.

This information about Leinberger's undramatic doings was interlaced with a second element, description of Mechtild's own state of mind and feeling. She was fond of Kaspar: she believed he had feeling for her. At present she found it difficult to distinguish in Kaspar between a general reticence and some purposive concealment. But in the last couple of days, since the quarrel with Briggs at Urnäsch, she had thought a lot about Kaspar. Kaspar was behaving a little oddly, even for him. There might be some complication, and it might be something that involved Fritz and Bernhard. She had never quite understood the familiarity between him and them.

What had triggered the third element in what she told Briggs – her constructive speculation about all this – was a fact Briggs did not know. Fritz and Bernhard owned an ex-Swiss army jeep, still khaki-painted but with the military markings blocked out, and fitted with a small powered winch at the front. She had seen it briefly two or three weeks before when they had been delivering something (she supposed) at the house, and Kaspar had gone out to admire their new vehicle's points. There had been talk out there and, from Fritz, laughter. But she had not taken much notice at the time and had not seen the jeep since.

That was one thing. Another came out of matching the jeep with Kaspar's asking for the key of the hut. It reminded her of the fact that this patch of country was Swiss army country. It was part of an important eastern frontier zone. If a foreign enemy were to come from the east, from the direction of Austria or along the Rhine valley from north or south, as foreign enemies had come in the time of Napoleon, the valley of the Walensee would be critical – a narrow corridor leading west through the mountains straight to Zurich and central Switzerland. This corridor had been dug by the River Rhine before it elected to keep on and go through Lake Constance instead. It was also very defensible. Twice a year, she knew, the Swiss army held elaborate manoeuvres here, mainly on the valley floor but sometimes ranging up into the mountains each side. The autumn manoeuvres were due now.

That was why she had called for Briggs. She had formed an idea of there being some enterprise under way in which the hut would be base and the jeep both transport and tool: with suitable tyres it would negotiate the rough track to the chalet, and with military markings replaced it might well be able to move about a temporarily militarized zone. The key to the hut was probably for Fritz and Bernhard. She had telephoned to the mill and discovered that they were away for the week. She did not know what the enterprise was. But Briggs was the only person she had been able to think of, to come with her. What she wanted to do was to approach the chalet from behind and above, to observe.

'Depending on what it is', she said, 'we can either stop it or join it.' For the first time she laughed.

By now they had climbed a couple of thousand feet or more through the forest and Briggs had found some sort of second wind. They were walking slower than at the beginning, but steadily. And within a few minutes three kinds of change came in close succession. The gradient eased a little and the path straightened. The trees first thinned and then gave out altogether. And from one moment to the next they found themselves above the cloud. It was a high romantic moment with all the lightening of burden and sense of revelation and trumpet-calls such a moment should have. It was splendid.

Twenty minutes later they were reclining like Roman diners on a sunny minor summit and looking around. Rising gradually to the south were the rolling hills of the moorland table, their coarse and sour dry grass tawny in the mountain light. To the north and the east were the cloud-filled valleys of the Walensee and the Rhine, with high rocky summits in sun beyond, pale but sharp. Much of the cloud surface above the mile-deep void of the Walensee valley, nearest them, looked almost walkably flat and reflected brightly upwards, though here and there were a few clefts giving vertiginous glimpses of dark grey vapour and space below. The dank and stuffy woods of the slope they had suffered up were no longer present, doubly gone, down in the cloud and anyway out of line of sight. Here, by contrast, there was a delicate warm breeze and everything was dry. But visually it was an austere Apollonian world made of light and reflection of light: bleached gold all around and dense white below and, above, the caerulean of high-energy light being scattered by an atmosphere. The change was total.

Briggs studied the map, which was the skier's kind, four centimetres to the kilometre and ski-routes marked in red. Mechtild pointed out where they were, where the chalet was, and also her intended observation point. Briggs noted that they had climbed a good thousand metres from Oberterzen. Then he looked at the placing of the chalet. It lay on an isolated platform facing east, with a very small lake of its own, half a mile and a couple of hundred metres in elevation above the Flumser Alp – a small skiing station above Flums itself, where they had left his car. In effect, what they had done in the last three hours was to go round a corner of the table-land and so approach the east-facing slope from the north-west.

'We could have just driven up to the Flumser Alp and avoided that forest slope', he said. 'Then we could have simply circled round.'

'No. We might have run into Fritz. And the people at the Flumser Alp inn know me. It's where we usually leave cars. Let's get on.'

They moved off, sluggishly at first, but the going was easier now. On rough grass they went quickly down into a small valley, across a stream, then up over a considerably higher rounded ridge, down again a little, past a small tarn, and then up a last short slope. The rucksack was dumped just below the crest of this and, at Mechtild's insistence, the last few yards were covered at a crouch and finally with a crawl. It was not the brow she thought it was, but a false summit, so they stood up again. Briggs went back for the rucksack, and they walked cautiously on over a minor dip to the next horizon, which was the one she intended. Here they settled, secure enough, and looked down at Kaspar Leinberger's skiing hut.

There must have been something lucky about the angle of their point of arrival, because the view down had a subtle asymmetrical balance about it. The platform was at the bottom of a shallow half-bowl or deep half-saucer recessed into the eastern slope of the table-land. Offset to the right was the small lake, perhaps three hundred yards long and two hundred wide, so that its right edge and near edge met rising ground and to its left was a lawn-like level. The shape of the lake was an irregular oval.

It was shallow enough for the bottom to be clearly visible from above – no underwater installations here, certainly – and in its near left quarter was a small crescent-shaped island only a few yards across, evenly covered with grass. The existence of the lake was due to the platform being rimmed on its outer side by a low ridge of rock, nowhere higher than six feet above the level of the lake, and falling on its right side to a point where the lake could drain downhill into a stream. On the left half of this ridge stood the hut, really a small house – a small, squat, low-roofed chalet evidently of some age, shielded on the north side by a stand of a dozen dishevelled firs. Beyond the rim were, to the left, distant mountains across the Rhine and, to the right, the escarpment of an outlying ridge of the table-land. Centre, there was the sea of cloud.

26

It was about now that Briggs began to come to terms with having, somehow, lost all confidence in Kaspar Leinberger as a villain.

Mechtild had dragged the rucksack back a little below their crest and was taking things out of it. He saw a bivouac tent, and then a short length of what looked like strawberry netting.

'What is that net?' he asked.

'A hide. You weave in bits of the local grasses and so on, and it will conceal you on open ground. English boy scouts must know about that.'

'I never was a boy scout. My parents thought they were fascist.'

'My father didn't let me join the Party youth movement either. He thought them vulgar. But my friend Jutta was a *Jungmädel* – that was the girls between ten and fourteen – and I made sure from her that I learned all the skills. One was how to pack for journeys. I still pack well. Adventurous journeys were a special thing for the *Jungmädel*.'

'I see.'

'And you had to be able to run sixty metres in ten seconds and swim a hundred metres, but I could do those already. Proper bed-making was important too. There are right methods for making beds and I still know them.'

She said this with a fatuous prissiness that melted Briggs, and he turned away.

He looked back down to the house by the lake. His change of mind was not a product of thinking. The fable they had worked up last night in Pavia, the tale of bullion vaults and symbolic justifications, had covered many of the facts known to him, as Pasquale had said. And it might be argued that what Mechtild had told him on the forest path fitted in quite neatly. Nor was it just a matter of atmosphere or mood, though the almost emblematic balance and sanity of the scene below may have been a cause of the already latent shift declaring itself at this particular moment. It was more a matter of a change in his sense of the pattern in things.

He no longer felt the same *pattern* in the bits and pieces presented him. Connections and continuities and closures found before no longer registered. What offered itself now he was still not at all sure, but the change was primarily one of lost centre. He could no longer see Kaspar Leinberger as the point to which the bits and pieces had primary relation. Things must be allowed to settle into a new pattern, with a new centre. But what – or who – was that centre?

Mechtild was now lying on her stomach nearby, uncomfortably arched backwards, observing the obviously empty house through a pair of binoculars mounted on a low but sturdy tripod. And the rucksack still looked full. The binoculars would enlarge but foreshorten. Briggs began and then at once stopped an ironic remark about this.

'I am just going to run back down to that last tarn', he said instead, on impulse. 'I feel sticky after the climb. I need to bathe.'

'All right', she said, not turning. 'I'll keep watch here for a time.'

He went back across the false crest and ran, as he had undertaken, down the hill-side to the tarn. Within five minutes he was in the water, which was on the temperate side of sharp, peat-bottomed and just deep enough away from the edges really to swim in. The cleansing was blissful. But he chose a bad, soft place to climb out and muddied himself so much that he went back into the water again, and then decided to swim whatever he reckoned was a hundred metres, in a circle in the deeper water. After accomplishing that he felt a little chilled at last, got out of the tarn at a firmer place and lay on a combination of rock, moss and his jacket – eventually without too great discomfort – to dry in the sun. Cherished by Apollo, kissed by Zephyrs, he would have gone along with being surprised by a Nymph, but none turned up. He may momentarily have dozed. But after a time he made himself get up and into most of his clothes. Carrying his jacket, necktie and socks, he picked his way slowly up the hill-side to relieve Mechtild on her watch.

She was lying on her back by the tripod, asleep. He had been away longer than intended. Nothing had changed below. But the rucksack had disgorged again and to one side were a tidy array of cooking things – a compact camp-stove and a saucepan with folding handle and so on. He should have brought water. Closer to Mechtild a small cloth was laid out, with a long loaf, some tomatoes, two apples, three packets still in grease-proof paper, cardboard cups, a super-heavy-weight red Swiss-army knife, a bottle of wine, claret-shaped. The *Jungmädel* had evidently made their adventurous journeys in style. It seemed ungenerous to wonder if they carried their own packs.

Briggs did not wake Mechtild. She had taken off her windproof, walking-boots and socks, and lay there bare-foot in a grey sweater and black ski-pants with an arm half over her eyes. He sat beside her and watched her breathing. Her mouth was relaxed, not open, and he studied the lines of her lips and her jaw again, and the relation of her upper jaw to her ears. Then he noticed her toes. They were quite exceptionally long, almost like fingers. They were extraordinary, even uncanny. He found himself visualising these toes turning on bath-taps, then feeling for soap. The familiar waves of conflicting lust and tenderness – the Briggsian self-locking system – washed through him.

He rolled away and looked down to the house and the lake. Nothing stirred. Possibly the cloud in the Rhine valley was thinning a little, or perhaps it was diffusing upwards. He could even hear distant noises in the valley bottom.

He brooded.

Mechtild woke twenty minutes later and sat up, discomposed and on the edge of out-of-sorts.

'You should have woken me.'

'No need. Nothing's happening.'

'We should eat. It's nearly three.'

'Right.'

'Open the bottles, would you?'

She unwrapped cheeses and paté while Briggs found his way round this particular Swiss-army knife. The cork-screw was easy, of course; but it was best to discriminate carefully between bottle-opener and can-opener – neither of them, in his view, clearly conceived.

They ate in silence, apart from occasional politely appreciative comments from Briggs.

'Well?', Mechtild said at last. 'So?'

'Yes.'

'But what do we do now? It will be getting dark in an hour. We could pitch the tent here, of course, but might it be better to be lower down, nearer? Or should we go down now and check out the house? We don't know nobody is there. People might be sleeping, if they intend night work. I'm worried that if we just settle down here we may miss anything that *does* happen. The cloud is quite liable to rise up to this level, you know, late in the day. I think it already is rising. Be a bit more help!'

'Mechtild', Briggs began ponderously. 'I'll tell you what I think we should do, but let me say what and why first, and we can argue after. And there are a couple of things I want to ask you about.'

'Oh, for heaven's sake! Get on!'

'Right. I think that quite soon, when it is beginning to get dark, we should curve down leftwards to the house, keeping out of sight from it on this side of the crest, and taking the rucksack and stuff with us. We'll get down there behind those firs. If we haven't seen any sign of anything, we then check on the house – door, lights, anything else we can. If it is dead, we then go down to the Flumser Alp inn and check on that. After all . . .'

'I said: the people there . . .'

'But they don't know me. I could have come up on the Post Bus or anything. After all, even if Fritz and Bernhard or whoever were going to use the chalet in some way, they might prefer to hang out at the inn, before, for any number of reasons – telephone, for one. But if the inn is clear, I am going to make a couple of phone calls myself. If you are prepared to appear, you could usefully make a couple of calls too, but we needn't wrangle about that now.'

'Who would I call?'

'Your husband, first.'

'Kaspar?'

'To see where he is. In Ravensburg, no doubt. But let me ask you – is your husband the sort of man who mislays keys? He doesn't sound it. Has he ever lost a key before?'

'Anyone can lose keys', she said impatiently. 'I do.'

'I know. That's it. But suppose he wanted you safely – *safely* – out of St Gallen for a day or two while he had to be in Ravensburg. Did you ask him, at all, about Fritz and Bernhard?'

'Not really. After our fight at Urnäsch, when you had talked about them, that evening I asked why he indulged Fritz so much. It had come up naturally because Carlo and Concetta had complained about the noise and smell Fritz made, tinkering in Kaspar's workshop. He said, as he has said before, Fritz was an old friend and a true friend, and a man of "untutored but natural inventive enterprise" or something. As I had just been thinking about it, I made a joke about what sort of enterprise he would need a jeep with a winch for – but quite lightly.'

'Suppose the key was a decoy. Suppose he wanted you out of harm's way.'

'What harm?'

'I don't know that.'

'He lied? To me? You have the nerve to tell me *my* husband was lying to me?'

'It would hardly be a lie. He just asked for your key. You contributed the rest. It would simply be like diverting a . . .a . . .'

'Child? Like diverting a child from something unpleasant, you were going to say. You see me as standing in a child-like relation to Kaspar. You are wrong.'

'Take it up with me later. We have to agree on a course of action now. It's getting on for four.'

For a moment it was not clear what she was going to do. Presently she turned and inspected the view below again, first with the binoculars – which cannot have yielded much in the weakening light – then without. Then she started unscrewing the binoculars from the tripod.

'Very well. You are a shit but your plan is the correct one', she said flatly. 'I will pack up the bag. No, I don't want your help.'

She deftly started to recompose the rucksack, her tongue poking her cheek as she slotted unused gear – tent and cooker and hide and all – into place. Briggs put on his socks and shook small twigs and things from his shoes. The cloud in the Rhine valley was both lifting and thinning and the faint, nondescript noises heard earlier were now clearly some sort of gunfire.

'Do the army take over the whole area during manoeuvres', he asked, 'or do they just have ranges? Would we be stopped if we went down?'

'They take over parts, which you have to keep away from, but you can get around on most of the real roads if you need. The bag's ready. Let's go. Remember, if we show ourselves on the horizon, the light will be behind us.'

It was very easy walking down the left slope, and not much more than ten minutes to the firs, but down here and in that time it had become much darker than on the tops. They inspected the house for a while from the firs before they came out to peer through shutters for a glimmer and first gently and then firmly try the door, but the place was clearly empty and tight closed. They would both have liked to go in and Mechtild was for breaking in through a window, but there seemed no sufficient purpose to this and they turned away.

The way on down now began as a steep, rough cart track – probably negotiable by a jeep with a confident driver but certainly not by a car – winding down the slope. They soon found it better to leave this and cut directly across towards the Flumser Alp inn, which was showing lights. It was steep but the ground was so even, one could have slid down it on a hay-sled.

The descent was strange because they seemed to be going down towards some spectral battle-field. The cloud of earlier had thinned into a general light mist. The noise had grown and diversified: not just dulled bangs and thumps but distant vehicles urgently revved and occasional remote shouts. And in the valley leading from the Rhine to the Walensee the mist intermittently glowed with diffused flashes and glares.

When they got near the inn, they stopped to discuss procedure. There were five vehicles outside, none of them a jeep but two of them large saloon-cars in military camouflage colours. A van and an old Simca belonged, Mechtild thought, to the innkeeper – certainly the van. The remaining car, a neat plump Auto-Union with Zurich plates, neither of them recognized as belonging to anyone they knew. One might reckon on Swiss soldiers and perhaps a tourist being in the inn.

It was agreed that Briggs should go in alone and cautiously prospect. If conspicuous wrongdoers were there he would come straight out and join Mechtild, who would have moved down fifty metres to where the trees began below. They could evade anyone down there. If there were no such people, so far as he saw, he would make one or perhaps two phone-calls, by which time he would have got a better sense of the company. He would then come out to report to Mechtild. She might come in or she might not. She would think about that while she waited. Briggs took off the rucksack and gave it to her, walked the last few yards to the inn door, and went in.

Inside, having gone through a small lobby and pushed past a heavy maroon baize curtain, it was difficult to scrutinise the whole room at a glance. It was a compartmentalized space with rather contrived nooks here and there. No one was either at or behind the bar, but half-a-dozen dapper officers sat talking at a long table raised on a one-step dais at the end, with wine-glasses in front of them.

The phone had been on the wall in the lobby, outside the curtain, and he went back to it to make his first call. No reply: Maria was not in. His second call was to be to Munich and for this he would need change or more likely participation from the innkeeper, whom he now heard returning. He pushed past the curtain again, greeted the dour stocky man replenishing something behind the bar and asked for a light beer, preliminary to negotiating to make an international call. There were stirrings in a recess behind him, and he turned to look.

'Hello, Bill old boy!', said an indefinably seedy-looking man, in English. 'Well met by moonlight, or whatever it is out there by now! Bring your glass over. Haven't seen you in an age.'

Briggs was appalled; but the call to Munich would not now be necessary.

27

The man was Christopher Penney, whom Briggs had originally suggested to Charlie Livingston as a more suitable investigator of St Gallen than himself.

'Well, Christopher', Briggs said blankly.

As he waited for his beer, carried it over and sat non-committally at Penney's table, he tried to clear his mind or, better, let his mind clear itself. He would go very slow.

Being with Christopher Penney was always an odd sort of continuous double-take. He alternated between being a character and being a person. The character was a somehow contemptuous cliché: the former RAF junior officer with some airs taken over from admired senior officers. The person was pure rodent – quick soft brown eyes and wary twitching curiosity – part ingratiating, part ironically played through. These two faces were almost wilfully kept in unstable relation.

Penney was going on about the limited interest of mountain scenery: he was and had always been a man of the city, and so on.

Briggs knew practically nothing about Penney's past except that he had spent a surely discreditably long time with the British occupying authority in Hamburg in the late 1940s. He had come to know him slightly a couple of years ago through Livingston. Nowadays he was a part-time agent on retainer for two American banks but also a more general purveyor of commercially serviceable information, partly a bespoke snoop, partly freelance peddler, and partly independent lifter of stones for the fun of seeing and then showing what was beneath. He loved finding Germans out.

And he was not ineffective. He worked a latent advantage in being a stage Englishman in Munich. To the Germans he was at least not American, not formidable, just a bad English joke. To some Americans he was a conveniently English-speaking European, a sort of semi-native informant. And in the large eastern-European community in Munich, involved with Radio Free Europe and the like, rich in special kinds of scuttlebutt, he moved easily because he was a conventional figure, familiar from BBC and film: it must have been somehow comforting to find such people did seem to exist, like encountering Squirrel Nutkin at a Schwabing party – which was where Briggs had first met him. He spoke fluent German with a voluntarily English accent.

Livingston used him, Briggs knew, but reluctantly and selectively because he considered him wild. Livingston had once said he used him to prod rather than probe. And so Briggs was appalled.

'I was cursing my luck', Penney said, 'getting bottled up for three hours here by these chocolate soldiers when . . . in you come! Couldn't be better. We'll have a few glasses and discuss life and letters. It's been too long since we talked.'

'How do you mean, "bottled up"?'

'You didn't know? The road down and area below are closed, from three to seven. Bang, bang. That oaf of an innkeeper told me. The rum-truffles over there are waiting to go down and assess. It's a farce.'

Briggs looked over to the officers on the dais. One was arranging with the innkeeper for Bauernbrot and the rest were relaxedly discussing a map. They might spend most of their lives as bankers or lawyers, but they looked competent men to him, whatever they were doing.

'I think there's a lot to be said for armies being commanded by people with normal social experience', he opined, partly with a view to buying time. 'I think the Haigs and Harrises were disasters partly because they never had occasion to be tested by a social reality at all.'

But Penney did not take the bait. He smiled sadly and let it pass.

'Well, now, you'll be wondering how I come to be here', he said instead.

'I know how you come to be here.'

'No, you know why – we needn't be coy about that – but not how. I heard about the house from a man in Winterthur and made a little deviation, as I was passing below. Haven't been right up to look at it, rather too late, but I was able to make sure that folk weren't there at present, from the innkeeper. I see you have been up. Mind-if-I-say you could do with a brush?' Penney flicked some lichen from Briggs's sleeve. 'Anything worth sharing with our friend Charlie? He's just a little miffed with you, actually, though he doesn't even know you're still on the job. Gone independent? Bit hard on Charlie, isn't it? I really am ready for another of these.'

Briggs sat trying to locate the source of Penney's elusive seediness. There was a physical component as well as the more internal one, but it was not a matter of dandruff and frayed cuffs. The man was oppressively neat, in fact, with his thin, sharp-edged moustache, and his thinning hair swept back. It seemed something to do with colour, some vicious relation of tone and hue, the tones too dark for the deep saturation of the hues, both in the person and the clothes. The rich dark blue and crimson silk scarf now tucked into the neck of his white shirt had it, and so had his brown eyes and auburn hair and fresh complexion, and the same bad relation of tone and hue was all over the man. It was subtle but it was a sort of seediness, no error. Or if it was not quite seediness, it was some cognate quality without a name. He was dreadful.

'Don't be absurd.' Briggs wanted to get word to Mechtild. 'I'll get you another drink. But first I ought to get my wallet from outside.'

'Old chap, your car isn't outside. It's at Flums station. M-58198. Volkswagens antique enough to have one of those divisions down the middle of the back window are becoming something noticeable, you know.'

'No, I mean from my rucksack. I left it out there.'

At this moment Mechtild pushed past the red baize curtain, looked round, familiarly spoke a few words with the innkeeper, and went to a table on the other side of the room. She was lugging the rucksack along with one hand, and dumped it beside her chair. Penney had leaned forward a little to watch, looked quickly at Briggs for reaction, but said nothing.

The innkeeper took a glass of wine across to Mechtild and they again exchanged words, at one point looking across towards Penney. Both looked amused at something as he went back to the bar.

One of the officers got up and walked stiffly over to Mechtild, as if to ask for the next dance, but instead was recognized beneath his uniform as an acquaintance, with adequately delighted surprise. They shook hands. He indicated his five colleagues, who half-stood up and bowed and sat down again, and after a few more words he rejoined them. Mechtild then sat pensively with her hand on her glass, without drinking.

'Somebody should start singing now', said Penney, and hummed a snatch of an operetta tune. 'Slow waltz-time, I think. A part for you, my boy! Well, I really do want another of these and as you don't seem to be buying I'll treat us both. Herr Ober!' He signalled in pantomime, and the innkeeper nodded sullenly.

Mechtild glanced over at them with indifference and started sorting coins in her hand. Then she got up and went off to the telephone behind the curtain. Penney moved his horrible florid brown eyes with mock meaningfulness to and from the rucksack, like some degenerate hamster. The innkeeper slapped two glasses down on their table without looking at them and moved on to attend the officers on the dais.

'I'll get my wallet from outside', Briggs said.

'You will? Well, I'll just take a quick leak then. Be kind to your B-ladder and B-well hope your B-ladder will be kind to you, as the steeple-jack said to the new man. Hurry back.'

Penney went towards a presumably appropriate door at the side of the room and Briggs went towards the lobby at the front.

Once in the lobby he said 'Pst!' to Mechtild at the phone, opened and shut the outer door once, muttered urgently: 'The area below is closed till seven – keep away from me inside – go out later and wait for me, well before seven', ignored her beginning of a reply, opened and shut the outer door again, and went back in through the curtain, extracting his wallet from his pocket.

Penney was well on the way from his door, but veered with a good grace back to their table when he saw Briggs coming.

'You were quick, old boy', he said as he sat down.

'We were both quick.'

'Yes. "'Nless it be that Nature *strongly* calls, waiting palls." Albert, Lord Wordsworth. I think we should talk.'

'Okay.'

'Talk about things as from now on. I'm not going to tell you what I know about Leinberger & Co., and you're not going to tell me what you know, we both know that. But I almost half-fancy you may have gone over to the other side – no, don't blather – gone over in some half-arsed starry-eyed way may be, but gone over. Something's up, and I think I have an idea what. I am going to open it up. *I* am. And dirt is going to spatter – bound to. Some of the Ravensburg people are going to be hosing themselves down for a time. So get out, and keep away. I'd be sorry to see you caught in it.'

'I really don't know what you are talking about.'

'You don't? Then that's all right then. Let's discuss life. Or the weather. A bullion broker in Lausanne told me it has turned worse, there. Know anything about that?' And Penney sat back and folded his arms, to watch.

For Mechtild had come back in to her table and now sat facing them. She was glaring angrily at Briggs and taking gulps of her wine, occasionally raising her arm to look exaggeratedly at her watch.

'You should have sung, old man. Missed cue.'

'You talked with Leinberger?' Briggs asked.

'Yes, and we had a little chat about the textile industry. Leinberger's all for it. He told me about that at length, but not with much detail about his own ploys. I took the liberty of raising your name, as a distinguished fellow-enthusiast in town for a time, as I thought – wrongly, I later gathered. I was surprised to learn you hadn't met. Astounded. So now I get to ask one. Where have you been for the last couple of days?'

'Oh, well, here and there. Stumbling about in mists.'

'Not a very specific answer. I get a supplementary, I think. Stumble on a ten-tola, by any chance?'

'On a what?'

'Ten-*tola*.'

'Spell it.'

'You're just not playing fair, my boy. I quit. By the by, the lady's impatience is becoming almost embarrassing, to a sensitive onlooker.'

Briggs was saved from a deteriorating situation by the Swiss army. It was half-past-six. For some time the noise outside had been reaching a climax, and the officers from the *dais* were going out to watch some conclusion from the terrace before finally leaving. Mechtild's acquaintance gallantly invited her along, and the innkeeper presently also went out to look. Without discussing the matter, Penney and Briggs got up to watch too.

28

It was a spectacle. The mist in the valley below was almost gone but it was very dark there. Above, the sky was clear, still with no starlight and no moon. But though the valley was too dark for its limits or form to be directly seen, the military exercise taking place in it was being conducted with tracer ammunition.

The valley was criss-crossed with lines of white light in various directions and at various angles. Though there was general continuity, there was also constant local change, individual lines of tracer ceasing and being replaced for a time by others, none persisting for more than a few seconds at a time, though they might recur. These lines were like some sorcerer's survey, bearing-lines which, if grasped as a whole and in relation, would give a plot of the shape and extent of the invisible valley. In addition, there were occasional much more diffused global flashes of much less intense light, too diffused and brief to illuminate the lie of land to the point of actual perception but giving rise to intuitions of possibility. It was all like some great act of constructive inference, Keplerian or Newtonian. Or it was a masque of the operations of such an act.

It stopped quite suddenly, no straggler persisting more than a few seconds after the majority had given over. In the new silence distant motors or voices surfaced, individual and small after the impersonality of the light show.

Briggs had been rapt and was the last on the terrace to stir himself. Four of the six officers had already gone off, presumably to drive down to their business. Penney had disappeared too. The innkeeper was going back into his inn. Mechtild came over from the remaining two officers and said that her acquaintance would give them both a lift down to Flums if Briggs was quick.

He went to get the rucksack. In the car-park he noted that the Auto-Union was gone.

On the way down, nursing the rucksack in the back of the big saloon, he was silent while the others discussed the merits of various skiing locations, and spoke only to thank the men again, who courteously insisted on taking them right to Briggs's Volkswagen. And as they were starting to drive off to whatever rendezvous theirs was, they stopped, reversed back, and Mechtild's friend put down his window for a moment to suggest Briggs check his tyres. At least one of them looked to him a little flat. But good luck!

When they had finally gone Mechtild leaned against the front of the car and started giggling, as Briggs went round looking at wheels in the dim light of the station forecourt.

'Rudi Hahnloser will have a story to tell. Ending with my delivery to a flat-tyred Volkswagen so old it has a Romanesque rear-window. Elegant! Are they all flat?'

'No.' Briggs was huffy. 'Only the two back ones, and I think they've just been let down. Move yourself and I'll get out my foot-pump. Penney would just have had time to do it after coming down, but I bet he did it before going up.'

While he inflated the tyres he replied to her questions about Penney. Her giggling persisted, in spite of the implications he spelled out. He was disadvantaged by the grotesque attitudes of the foot-pump user who is also having to talk. But twenty minutes later they were on the road.

From Flums to Unterterzen they talked mainly about Briggs's engine cutting out when going down-hill – not an entirely new trick but now worse, he had to admit. But the bracing climb up the steep road from Unterterzen to Quarten and Oberterzen banished the stuttering for the moment.

'By the way', Mechtild asked, 'your important phone-calls? Productive?'

'No.'

'I made three, myself. I spoke with Kaspar at the office in Ravensburg. He was there and is to have dinner with colleagues. I spoke with Concetta at home. Fritz was making smells and smoke in the workshop again today. I said I would be staying with a friend tonight, not coming home.'

'Oh? Where are we going?'

'"We?" Well, *I* am going to Maria Fleury's. That was my third call. Klaus is away with the army somewhere in the Vaud, but Maria had just got in. She and I are going to spend a long evening discussing our marriages: it's an old plan, but we hadn't fixed when till now. In fact, I suppose I never got round to mentioning you to Maria – you broke in on me in that absurd way. But I'll be sleeping there, so there won't be room for you. It would be inappropriate anyway. You'll find a hotel.'

They drove into the ski-lift car-park. It's desolation was hidden by darkness, but known. Mechtild got out, took the rucksack across to her Porsche and threw it in.

'Call me tomorrow at home – but after eleven, say. I hope your car behaves itself.'

She drove off in a confident noise. Though Briggs felt like sitting and thinking or even sleeping for a while, he did not want his engine to cool much. Both hot and absolutely cold it was fine, usually, but half-hot it could be the devil. He set off down the hill.

The car went more or less all right for a time, but after a dozen miles, before most of the main climb over the hills to St Gallen, it had become clear that whatever it was was seriously disabling and he would not get anywhere far. Much use of what remained in his battery got him to yet another railway-station forecourt: Kaltbrunn.

But Kaltbrunn station was an isolated one, its existence due more to a tunnel-head than anything else. Briggs got out. It was impracticable as well as unbearable to think of arranging diagnosis and repair here tonight. Platform lights were on in the station but there were few others.

Unlike Bad Ragaz and Flums, this was not the Swiss Federal Railway system of the valleys but the Bodensee-Toggenburg-Bahn, an independent line that takes an eccentric hundred-kilometre course across the grain of north-east Switzerland. From Arth-Goldau on the main Gotthard line in Schwyz it climbs up and then down and across to Rapperswil at the dead end of the Lake of Zurich; and then up again and on through the long tunnel at Kaltbrunn to wind its way eventually to the Lake of Constance – by way of St Gallen, among other lesser textile towns.

He looked west. The lights of a train were indeed snaking slowly up along the side of the valley from Rapperswil. The decision made itself. That train was going to St Gallen and for all he knew it might be the last that night. The car, such as it was, would be as secure here as anywhere and easily retrieved. He grabbed his bag from the back seat, hid the car key down the side of the cushion, and made for the platform. No one was about. He would get his ticket on the train.

When it arrived three minutes later, nobody got off and only he got on. The coach was almost empty and the train immediately started into the tunnel. The conductor came, with his ticket-bag on its long red-lacquered strap, and Briggs bought passage to St Gallen. He lay back on his seat, suddenly tired. The bright lights in the train were an assault.

The conductor, a haggard middle-aged man, had sat down on the other side of the carriage to write out the ticket and still sat there now for the blank five-mile run through the tunnel. He had taken off his spectacles and was slowly rubbing the bridge of his nose. Without the spectacles he looked different, the face not socialised and functionary but private and troubled. Their eyes met for a moment and Briggs weakly felt the need to say something: not to, once eyes had met, would not be polite.

'My! It's good to sit back and let your train do the work', he said.

The man smiled formally.

Briggs had done his bit and lay back again, closing his eyes this time.

'"Work"?' the man's voice came to him after a little, not so much questioning as quietly exploring a theme. 'Work in the sense of productively directed energy? The train's controlled energy as work, you mean? The energy is water-power – which is an extension of gravity, really – mediated along wires by electrons. And constraining steel rails on a constructed base are the control. Naturally I've had occasion to wonder at times, but a train is not really a good analogy for human action within conditions. The rails are calculated bonds contrived years ago by people outside, for their purposes, not necessarily altruistic by the way . . . the point is that the energy and the control are not integral with each other. It won't do.'

A pause.

'No, the interest of these trains is different. You know their secret? To go up hill their motors use energy taken through the overhead wires from the source. But going down hill, as they presently always do, they use the resistance of their motors as a brake and the motors reverse their function and become dynamos themselves, making energy they send back through the same overhead wires to the source. That's one thing.'

A shorter pause.

'The other is that two facts of the world, two circumstances of existence, that deny the train recovering all the energy in this way are: friction and mass. That is, let us say, jarring against damned ambience and bearing damned burdens. One of the main burdens is its own damned substance, of course, and some of the most grating ambience is within that same substance too.'

'We are approaching Wattwil. I must go.'

Briggs slept.

When he woke an hour later the train was running into Romanshorn on Lake Constance, the end of the line. He had missed St Gallen. The conductor, bespectacled and remote, had woken him and was writing out a supplementary ticket. Briggs did not care much. It would only take twenty minutes to travel back to St Gallen and he would not even think of that till tomorrow. If then.

He left the train and the station, settled for the first plausible-looking hotel, took a room, and went to bed.

29

Romanshorn is the chief port of Switzerland on the Lake of Constance. It lies half-way along the Swiss south shore, the German border city of Konstanz being fifteen miles away to the west, and Austrian Bregenz twenty miles to the east. Ten miles across the lake on the German north shore is Romanshorn's counterpart, once – and, to Briggs, still – the ancient Imperial City of Buchhorn; this was unacceptably renamed Friedrichshafen by King Friedrich of Württemberg in 1811, and is where Count Zeppelin made his zeppelins. Both Romanshorn and Buchhorn became railheads in the nineteenth century and the ferry traffic between them is the principal traffic on the lake. Ravensburg is about ten miles north of Buchhorn, and St Gallen is about ten miles south of Romanshorn: the pattern is easily kept in mind.

A point about the Lake of Constance is that formerly, when the glaciers of the Ice Age had receded south into the Alps, its waters were eight hundred feet higher than they are now. The Rhine has taken time to dig down to its present draining course to the west. This means that the slopes round the lake are its former peripheral bed, very gradually left behind as the lake itself has progressively but slowly fallen back. Many of them now take the shape of rich gentle inclines, meadows and orchards running down to the water in a peculiarly neat way. They are one thing that gives the lake its distinctive look and feel. Another is the large number of small old towns on its banks, usually tidy and often doggedly picturesque. Romanshorn, a no-nonsense place with a practical but narrow agenda, is not one of these.

Briggs next morning, with an expansive late breakfast in mind, had decided to take the small shore-running launch one stop east to Arbon, also a working town but one which he liked for its subtle balance between a medieval and an Edwardian aura. He had slept for ten hours, lazily bathed and shaved, taken stock of what was in his bag, and dressed in his last clean clothes – an oddly matched ensemble, as it had turned out, but never mind. With two phone-calls he had located and engaged a garage in Rapperswil to see to his car: they would be ready, they said, to report by early afternoon. He had left his bag at the hotel. He felt lethargic but in order. The last few days seemed long ago.

He spent the twenty-minute voyage to Arbon leaning on the rail and looking mainly northwards, away from the Swiss shore, towards sunny haze on water and a few boats. He was reminded of the similar weather six days earlier, when he had sat in the beer-house at Bregenz and had thought in a preliminary way about the matter of Kaspar Leinberger. It was striking how little he had progressed since then, in the sense of getting the information Charlie Livingston had asked for. But his firm feeling was that the matter was a mare's nest. Florian Schulte's pursed lips and 'singular man' must come out of his experience of Leinberger at the Collegio Praga, years ago. Leinberger had his problems, perhaps, but they were hardly of a kind to affect Ravensburger-Humpis stock prices. He owed it to Charlie to call him, when he was back in Munich tomorrow, to offer this impression, even if Charlie received it coolly.

He owed it – he was coming to think – to Leinberger, Mechtild and himself to make a sharp break out of the whole situation and clear off. He could no longer pretend he was playing the protective role he had inanely formulated for himself at Urnäsch. As for himself – to put the matter crudely, as he was programmatically doing – entanglement with another hoyden, and a married one at that, was something a prudent man would extricate himself from as soon as possible. Pasquale had called his position inelegant. It was worse than that.

As for Penney, Penney no doubt would and could prod away. If anyone wanted Briggs's opinion, Fritz and Bernhard were cheerful petty thugs and probably involved in some cheerful petty thuggery, which Penney would probably uncover. And Leinberger probably knew something or even all about it. But Leinberger was unlikely to be himself an active party. Perhaps he was just keeping quiet out of old loyalty or sense of debt to Fritz: Fritz had clearly covered up for him in Pavia. At most Leinberger was lending a workshop and a blind eye. The one complete blank in his mind was Eberhard Vogt . . .

But Briggs was no longer urgently interested in all this. The mess had lost its glamour. When the ferry throbbed into the pier at Arbon, he was listing in his mind the few phone-calls he should make to clear decks if his car was ready for this evening.

As you come off the ferry pier at Arbon there is a garden-like area with trees and benches on which people sit and look at the lake – making a strange impression, since the lake offers a wide prospect and they are all looking in different and shifting directions, as if collectively perplexed. A man got up from one of the benches and walked over.

'Good day, Mr Briggs! How unexpected but how good to meet you here. But then, one might say Arbon is, in a sense, St Gallen-Plage.'

It was Lorenz, Hanspeter Hefti's counter-type at Sybille Röösli's. Briggs would not have spotted him because – picking up the Edwardian rather than the medieval tone of Arbon – he was wearing an idiosyncratic straw hat, a kind of shallow or boater-ised panama. Otherwise he looked much the same.

Lorenz, it was soon explained, was at a loose end. The college where he and Klaus Fleury taught was a depressing limbo during the autumn manoeuvre season. Lorenz himself and the Swiss army had long ago agreed not to go on manoeuvres together: he paid the substitution tax and stayed home. He had come down to the lake today with a desire for some 'air': high up and enclosed in its valley, St Gallen does bring that feeling on. Hearing now that Briggs was looking for a late breakfast, Lorenz said that he knew the one good place where that could be achieved in Arbon and, if Briggs was agreeable, he would join him and enjoy the excuse for an early aperitif.

The place was a hotel terrace, which was prepared to provide an expanded *café complet* for Briggs and a Suze for Lorenz, and had a fine panoramic view of the haze.

'Time', Lorenz said, fitting a cigarette into a meerschaum holder. 'The Lake of Constance – I just cannot call it the Bodensee, even when, as now to you, speaking German – the Lake of Constance always makes one think about Time. But, as it happens, at the moment you disembarked like some Arthurian knight from the mist, I was thinking about Time-*ing*. Timing. And about a man called Caminada. You will not have heard of Caminada? No, few people know the name now. I do so only because he was a friend of my father. Shall I tell you about him? Then you will be able to pursue your breakfast without having to make conversation.'

He lit his cigarette carefully with a match.

'Well, Caminada was a Lombard and an engineer and a man of bold vision. A true Milanese. In the years before the First World War he produced a then much discussed scheme, a carefully surveyed and costed scheme, for a great canal from the Lake of Constance to the Mediterranean, at Genoa. It seems fantastic now, doesn't it? Greek coasters sailing through the Alps and chugging past us at Arbon here to Romanshorn, to unload . . .well, unload lemons, perhaps.'

'It seems fantastic. But consider. It was an age of great ship-canals – Panama, Kiel, Corinth. The technology – the new explosives and excavators and powered locks – was established. The money markets and the governments were habituated to raising funds for such enterprises. The success of Suez was a particularly powerful lure. And the advantages would have been real. The Lake of Constance is the nearest thing Europe will ever have to an inland sea. The Mediterranean would have been taken into the centre of Europe. Germany and Switzerland would have had Mediterranean ports. Fresh, cheap figs! Olive-wood in newly plentiful supply!'

'And Caminada's plan was ingeniously economical. By driving a bold first tunnel under the hills above Genoa he took his route quickly from the sea into the Lombard basin and its existing waterways, and passed through Milan – with all that trade added. And this then took him quickly to Lake Como, fifty kilometres of deep water, ready-made, running deep into the Alps. Then up with locks to the second, longer tunnel under the Splügen pass to cross the Alps – fifteen kilometres long, but that is less than the Simplon railway tunnel. Then down to a tidied-up Upper Rhine and the lake here. Much of the route followed existing rivers and lakes.'

'My father – who was what one would, I suppose, call a financier, though on a rather more modest scale than that word somehow suggests – used to say that the failure of his friend Caminada's scheme to get under way was due to the multitude of agents. It justified my father to himself, I think: it fortified him as lone entrepreneur. The trouble, he felt, was that the canal depended on too many governments with too many different interests, as well as too many too various commercial institutions, all these consisting of councils and committees which change their collective minds from one moment to the next. One did not argue with my father, and also in a way he was right.'

'But I cannot help feeling that further analysis takes one to some more intrinsic malaise of Timing within the scheme itself. I mean that the contingencies around the canal – the technologies, the unified political will of this state and that, the readiness of the various capital markets, the buoyancy of trade here and trade there, the advantage to strategic interests of different nations, the diplomatic alignments, even the desirability of the intended size of the vessels – each of these can be found in favourable versions at some moment during, say, the quarter-century before the First World War. But there is no one catalytic moment, no happy conjunction when all of them were tractable at the same time.

'Worse – and this is really my point – the scheme involved a set of internal relations that ensured there could be no such moment. Buoyant trade, as an example, usually meant scarce capital in those days, at least for the moment: and scarce capital means narrower canal and smaller vessels, and that means inability to serve and profit from buoyant trade. Or consider the complexities of the German relation to Austria, with its expensively developed Mediterranean port of Trieste. Or again, precisely the electrical technology that enabled massive lock gates at Kiel and Panama was beginning to be installed by the Swiss to transform their railways, the alternative to the canal. And so on. The scheme was systematically unviable. It seized up. It jammed on itself. Sad.'

Lorenz leaned forward to put out his cigarette and extract the butt-end from the meerschaum holder, which he then examined. Though Briggs had been listening and eating, he had also been thinking about Lorenz. He remembered that at Sybille Röösli's Lorenz had tried to ask him some question he had never had a chance to complete. And he remembered being surprised when Lorenz greeted Mechtild as 'Mechtild' – more familiarly than one would expect from someone so formal, unless he knew her quite well. But, except that he was a sort of physicist, a viscosity man, Briggs knew nothing of Lorenz, who had now put his cigarette-holder away and was continuing.

'The story interests me, because part of everyone's mental life consists of constructing courses of action in complex fields of contingency, and then either following them or not. Don't you agree? And people characterize themselves by their style in doing this. Some simply seem to have an intuition for the viable and act on it. Some similarly for the disastrous. Some press on and try to force the last contingencies into place, a few successfully. Others cannily wait for a least unpropitious moment and jump in then, and over time they come out all right, on average. But some are simply frozen. After all, the process has two phases – constructing courses and then deciding whether or not to follow them. These people keep constructing Caminada schemes but will not move unless everything is right. It never is and never will be. Tell me, Mr Briggs, why are you interested in Kaspar Leinberger?'

Briggs had felt something on the way – though hardly something as direct as this – and could answer with reasonable evenness.

'Kaspar Leinberger? Yes, I was interested in Kaspar Leinberger. It was a matter of a friend's investment. Its security seemed to depend on Leinberger's reliability. I think now that I was wrong. I mean, I was wrong about the investment's security depending on him. So I am not now concerned about him.'

Lorenz stared at him with unblinking black eyes. He had either lost or dropped his quizzical manner.

'I *hate* witch-hunts and lynchings', he burst out with a sudden hissing intensity, 'even the little everyday victimisations of odd or awkward individuals by groups. That happens all the time – in play-grounds, mills, model-railway clubs, geriatric hospices. It is nauseating that humanity seems unable to evolve away from its origin in packs. Jackals. But we are in serious witch-hunting country here, remember – the last witch trial in Europe only fifty kilometres away south. 1782 in Glarus: just some poor servant-girl tried and beheaded for being odd and awkward. I have been sensing persons poising themselves in a sinister way round Kaspar Leinberger. It was you enquiring about conversions to tola?'

'No. I don't even know what tola is. What is it?'

'I assure you, Mr Briggs, that Kaspar Leinberger is incapable of carrying out any course of action within contingencies as equivocal as those surrounding an illicit enterprise must be. He is incapable of it almost to the point of a disability. I offer this, on my word of honour, as what would in another context be a personal guarantee. Please leave him alone.'

'This is embarrassing', Briggs said, trying not to lose his temper. 'I could readily undertake to leave Leinberger alone, because that was already my intention. But if I do, you will either not accept that it is my intention or mislead yourself into believing I respond to what you have just asked, which I would prefer you do not do. I am not part of a pack. I wish Leinberger as well as one can wish someone one does not know. I am not enquiring into tola conversion. As soon as my car is repaired – I hope this afternoon – I intend to leave this over-reverberant region of yours and drive back to Munich, which I much prefer, and to my books and papers.'

They were silent for a time. Around, people were beginning to drift in for an early lunch. Lorenz oddly hunched his shoulders for a moment, sat back, and smiled with his old ironic urbanity.

'I really must apologise. One should not vocalise one's anxieties during other people's breakfasts.'

'No matter. Shall we go?'

They got up, left the terrace, and started walking slowly together under the trees bordering the coast road here. Neither spoke, and only some of the tension of the last minutes had eased. Near the water-police station, with its pier and launches marked *Wasserschutzpolizei*, a large BMW motor-cycle was parked. Lorenz walked over to it and took off his hat.

'My vehicle', he said. 'I leave it here under – hopefully – protective eyes.'

He opened one of the pannier boxes, took out a pair of gloves, and dropped the hat in their place. The boater-ized panama was functional. From the other pannier he took a belted black-leather jerkin. As he shook it out he paused for a moment, as if to admire some boat that was passing at that moment on a trailer, and

Briggs reflexively gestured to hold the jerkin for him to get into. It turned out a sort of act of truce.

'Thank you.' Lorenz began fastening buttons and buckles. 'These things are ungainly but necessary. Again my apologies, Mr Briggs. I accept your assurance that you are not pursuing Kaspar Leinberger. Someone, I believe, is. He is a decent, vulnerable, clumsy man I have come to esteem. But in the end . . . well, I wish you good journey back to your books and papers.'

'I wish you, too, good journey', Briggs said formally, and then on impulse added: 'But, Lorenz, what *is* tola?'

The motor-cycle had a self-starter, and Lorenz mounted and started the machine with easy competence. The engine was powerful enough to purr, not roar. He pulled on gloves and adjusted goggles.

'To save you getting down your Brockhaus, once you are back with it in Munich', he said finally, 'a tola is an Indian measure of weight, a very small measure, little more than ten grammes. A ten-tola bar is – as everyone else knows and as I still find it hard to think you do not – a very small square bar of gold. The volume of a very small marron glacé, perhaps, but weighing a hundred grammes or so – four of your ounces. One will cost you only a hundred dollars in Lausanne, rather more in Bombay. Good journey, again.'

He waved curtly and purred majestically off along the coast road.

As Briggs watched him go, the same boat on the trailer was coming back again, in the other direction. He saw now that it was drawn by a khaki-coloured jeep with a winch on the front. Fritz was driving but, as he passed, he did not see Briggs because he was looking towards the *Wasserschutzpolizei* launches. And he seemed extraordinarily pleased with himself.

30

It was early afternoon and Briggs was sitting by the lake at Arbon. He was waiting for Mechtild Leinberger.

He had telephoned to Rapperswil. His car was not ready. It was a new distributor head it needed, they said, and as the car was so old this was not a stock type: it could not be got from Zurich before tomorrow. He had not telephoned Maria or Pasquale since they would be out during the day. He had telephoned Mechtild. His other accomplishments had been to buy a large-scale 1:25000 map of the lake and a ham sandwich in place of lunch.

He had found himself unable to do anything very purposive with Mechtild during their conversation. She had been effusively warm, apologetic about yesterday and urgent about meeting today. He wondered about the discussion of marriages last night with Maria Fleury. But he suspected it might be less his presence in Arbon that was bringing her down there than the presence of Fritz and a boat. He had mentioned this when she had remarked that he and Bernhard were not in Kaspar's workshop today, and she had latched on to the news with delight. She was now half an hour late.

He had eaten the sandwich and was looking at the map, not with any very definite purpose but to get a firmer sense of the lake, particularly its more complex west end – which was German.

Maps were fine but they were also a bit confused about their language. Over the last five centuries they had become macaronic. They seemed to offer themselves first as simplified bird's eye pictures. Blue for water, light green for grass, dark green for trees, red for roofs of buildings; roads were wide or narrow. But then there were numbers, for elevation, and letters for names, different symbol systems, and discrete: but then again the letters were semi-picturised, varying in size according to the importance or size of the feature. Contour lines were a different sort of hybrid language again: it was hard to say what sort. And in this map contour lines were reinforced by shading to bring out the hills and valleys, a super-picturised thing, since shading is of the moment and supposes a particular light. But in fact the shading here supposed a light at the top of the map, which was north, the one point from which the light would never come. It was pseudo-super-picture. The map as a whole was a polyglot account not of the lake but of some useful kinds of knowledge of the lake, and not others. Many inward things of the territory were left out of this map, or at least not directly addressed . . .

'Good, you've got a map!' It was Mechtild. 'Look! I've borrowed the keys for Lothar Frischknecht's boat. That's why I'm late. I've borrowed it a couple of times before, for small trips, and know it. What we have to do first, though, is find where those two get their boat into the water. It should not be difficult. There are only a couple of places round here with ramps for trailers, and that jeep sticks out. Then we'll take Lothar's boat – he keeps it in the Frischknechts' boathouse and it hasn't been beached for the winter yet – and stalk them.'

'Who is Lothar?'

'Ida Frischknecht's son. He is a disappointment, you know. A rather fat playboy, always off somewhere trying to meet smart people, which is *not* the St Gallen way. He's at Ischia at present, for some reason. Poor Ida likes lending me the keys because she is shocked by Lothar's extravagances. He buys flashy things he doesn't really use because he loses interest. Though his boat is a modest one, in fact. I don't know how far it will be up to chasing Fritz's – what's it called?'

'*Liebchen IV*, it said on the back.'

'My God!' She laughed. 'Lothar's is called *Franz Sternbald*, I don't know why. Let's go and locate *Liebchen*, then. The car is over here.'

Mechtild was right about finding the *Liebchen* easily. It was at the first hard they tried, still out of the water but with Fritz bustling about doing things of a preparatory kind.

They kept their distance and watched.

'It is one of those new glass resin boats, mass-produced', said Mechtild. 'I have seen the type before. Nothing special – it will not be very fast. Let's get to the boathouse. It will take us a little time to get the *Franz Sternbald* out.'

The boathouse, an incongruously sawn-off chalet just off the road, was a couple of miles back towards Arbon. Mechtild gave Briggs a basket to carry – 'bread and a few things' – and let them in. There was a hollow noise of lapping water and a damp smell. The vessels inside were a casually beached dinghy, a handsome old-fashioned cutter with its mast unstepped, and the rather smaller *Franz Sternbald* – a staid clinker-built and varnished launch perhaps twenty feet in length, with a low cabin roof ahead of the well. To get to it they had to cross over the cutter which lay next to the walk.

'So! You fuel it up – here – with one of those cans from back where we came in. Put in a whole can, and bring a spare too. Then we must get the battery from the charger. I will be opening the boat-house doors. Then we can start the engine. That can take a little time.'

It did take time. Briggs, once he had brought the battery and attached the terminals, laboured at an awkwardly placed starting crank low-down in a casing at the front of the cockpit, while Mechtild stood behind him and jiggled the throttle lever.

'It must be damp. It has always been summer before.'

'I see how Lothar could lose interest in this boat.'

'Oh, don't grumble! Or do you want me to turn it?'

Briggs persisted, eventually the engine stuttered, and Mechtild, with showy manipulations of the throttle, coaxed it to full life. After naming the three control levers to Briggs, she went to ward off while he reversed the launch out. When he engaged reverse gear and moved the throttle the boat kicked sharply sideways, leftwards, with its stern. Mechtild, busy holding on and warding off from the cutter, was startled and looked back, but said nothing. The *Franz Sternbald* emerged untidily but safely from the boathouse, and Mechtild came back down into the well. Briggs moved the reversing lever to neutral.

'Now what?'

'We'll cruise that way – east-north-east, I suppose – and hope to pick them up. I should have brought my own binoculars but there are some somewhere in the cabin.'

She went to find them. Briggs put the lever in forward drive, eased the throttle gently up and took the boat slowly round to head roughly north-east, which meant along and gradually out from the shore. He was unsure about the handling of this boat. It felt rather like a very slow car with two flat tyres on the same side. He veered experimentally with the absurd small steering wheel, trying a little more throttle. Presently Mechtild came out of the cabin with a small pair of glasses.

'Got them! But they are more like opera glasses. Why were you zig-zagging?'

'Just getting the feel. It prefers turning right to turning left.'

'You are not used to a single screw?'

'I have never driven any sort of motor-boat before.'

'I was wondering about that.'

'There does not seem much to it.'

'Not much.'

She put her elbows on the cabin roof and started earnestly scanning the horizon through the glasses.

'I can't see a white launch', she said after a while. 'With this haze we shall have to work from close. We had better go on towards that hard. I hope we have not missed them.'

'I suppose', Briggs said, 'the haze should get worse as the sun goes: the air cooling faster than the water, I mean.'

'No.' Mechtild turned and put the glasses down. 'It does not work like that here. For one thing this lake water is still warm from the summer, not like the sea: that is why there is so much haze during the day. And then it is a matter of levels. When the sun goes the haze will thicken but rise a bit and concentrate some metres up. Down here at water-level it is likely to be clearer. You don't believe me? You'll see! This is a strange lake, you know. Sometimes when it is quite calm there is a sudden big wave like a tidal wave, the *Ruhss*, a metre or more high – to do with un-evennesses of the water-level gradually building up and then all at once evening out, they say. Yes, I have seen one – only once, from the shore, and not the biggest – but I have seen one. And then sometimes there are very mysterious noises . . .'

'Achtung! White boat!', Briggs said.

Mechtild snatched up the glasses and inspected the white speck Briggs was indicating. It was something like half a mile ahead and coming towards them, crossing their bows from right to left. It was going down the lake in the Konstanz direction.

'It must be them', she said. 'I cannot see clearly enough to be sure, but we must assume it is them. There is little enough else out today. Keep going, a little slower – we are Lothar out with a floozie – and we will let them pass, and get a look at them. Then we can turn and follow.'

The white launch passed, three hundred yards away, and though there was only one figure in the cockpit it was clearly the *Liebchen*. At the stern it sported an outsize flag with the bear of St Gallen. Soon Mechtild made out the name on the stern. After another minute or two, with the *Liebchen* still well in sight, Briggs turned the *Franz Sternbald*, turning clock-wise right and looping with more than a half-circle so as to give a general impression of making shorewards.

'Clever!', Mechtild said. 'Now nearly full throttle.'

'Let our course be nor'-nor'-west, half-west, and Arcturus be our guide', Briggs said to himself in English, and then aloud in German, 'This seems about the fastest this boat will go.'

It was not very fast. Briggs reckoned it was a trotting pace, six or seven miles an hour, but the *Liebchen* seemed no faster, at least at the moment. The lake was not a place of speed-boats on the whole, the various policing forces apart.

After ten minutes it was clear they were gaining. They occasionally used the margin to vary course a little, though there was little chance of being spotted at this stage. The white hull of the *Liebchen* showed up against the late sun while the *Franz Sternbald*, brown and eastwards, must be unobtrusive. Twenty minutes later again they decided to close up a little, not to lose the *Liebchen* if the light failed. It looked as if the course was for Germany. They motored on into, or perhaps a little to the right of, the sunset.

31

An hour and a half later Briggs put the reversing lever into neutral and eased the throttle to an idle.

It was dark. Something like the change in conditions Mechtild had predicted was under way but had not yet run its course. Mist had certainly risen to form a blanket some metres above lake level: there were no stars or moon. But there were still also islands of mist on the water here and there, floating like ghost ice-bergs. They became aware of these mainly by passing through them. They were seeing very little at all.

'Let us consider', he said. 'We do not know where they are. We do not know where we are. We do not know where they are going. If this little compass is any good at all, we do know roughly where north and so on are. When last sighted the *Liebchen* was still on a course the compass said was north-north-west, about. That was twenty-five minutes ago. During that time we have been roughly matching their then speed on their then course. Roughly. Fifteen minutes ago we also got a glimpse of lights on the north shore which gave us both, we agreed, a sense of being about a kilometre and a half off Meersburg, but south-east a bit. Fifteen minutes at about ten kilometres an hour is – oh! say three kilometres including their distance from us. Noting the time – seven-fourteen, minus one minute for the time I have been talking, makes seventhirteen – what we now do is take a look at the map. With a pencil.'

He fumbled in a pocket.

'You have been talking', said Mechtild, 'but they will be getting even further away. Surely it would be better if I keep us going as before while you draw your lines.'

'The risk of ramming Germany is on my mind. But yes, you are right. At our speed that wouldn't be such a great matter. We are now about three hundred metres plus nearly two minutes behind them – say six hundred metres. Notionally.'

Briggs went into the cabin, where the map was on the table, and turned on a torch. He quickly made a mark about six centimetres off Meersburg and from it drew a line free-hand a bit west of north-north-west, about fifteen centimetres or three and three-quarters of a kilometre long. This took him to a point round which he drew a rough circle the size of a saucer and scribbled the time. After half a minute dubiously looking at this zone and the area around and beyond it he turned out the torch and went back to the well.

'The odds are on our being somewhere near the mouth of the Überlinger See. We might gamble on doing another ten minutes on this course. Then we should turn north for a bit. We do not want to hit Mainau. It has a hard masonry edge.'

They motored on.

At its west end the Lake of Constance divides into two very different offshoots. To the south west is the Unterer See, an intricate body of water reached only by the narrow channel running through the city of Konstanz itself. It is from this branch that the Rhine runs. To the north west is the more truly continuous Überlinger See, a sort of very elongated bay a couple of miles wide but ten miles long, complicated only by the palace island of Mainau near its neck. This neck was what Briggs guessed they were approaching.

'How long have we been going since you said ten minutes?'

'Six minutes.'

'I think this is becoming pointless now. They have certainly turned off somewhere.'

'I am afraid so.'

Mechtild idled the engine and plumped down on the cockpit seat.

'It is so weak', she complained, 'just to lose them and then go back without doing anything. Have you no ideas?'

'As we are here I suppose one thing we could do is turn off the engine and listen for them. Sound travels on water, they say.'

'If you like. I only hope the motor will start again. But yes, we ought to do that.'

She pushed the small stop-run lever to off.

The stillness was a positive force after the last hours' engine noise and vibration. The water was so calm, there was scarcely even a lapping against the hull. Mechtild sat on the cockpit seat near the wheel, Briggs stood leaning against the cabin wall. After a couple of minutes' deep quiet they both sensed something, not quite a sound but some remote activity on the very edge of hearing. Then, abruptly, a sort of distant animal noise came out of the murk and Mechtild jumped up.

'That is Fritz's awful laugh. I am absolutely sure.'

'It came from that direction, there.'

'Or a bit to the left.'

A faint snatch of talk, not comprehensible, now followed the laugh and confirmed the bearing.

'All right', Mechtild said. 'What do we do?'

'We can only motor. Their engine must be running or they wouldn't be talking so loud. I will try and start with almost no throttle. The engine is still warm. And we will go slow.'

A couple of turns of the crank and the engine took.

They moved towards the sound at less than half speed and quite soon ran into a mist patch, welcome at first as cover. But as they inched nearer the target it became frustrating. Things were coming to some conclusion there and had been further off than they had sounded. Farewells were being made, a motor was being revved, and there was a light somewhere, here diffused by the mist. Nothing could be seen. Briggs hastily turned their navigation lights off, risked more power and suddenly the *Franz Sternbald* emerged from the mist patch.

They were only just in time to make out one dim shape disappearing into mist and darkness, eastwards. But a second boat was still clear to see fifty yards off, lit up by an occupant moving forward from the stern into the well holding a large hand-lamp. Almost at once the lamp went out, the engine noise rose, and this boat too left, apparently in the same general direction.

The *Franz Sternbald* followed. Mechtild put down the glasses.

'Damnation! It was the other one we really needed to see. That was just Fritz, with the lamp, and *Liebchen*.'

'I saw the name but did not recognize Fritz. Was he carrying something in his hand – not the lamp, I mean, his other hand? I got the impression . . .'

'Just something a bit long and pale. It looked like a small flag-pole, or perhaps a rolled chart. It was just Fritz.'

'No glimpse of Bernhard?'

'No. But it was only a few seconds.'

'I cannot hear their engines now and we don't have a compass course this time. We are going to lose them.' Briggs turned the navigation lights back on.

'This mist should all rise soon. Let's keep going south-east, and hope. I'll steer for a spell to bring luck.'

Mechtild was right. Five minutes later, as they came back further into the main body of the Lake they began to see twinkling but clear lights to the left, on the north shore, and another five minutes after sparser lights to the right too. The mist had consolidated fifty or a hundred feet above. They saw they had been further west and very much closer to the south shore of the Überlinger See than they realised.

After some scanning and searching for the two boats they agreed that an object showing up against the lights on the left bow was almost certainly one of the two, making a line as if for Buchhorn (or Friedrichshafen) to the west along the northern shore, but would be too far ahead to catch before it lost itself somewhere. They also decided that a more ambiguous feature tighter on the right bow might be a boat going round from the Überlinger See, south, as if for Konstanz, and in that case would be nearer than the first. And, thirdly, it was clear that any boat going straight back up the lake towards Arbon would not show up as a mass at all, due to lack of shore lights in that quarter.

They were inclining to the southern option when the engine coughed, faltered, recovered, choked, and stopped sharp with a noise like a plumber's plunger.

'Shit!', Mechtild said. 'The fuel tank should not be empty yet. I hope it is not water in the petrol: that happens and is hell's work to put right.'

The tank was under a cockpit seat. There was no gauge, but it did not seem empty. Briggs topped it up, anyway, and then went grimly to the crank under the casing and got to his knees.

The next hour or so was very bad and at the end things were worse rather than better. A climax of temper had come with a bungled effort by Briggs to clean the fuel leads. Finally they agreed to give over, at least for the moment. They cleaned themselves up a little with lake water and went into the cabin.

'I am sorry I said that about going to sea with a fool', Mechtild said. She collapsed on to one of the two seats running along each side of the cabin. 'It is just that I am used to people who understand motors and you do not know a jet from a point. And the other thing – when you were trying to explain capillary action in that futile way – was foul. Sorry.'

'I apologise for my remarks also. I do not remember their detail.' Briggs sat down opposite and sucked a grazed knuckle. For the first time he looked round the cabin.

'Lord!'

'Yes. Ida Frischknecht calls it a tart's parlour, but I suppose that is a way of speaking. It is mainly the red plush – isn't it? – and that bronze nymph. Why is she kneeling like that and what is she looking at over her shoulder? Lothar? The berth you are sitting on pulls out into a double, by the way. Poor Lothar! I cannot believe he ever gets anywhere. Not that I know about all that, personally, since he is frightened of mature women.'

'*Mature* women?'

'Well, married women then.'

'Oh. So am I.'

'Do not be so unfriendly, *Liebling*. Move the map and pass that basket and we can eat something – though I did not plan for a situation quite like this. The plates and things are in one of the cupboards your side.'

She began to lay out one of her neo-*Jungmädel* repasts. In a cupboard Briggs came across a candle-holder and some candles.

'I wonder if we should save the battery', he said.

'Fine. And candle-light will be snugger here. Are those the only wine-glasses? It seems absurd to drink Rhone red out of flutes. Poor Lothar!' They ate in silence. Both glanced intermittently at the map open on the other end of the table. In the mobile light of the candle it was a mediating third presence that demanded no conversation. But eventually their eyes met.

'Well, this is very nice', Briggs said.

'Yes.'

'Thank you for this excellent dinner.'

'Yes, that is due.'

Mechtild refilled their flutes.

'We must hope nothing runs us down', she said.

'It is too clear for that. But I ought to check that the lights are still working.' Briggs got up and went out into the cockpit.

The red and green navigation lights and the surrogate for a white mast-head light on the bow were all robustly glowing. The lake gave only the faintest hint of movement – not swell, just a suggestion of slow respiration. Briggs sat down for a moment on the seat over the fuel tank. At water level it was very clear in all directions. The *Franz Sternbald* was surrounded by a nearly complete ring of lights, frequency denoting settlement, and size and steadiness implying proximity. A single blank marked the forty-mile stretch of the lake south-east and here there were now half-a-dozen slowly moving faint lights of cross-lake traffic, miles away. From a scattering of lights one inferred a world.

He got up and stooped back into the cabin. Mechtild was looking at the map.

'We are quite safe', he said. 'Visible for leagues. Adrift a couple of kilometres off shore. And this is not a ferry route.'

'We are here for the night.'

'It does look like it. But tomorrow we will drift somewhere or someone will give us a tow.'

'I put it to you that it may get rather cold. Well, we must just make the best of it.'

'Whatever that may be, yes.'

'Come and show me where we are.'

32

'The sun is red but the mist is white.'

Mid-morning next day they were still adrift. No perceptible wind, no swell. Visibility at water level perhaps twenty metres.

Between daybreak and sunrise the surface haze had returned in strength. Rather later the night's blanket ceiling of fog above had dispersed. Now at mid-morning the sun shone strongly through the haze, a reddish disk that seemed only a few metres overhead. It was extraordinarily warm, a steamy shadowless world of scattered light.

They had tried the engine again and it was quite dead. They had bathed. Briggs was now more or less dressed and sat with his legs up on a cockpit seat. Mechtild was not and lay on the cabin roof.

'The water is green', Mechtild said. 'But the sun is red and the haze is white. The water is really green, I know, from acids and salts in the moors. But if the sun is red I do not see why the haze is white. It should be red from the red sun, like evening clouds. But why *is* the sun red?'

'I suppose the haze must deflect the sun's blue light more than its red light.'

'Then why is the haze white?'

'Because overall it evens out, I suppose. The deflected blue light has to go somewhere, inside the haze. It is different from red evening light falling on clouds from outside.'

'I do not find that very satisfying.'

'No.'

Later, there was a sudden noise like a roll of thunder, but it came from the water, clearly from far below the water. They both sat up.

'The Cannonade!', Mechtild cried. 'That was the Bodensee Cannonade. I have never heard it before . . . it is the lake bed settling or subsiding, they say, hundreds of metres down. This lake is strange. I wonder what it would have been like to be bathing when the Cannonade came. Perhaps one would actually feel it on one's skin. That would be really uncanny. But we were lucky to hear it. Now I have seen the Ruhss *and* heard the Cannonade.'

She sat with her arms round her knees and looked alertly about for a little, but presently half-lay again, propped on elbows.

'I wish I had been bathing in the lake when it came', she said, and stretched, looking at the muscles in her tensed thigh.

'I should like some dumplings', Mechtild said. 'I should prefer bread and egg dumplings, with liver perhaps, but ham dumplings would do, even on their own.'

Briggs said: 'Why, that day at Urnäsch, did you decide to provoke my going to Pavia?'

'Did I?'

'Yes.'

'Why might I? Let's think. Perhaps it would stir things up? Or perhaps it was just for the comedy? What do you think?'

'The first, and a bit of the second.'

'Let's settle for that.'

'Then why . . .'

'No, that is enough.'

Briggs stood up. He thought he heard a distant bell, some great bourdon bell, far off in no particular direction.

'I think I can hear a bell', Mechtild said, and sat up.

'Yes. That is a very big bell, a cathedral bell. It can only be from Konstanz. Can you tell where it is coming from – from which direction? I cannot.'

The bell seemed to sound at slightly irregular intervals and Mechtild strained to hear three more of the remote baritone strokes before replying.

'In fact it just sounds to me as if it were coming from above, I think – from above the haze.'

'Yes.'

The bell continued to sound, off and on, for another twenty minutes and even in that short time it became – they felt – a little louder and so, perhaps, nearer.

'If the lake shallows towards Konstanz', Briggs said, 'which it must do, there will be drift or current towards the channel, through to the Unterer See and the Rhine. We may be feeling it. It would increase as we approached the channel – that is only a hundred metres wide at one point, after all. We may want to paddle the launch towards one side or other at some stage. I think I ought to unscrew a couple of bed-boards from the smaller berth.'

'In order', said Mechtild and lay back again.

By mid afternoon they began to sense a city somewhere. At first it was a remote and undifferentiated murmur, a quiver more than a sound. Later, occasional isolable but uninterpreted events surfaced – twice a sort of short sharp whistle, once a hollow clang like someone dropping a large steel tank, and once a screech, like sheet metal being afflicted. There were people out there. Mechtild had shivered, and dressed.

Later again, though the direction of particular sounds was still indeterminate, they had a general sense of the sum of sound starting to envelop them, sound coming now from both sides. And it was evolving into an almost human thing, one part of it being voices – a sum of voices, but now and then with some aggravated accent that almost suggested an individual voice – and another part being machines.

The sun was lower, ahead now, and weakening. The green water and the red disk were losing their hues, and the white haze was losing its subtle lustre, greying. Briggs fidgetted with two bed-boards he had propped up in the cockpit. Mechtild sat silent on the seat opposite.

Shockingly closer, the great bourdon bell suddenly struck once and then continued to toll, slowly. It was a compound sound, shaped and layered – a first briefly dominating strike tone which could not persist, accompanying hum tones which hung loyally on, and late-arriving overtones, sympathetic but never quite tame, always with the potentiality to buzz. To heed one tone out of the complex was strangely to lose the others.

'There is something above the haze over there.' Mechtild pointed twenty degrees up, left of forward, to a looming shapeless darker patch. Because they could not assess the distance of the thing it represented they could not gauge its size: and because its size was unknown, they could not make out how far it was.

'I think this is the moment to paddle', Briggs said. 'We may as well go towards that thing, if only as a constant bearing.'

They knelt on the cockpit seats and set to work with the bed-boards, Briggs now and then muttering a count for timing. It was several minutes before they had any sense at all of the bulk of *Franz Sternbald* moving through the water. Even then it was pitifully slow. But after ten minutes' more and more painful labour they saw a real goal ahead, an actual low wall of masonry at the lake's edge. This spurred them on, partly because they now recognized that they were drifting rightwards, presumably towards the channel through to the Unterer See and the Rhine.

The bell had fallen silent.

In the five minutes of paddling that followed, the original patch of darkness somehow disappeared into a more general murk increasingly studded with local lights. They never knew what it had been. An elderly man with a queerly docile dog and a walking stick spotted them and – pleased to represent decent people whose engines do not fail – watched grimly until they reached the wall and manoeuvred a few yards along to a rusted iron mooring ring set in the masonry. Then he and the dog walked away.

Briggs tied up and they clambered from the cabin roof on to the top of the wall. And as they stood and looked about in the early dusk, street lights came on.

They were on a brief stretch of a sort of promenade, separated by two rows of trees from a wide and fairly busy street with street-car lines. Across this were substantial nineteenth-century buildings, withdrawn from the street behind a single row of trees and a broad pavement. And here, almost opposite them, was a quite serious café with a zone of outside tables, lit up but sparsely occupied.

'Fate!', said Mechtild. 'First we eat, then we telephone.'

They crossed, took a table outside and read menus.

'Be a friend in need – go in and get some cigarettes and hurry things up.'

Briggs went inside, bought a pack of Zanussi at the bar and mentioned they were ready to order. On his way out again, he glanced right and stopped short.

And that is how he came to witness the end of Kaspar Leinberger.

33

What had stopped Briggs was the sight of Christopher Penney. Penney was standing ten yards away, in the doorway of a yellowish Wilhelmine apartment house – out of which he had not necessarily come – staring across the broad sidewalk pavement at an angle, towards the street. Following his gaze, Briggs saw only a man whom he did not know standing by the kerb, not far from the chairs and tables of the café. This man was looking back at Penney but glanced about once or twice, as if choosing a line by which to avoid him.

Mechtild was reading a menu and unaware, her back to the street.

The man's gaze stayed on Penney as the apartment-house door opened and another man stepped out. This man was Fritz, who looked at Penney – as rather encumbering his way out – blankly and with no recognition at all.

But Penney now entered on a brief pantomime. With one arm extended and open hand he indicated Fritz to the man on the kerb, and with the other he made a florid gesture of invitation or presentation. And then he bowed.

'Well, Fritz!' Mechtild called suddenly, having just put down her menu and seen him.

For the first time the man by the kerb noticed her, though she was still facing away and did not see him. His gaze went from Mechtild to Penney to Fritz, first rapidly then slow. He took a step backwards – in retreat or in dismay or for whatever reason – and then another, and with the second step a foot passed the kerb edge behind him and he lost balance. He simply lost balance and fell backwards. Slowly, it seemed, and with his arms out as if to soften a fall, he fell in the path of a closely approaching car.

The car had no chance at all of avoiding him but in some reactive attempt to do so veered sharply and, after striking the falling man so that he was thrown rightwards – almost back on to the sidewalk, eight or nine yards along – it swerved leftwards into collision with a streetcar coming fast the other way. The iron mass of the streetcar chassis struck the car violently side-on, so that it shot back along the street, turning over twice, coming to rest right way up, bouncing on springs. Its door opened and something or someone began to topple out, but then stayed.

The car or the streetcar or both resonated after the impact like some huge and elaborate gong, and by a trick of attention all other sounds of the city were stilled for a moment, and time extended. The only sound to hear was the always diminishing yet endless gong chord. Then, after a long pause, the beginning sound of running feet.

Briggs ran too, past Mechtild, who was looking round in bewilderment – 'Stay, don't move!', he shouted to her roughly – and ran to the man lying in the street: dead, broken in several quite distinguishable ways, and wide-eyed. It was no one Briggs knew but he was clear who it was.

The noises of the city had returned and people were now shyly arriving, whispering and exclaiming. Briggs straightened and met the eyes of a man standing next to him. Lorenz stared back, blank-faced with loathing. Briggs looked about for Penney and Fritz, but they were not to be seen.

He turned to retch into the gutter, and then went to take Mechtild away.

IV

October 25, 1956

34

The death of Kaspar Leinberger was on a Thursday. Through the activity of the rest of that day and the day following – looking to Mechtild till she went, as she insisted, to her father's house; dealing with Eberhard Vogt's driver, with cautious but pressing police, then two capable people from Ravenburger-Humpis, and somebody already worried on a point of insurance, with the Frischknechts' boat man, and others – through all that time Briggs still often thought to hear the gong, always fading.

In Konstanz on Thursday Mechtild had withdrawn. She would go to her father's. She wanted nothing from or, it seemed, of Briggs. Her father had sent a car.

On the Friday, early afternoon, Briggs called her father's house, leaving a message that he would still be for the moment in Romanshorn, at the hotel where his bag was.

On Saturday he collected his car from Rapperswil and visited Maria Fleury in St Gallen. When he got back to Romanshorn late on the Saturday evening there was a message asking him to call Mechtild in the morning.

He did so. She was still remote. She was calling because her father would like to talk to Briggs, and she would like Briggs to talk with her father. Would he come up to the Arbon house at three, say? She herself would not be there, since she must go to the St Gallen house to see to things: Monday was fixed for the funeral, a corporate affair in Ravensburg.

It was a dingy morning, windless and overcast but very clear in the distant view, a day perhaps for cold self-assessment. Briggs wasted most of the morning on newspapers and reverie in a café, and then ate lunch on his own in Arbon.

When he arrived at the entrance to Vogt's he was rather early, but he did not feel like waiting meekly outside till the hour. He drove up the long drive, through sloping orchards and pasture with open outlooks to the lake, north, and to the hills, east. The house was a large old farmhouse, something like an atrium being formed on one side of it by two wings of stables and byres and steadings, expensively converted with self-congratulatory tact. There was no trace of husbandry. It was all very clean.

There were already four cars in the courtyard. A man he did not know was getting into one and drove off as Briggs arrived. Another was Mechtild's, newly washed. Vogt's driver – met on Thursday in Konstanz – was standing ready by another. They exchanged nods and the man then looked blankly at the Volkswagen.

As Briggs walked up steps to the small terrace in front of the door it opened and Mechtild came out, dressed for outside. She was clearly disconcerted to find him there.

'You are early', she said. 'I am just leaving.'

'How are you?'

'All right', she said after a moment of silence. She made as if to go on.

'Do you want to meet, Mechtild, when tomorrow and that is over? We have things to talk of. When you want to, just say.'

'No, I do not want to. What things anyway?'

Briggs found this too much.

'Sooner or later we are going to have to talk with each other about the last week. You will want to be open to me about things like your telling Kaspar I had gone to Pavia. I ought to tell you what I did there about Kaspar. We shall want things a bit clearer between us. Surely? This is not the time, but, when you want, just say . . .'

'Oh, the time is wonderful. I did not tell Kaspar. I told Bernhard.'

'Bernhard? But why?'

'He has balls bigger than a bull's.' She set off down the steps, then paused and turned for a moment. 'Or a bear's!' She laughed and went on down to the car, where the driver was holding the door.

Briggs stood and watched her driven off. Not herself. Not herself? What in hell did that mean? Not which self? Not the person preferred by him. Well, would this right self be alive without the other one crouching inside? He looked at the Porsche. He looked at the third car remaining and realised it was Leinberger's BMW, last seen the evening at the mill. What was a 'self' anyway? He turned and used the massive knocker on the door.

A youngish man-servant knew his name, let him in, and led him past the open door of what seemed even today, even in a country retreat, an active office, with one woman typing and another dialling. They passed on to a large room some way beyond – the library, the man said, and the Professor would be here in a moment. Meanwhile Briggs might perhaps like to pass the time with the books? He briefly tended the fire, bowed curtly and left, closing the door behind him.

Briggs resisted the suggestion to admire the books. To follow it would be to collude in some contrived *mise en scène* of the kind enjoyed by René Pfiffner. He looked about.

It was a likeable room. At the far end wide but relatively low windows looked out down orchard slopes over the lake, to Germany. One wall held a fireplace with a glowing fire of small logs and pine cones mixed, a deep chair on one side of it and a davenport on the other. Two long walls were devoted to bookshelves. There was space and there were various pieces of fine but serviceable furniture, including a sort of partners' desk, a neat five-step library escalier, and a massive nineteenth-century shallow-drawer plan chest. The waxed wood floor, only very locally relieved with rugs, gave a sense of comfortable austerity.

What René Pfiffner had described as a medieval statue of St Martin was certainly not St Martin. St Martin, Briggs knew, was the saint who is shown on a horse giving half his textiles away to a poor person. This statue was of a young man archly lifting an edge of tunic – its fall and folds suggesting the finest, at that date probably Provençal, linen – to reveal a sore on his thigh to a highly bred dog. St Roche, the plague saint.

René's old music-stand was not a music-stand but a baroque lectern for a standing reader. It might be useful for atlases and such. Briggs went over to see. On it, at the moment, were the *Frankfurter Allgemeine Zeitung* and the *Neue Zürcher Zeitung*, folded.

The cello leaning against the window-sill was indeed a cello, and a much used, creditably scuffed one at that. But wouldn't a serious amateur musician keep his instrument in a case? There was no case. This un-glossy object was a subtle touch, perhaps.

No pictures, but over the fire-place an old map of Swabia, with Lake Constance at the bottom.

Briggs went to this. It was an austere eighteenth-century map of a specialised kind, concerned not with distance but with time. Big towns, small towns and villages with post-stages were connected by straight lines, single lines for horse-back bridleways, double lines for roads that would bear a carriage. Short cross-strokes on the lines denoted half-hours, and winding roads and mountainous areas showed up only by their roads having many cross-strokes. It was like Tibetans describing distance in terms of cups of tea . . .

Vogt came into the room quietly – a sixty-year-old man of middle height, much the same height as Briggs, holding himself stiffly upright. He wore a country suit, a pale-grey Irish tweed, cut tighter than the English style. The trousers and the shoulders had raised seams.

'Herr Briggs, how good of you to come! I am sorry you have had to wait. Affairs pursue me, even today. I dare say you were able to scan the bookshelves? A sadly unsystematic choice to the eye of a scholar, I realise. Shall we sit by the fire?'

With a gesture he gave Briggs the choice of deep chair or davenport. Briggs chose the davenport and Vogt took the chair. Briggs was now sitting rather upright while Vogt reclined, but the other way round could have been made disadvantageous too.

'I wanted us to meet', Vogt said at once, 'because I feel you are due, in confidence, some explanation of these wretched events. I know from several quarters of your discretion in the last couple of days. I am grateful. And, to be frank with you, I would prefer myself to tell you what you want to know rather than that you feel compelled to pursue enquiries in a perhaps aggressive spirit. I gather from Mechtild that you are stubborn in enquiry.'

He smiled and waited. Briggs eventually turned a hand palm up in – he hoped – a meaningless way.

Vogt's manner was dry but combined with a generalised twinkle or sparkle that seemed to derive from the eyes, though not denied by a thin mouth quick to smile. As René had said, it was the head one noticed. From the side it was like an axe-head, with a high brow and a sudden fall at the back of the crown. And the eyes, behind spectacles, were kin of Mechtild's pale blue, with the same hint of the steppes. But the impression here was above all of a habitually focussed intelligence. The odd scintillation was something to do with agile attention. Only the smile enlisted it as amiability.

'Well, we shall see if we can satisfy you. If we can, I shall hope you will still be discreet. I gather you have friends in Munich with an interest in Ravensburger-Humpis. But I know you also have a concern with my daughter's welfare. Tattle about the affair can do Mechtild nothing but harm, as you realise.'

It was a question and, again with the smile, he was waiting for an answer. Briggs felt it was a moment for careful statement of a position, even at the cost of being pompous. Otherwise he would soon find himself committed to some Vogt-determined policy of suppression.

'Certainly I would not want to harm Mechtild', he said. 'I have a residual obligation to one man in Munich, which you will have heard about, but that is a matter simply of what bears on his investment – not detail about motorboats and ten-tola bars. But Ravensburger-Humpis . . . I must say I feel no immediate obligation to shield your company in any active way; but nor do I have any particular interest in injuring it. And in a secondary way I suppose it is likely to be covered by my wish for your daughter's well-being.'

He drew breath, sat back and crossed his legs. Vogt was looking at him without expression and continued to do so for some time before speaking again.

'I had not expected', he said slowly, 'such a warily itemised response. And '*particular* interest' – an odd emphasis. I have known for a time about Charles Livingston's intrusion: I had enquiries made.'

He smiled, and signalled decision by moving one hand lightly up and down to pat the arm of his chair.

'Well', he said, 'I shall go forward. I comfort myself with the thought that your care in qualifying assurances suggests scruples. In effect.'

He leaned back and, for the first time, took his eyes off Briggs. He paused. He was preparing for exposition.

35

'Sometimes', Vogt began slowly, 'an event can seem more complex than it is because a quite simple incident has had effect on more than one level. For the observer unaware of there being these different levels, it is easy to mistake the different levels of the single incident's effect for different incidents.'

He paused again and scrutinised Briggs. The pause lengthened and became awkward.

'As in chemistry', Briggs said at last, and immediately promised himself not to play up like this again.

'As *frequently* in the history of chemistry, yes. Very good indeed! Yes. But then I must alert you to a necessary distinction. In chemistry the event – some rearrangement of the atoms within a molecule, It may be – is real but the "levels" are a product of the human mind: good science often consists in modifying the product of the human mind to accommodate the integrity of the event. It disarms the "levels" and questions their standing, even if it retains them for the purposes of description. But in observing human affairs the case is quite different. The events themselves are in the realm of the human mind because the actors are human, behaving with human minds. Our analytic sense of "levels", for instance, then has a peculiar reciprocity with the logic of the behaviour – which may or may not have involved thought in terms of "levels" in particular, but was certainly systematically one with the general mental structure of which "levels" is a part. We can say that "level"-thinking then addresses "level"-thinking.'

And then we are in a right old bind, thought Briggs. Vogt sensed the coarseness of his audience. He sighed and went on more tersely:

'In any case, the affair can only be understood if we distinguish within it three . . . tiers. We can leave aside what their standing is.'

He raised a single finger.

'The first and lowest tier was a substratum of activity, simple incident, and I shall be brief with this. It was generated by a spirited but illegal enterprise of Friedrich Hauser, known to many of us as Fritz, who seems to have now gone to earth somewhere with his friend Pappalardo, Bernardo. You will know the background. In the Levant and near east and for some way beyond, outside the more sophisticated bank-using classes and for certain purposes also within them, the favoured currency for business dealings is the small ten-tola bar of gold; it is worth something in the range of thirty or forty English pounds – depending on place and moment and, doubtless, circumstances. The situation is quite different from Europe, of course, where if gold is used in a small-scale way it is in coin, and where bullion transactions are in the form of much larger bars – the four-hundred-ounce bars of the banks or the kilo bars of the private hoarders. But you know all this.'

'Not as well as I might.'

'Through the Italian Pappalardo – who had kept contact with disreputable war-time comrades – they seem to have established some relation with agents of people in Beirut, criminal or near-criminal people. These people were anxious to exchange funds in various currencies, God knows how earned, for ten-tola bars and they were prepared to pay for these at a premium. The two of them – it is charming! – simply decided to cut in on the legitimate business of converting large gold into ten-tola bars. That is a specialised business confined to a small number of licensed firms in Switzerland, above all the Bullion Exchange Company of Lausanne. Both men were used to working metal, after all, and technically the process was quite primitive. They could contrive access to suitable equipment in St Gallen. It is legal and easy to buy gold in kilo bars in Switzerland. But the crux was always the matter of transmitting their unlicensed ten-tola bars from St Gallen to Beirut, since this was necessarily clandestine. They did it through Germany.'

Vogt stood up and walked over to the window.

'Mechtild has told me what you two saw on the lake on Wednesday, and the police are being very candid to us about their own knowledge. It was the biggest consignment Fritz and the Italian had made so far, and the trick was simply to procure two identical boats of a commonplace kind. They registered one in Switzerland and one in Germany. It seems that the hulls of such glass-fibre boats must be given rigidity through a cellular system of low walls or bulwarks, often put to use as containers for water and so on. The gold was stowed in these in St Gallen and they were sealed with glass fibre panels: the glass is a material that can be worked with heat and pressure. The boat became the packaging.'

He returned from the window and stood in front of the fire, looking down at Briggs.

'You are with me?'

'What we saw would be the exchange of boats and names', Briggs said. 'Changing the names would not need much more than stripping a piece of paper off the stern.'

'Painted calico, the Swiss police say. ' Vogt laughed. 'They are very angry with Fritz. Someone, a diver with under-water equipment, disabled their patrol boats that morning by mutilating the propeller screws. They suspect him.' He laughed again. 'A spirited man.'

'But with all this the gold is still only as far as Germany', Briggs said.

Vogt nodded, and sat down, but said nothing. Briggs tried again:

'It is in my mind', he said, 'that in earlier times a usual method of shipping precious materials securely to the Mediterranean countries from the north was to pack them in the centre of bales or barrels of cloth.'

'The historian speaks.' Vogt spoke drily. 'The case is not quite as crude as that, but you make your point. Yes, their accomplice on the German side was an employee of our shipping department at Ravensburg. It was a matter of access to forwarding channels and, let us say, informal local agents, and most of all a means to fraudulent documentation – not actual bales and barrels. Beirut is our centre for distribution in the near east. The gold passed as machine parts. That much has emerged in the last two days. It is not yet public knowledge, but will soon become so and is an embarrassment. Kaspar, my son-in-law, seems to have first stumbled on it when he was in Ravensburg earlier in the week.'

There was a silence. Briggs looked expectantly at Vogt. Vogt looked back.

'Shall we move to the second tier?' Vogt said.

'If this is the moment.'

Vogt stared moodily at Briggs.

'It is difficult', he said then, 'to talk of Kaspar Leinberger to someone who never met him.'

'One or two people have spoken of him to me', Briggs said. This was dismissed with a gesture.

'Well, I shall soldier on. On this second tier one is in a world of artisans' fiction developed around the simple act: not interesting apart from one paradox. Simply, it sprang from Fritz's need of Kaspar's indulgence for what they were doing in St Gallen – the casting of ten-tola bars. But this was not much more than technically against Swiss law. You could almost say they were just neglecting the paperwork, the licence to convert gold. Neither the conversion nor the export is forbidden, as such: only regulated. That is the first element in the paradox. The penalty might have been a relatively moderate fine and admonition.

Serious illegality only began with the forging of documentation at Ravensburg – precisely what Kaspar could not and would not have countenanced. He would have seen this as a betrayal of the Company. And he would have despised the whole affair, from St Gallen to Beirut, as paltry and base – squalid money-grubbing. When he finally realised – on the basis of something said to him by a colleague – how Fritz was abusing Ravensburg resources he was outraged. It was Fritz he was seeking in Konstanz.'

'Kaspar knew nothing about Beirut?' Briggs asked flatly.

'Nothing. Fritz, who understood Kaspar very well, had fabricated a fairy-tale for him. The gold, Fritz said, was gold which *Obergruppenführer* Wolff of the SS – a not uninteresting man, by the way, though still incarcerated by the Italians – had moved to Switzerland from Italy in 1945. It happened that Kaspar, in his connection with military transport, had himself played a marginal role in such operations. The gold, Fritz said, was being abstracted by associates of Fritz from a secret hoard in a lake! Yes: kitsch! Horn-calls, *tremolando* violins! But notice that, unlike the reality, here would have been clear felony and risk for Kaspar in Switzerland. That is the other part of the paradox. Then, the tale was that the gold was being repatriated to Germany, to a trust – Fritz unimaginatively named it as the Arminius Trust – which was distributing funds to victims of the war and recent oppression, including anti-communist groups in Fritz's native Pomerania. Fritz was entrusted with recasting the gold to conceal its source.'

'That is not much of a story.'

'Perhaps not. No, certainly, it is not. You would not have believed such a story. I, when the time came, did not believe it. But Kaspar believed it, at least in three quarters of his mind. It was designed for him. It played on strong deep impulses of his, impulses you would recognize if only you had been acquainted with him – a longing for meaningful action, an old habit of trust in his sergeant Fritz, a desire to assuage a nagging self-reproach

. . . but this brings us to the third and highest tier, the level of spiritual movement. And here, I have to say, begins some agency from myself.'

Briggs was studying Vogt. The man – he had noticed – had some mild kind of tremor: the stiff straightness of bearing was partly a function of controlling this. But now he was starting to project the tremor through his voice, using it – Briggs was al- most sure – to lend a vibrant throb or pulse to those parts of his discourse seen as particularly significant. And the particularly significant parts tended to be those bearing on Vogt himself.

'The third, or metaphysical, tier', he now said resonantly, 'was the site of my problem.'

36

'*Your* problem?' Briggs said.

Vogt stood up and walked over to the lectern. He picked up the two newspapers Briggs had noticed, took a couple of steps to a square wood-and-brass waste-paper bin and dropped one of them in. The other newspaper he took back to the lectern, behind which he stood silently for a moment in thought. Then he returned to his chair.

'You have no clear image of Kaspar Leinberger', he said. 'How could you? Keep in mind, I suggest, that he was a student of looms. It was temperamentally defining. The loom is a serviceable device but it is not, as tools go, lucid in its relation to nature. It is not hands on clay; not an adze conversing with wood. Nor is it the hammer in its wonderful four-cornered game with iron and fire and water. It is an opaque tool that sets distance and mass and contrivance between man on the one hand and stuff on the other. The loom is to the adze or hammer as . . .as a Dutch steam-organ is to my cello.'

Vogt waved a hand towards his cello.

'And the loom is metaphysically null also because though it may itself be elaborate its achievement is not a complex operation – as the humble hammer's transformation of the crystalline structure of iron is a complex operation – but mere multiplication, the repetition many times of one simple operation, the laying of one thread across another.'

Vogt laid one forefinger across the other forefinger and made his face startlingly mindless for an instant, to signify even to the dense a metaphysical nullity. Then he smiled his smile and leaned back.

'I am by origin a chemist', he said with a throb, 'as you may be aware. A pragmatic craft. But there are a number of moods to active chemistry, and not the least is the intuitive chemistry of signs, the reading in natural objects of the declarations of natural order. The benzene ring – it is a tired example but you will know it – is a clear message from God. Entities in a flat pattern of primacies and bonds and energies: this, it tells us, is one way in which God thought of his world. And it also induces in us wonder, a wonder that can take us out of our selves so that we may discern these selves in the larger domain. Such wonder Kaspar Leinberger lacked.'

Vogt shook his head despondently.

'In a sense, I have to say, Kaspar Leinberger was just loitering in the world. He had no sense of himself as a free Kaspar Leinberger. His activity was no more than to react piecemeal to occurrence. A spool jams? Oil it. Or better – and this, of course, was his usefulness – tinker until it will not jam. My problem, about which you have been good enough to ask, was to conduct him through to where he might realise an authentic Kaspar Leinberger.'

At this thought Vogt's face cleared.

'For I had decided I had the duty and also the right to become Kaspar's guide – not a spiritual director, but a friendly pointer-out of paths and a sounding-board and sometimes a necessary adversary-critic. I was the man to do this. He was the friend of my son, who died as a consequence of following a course of action – I will not discuss its correctness – that was certainly willed action of a kind Kaspar Leinberger had never brought himself to take. He was the husband of my daughter, for whom – as you, I gather, are perhaps too actually aware – he had failed to provide the proper frame of feeling. He was an intermittently awkward officer of my company. I saw him very clearly.'

Vogt was now looking at Briggs with open distaste.

'You are restless. How could I have been so confident in my sense of the man, you wonder? No, Mister Briggs, I feel no need at all to take correction on this matter. And (may I say?) if I did, it would not be from a person whose native tongue collapses intellectual grasp and real acquaintance into – allow me! – the stunted English word *"know"* . . . my dear sir, do let me speak! In mature cultures the distinction between information and experience must be recognised, has to be registered, cannot be evaded: in wholesome tongues there exists no sly or slovenly concept of *"know"*-ing to hide in. Every ploughman or kitchen-maid in Europe, in Europe proper, has had to choose since infancy between *wissen* and *kennen*, or *sapere* and *conoscere*, or whatever. Constantly. There is a firm fineness of discrimination in their very fabric. But you people are still picking away at a *"problem"* of *"know*-ledge" from which – after hundreds of years of provincial-baroque contortions – you still have not extricated yourselves. Like apes exasperated by a mirror. Ach! *"k-n-o-w"*: ugly! That is by the way, and I have no wish to be offensive. But please do not *you* question the clarity of my sense of Leinberger!'

The room was darkening. Vogt put out a hand and flicked on the lamp next his chair. He sat in mellow side-lighting and smiled pleasantly at Briggs before continuing more quietly.

'Well . . . we are both aware there are certain experiences, times of enlargement of feeling and of view, that can be occasions for self-realisation, paths to transcendence of the realm of the loom. Death, for example – acknowledgement of the fact of death? Much is made of the potentialities in our recognizing our own eventual end. But death I consider overrated here: most of us accommodate ourselves in very easy stages to the fact of being finite. I recall having fluently negotiated my own first anxiety over the matter at the age of five. Grief, then? That *I* have experienced. But, as it happened, there was no suitably fresh object for Kaspar's grief. A third possibility, they say, is awareness of guilt. Guilt? Ah!'

He slapped the arm of his chair.

'The man *flaunted* a sense of culpability. Then let it be guilt! You see, Kaspar Leinberger – I must say it – had an unattractive disposition towards displaying his wounds.'

He waved a hand towards the statue of St Roche.

'He liked to expose his sores. Was I a dog, to lick them? No! he claimed dignity from them. It was irritating. His sense of guilt was the sore he insisted on revealing with such intolerable smugness, as if it was his badge of manhood. So let guilt be the transcending predicament in which he could be *kicked* out of the limbo of his everyday!'

He caught himself up and leaned forward to throw a couple of logs on the fire.

'His sense of guilt, as he displayed it, was particularly about inertness – action not taken. The catastrophe of my son was much invoked. I worked – I worked very hard, Herr Briggs – on articulating and refining his sense of culpability, since this must first be firmly established for him on the moral and personal plane, fully and formally submitted to the judgement of his conscience, before it could be transfigured and made metaphysical.'

Vogt suddenly adopted a bantering tone.

'Yes, yes . . ."metaphysical" – you need not wince so elaborately. I took the point some minutes ago: you mistrust my use of the word. But by a metaphysical sense of guilt I mean – *I* mean – something plain enough.'

He looked at his watch.

'I might say: I mean an induced awareness of our bond with humanity in the eyes of God. But how crisp is your Absolute, Herr Briggs? I am far from sure.'

Vogt's pace was quickening.

'Now, it was about this time I learned – no matter from whom – about Fritz's fiction of the gold from the lake. I found it

232

preposterous from the first but I let it run because it might well prove to the purpose. And indeed Kaspar apparently took pleasure in weaving it into his display. It added colour. It was a token, he felt, of culpability actively acknowledged. It was action redeeming earlier inaction. But I had something else in mind. The tale was, I could see, a mine that could be detonated at any time, simply by exposing its falsehood. I did not know precisely what Fritz was doing, but it would clearly be some commonplace roguery which I could quickly and quietly have inquired into, and then discover to Kaspar at the useful moment. I needed a means to *shock* the man.'

Vogt, this time, had hit his chair arm with a closed fist.

'You see, he had fingered his guilt till it was quite limp. He flaunted it, but it was like the rag that survives from a child's woolly toy that has been too long cherished – familiar, consoling even, but no longer representing anything in particular. Such a remnant was nothing that I could work with. My task was to reinstate live feeling here, and Fritz's fiction might offer an appealing means. Let Kaspar instal it as a positive element, a symbolically redeeming element, in his comfortable picture of self and then one might explode it.'

Vogt laughed.

'At least, it would be interesting to try – to see if the detonation might set off a larger reaction! In fact, a couple of weeks ago I put one of my people on to discreet enquiry, quite preliminary and tentative. The man quickly got some way – to the bullion purchases, to the Lebanese connection, to unlicensed ten-tola bars that were worrying at least one of the licensed converters – but after a few days he had also picked up in Beirut an indication that someone in the Ravensburg offices might be improperly involved. At that point I had to call a halt, temporarily, since this introduced a new and disturbing element which demanded distinct handling, through specified instruments at Ravensburg. The mine should not be detonated, clearly, until this complication had been appropriately resolved. But . . .'

Vogt raised a hand and let it fall on the arm of his chair.

'. . . Kaspar exploded it under himself. On Tuesday he heard from a colleague that recent dealings with Beirut by our shipping office were under scrutiny. By Wednesday he had put this together with other things, including something said by an agent of your friend Charles Livingston, into the truth. Foolishly he did not consult me. He went off in frantic search of Fritz and fell under a car with a confused mind. That is all.'

Vogt leaned back in his chair and twinkled.

'Now what do you think about all this, Herr Briggs? I would be interested to know.'

For some time Briggs had been asking himself whether Vogt was a lunatic or a smooth smiling master-villain, or both, or what.

'All this?'

The question first brought to mind a set of places: the Bar Vadianus and the Galerie Röösli, hills looking into Appenzell, a ravine with a humming mill; brick Lombard streets by night, Zanzi's and the Due Fiumi, quadratic plain and floodlit Aula, and the shadowed court of the Collegio Praga; the perverse moorland above Flums, the mountain inn and the tracer-lit valley, the great lake by night and in the sunny haze of day . . . people turned up in places. Leinberger had turned up dead on a sedate lakeside street in Konstanz. And one hollow man had never quite got to the point of knowing another hollow man.

'I think . . .', he began doubtfully.

'Rather too late', said Vogt.

The door was opening and Mechtild walked in. She stood for a moment and looked at her father, then closed the door and loped over to stand behind his chair. She rested the finger-tips of both hands, spread, on the chair-back and looked down at him.

'Done!', she said to Vogt. 'Done?'

Vogt did not turn his head but he raised a hand and briefly touched one of hers. He still looked at Briggs.

'Well, what do you think?' he repeated.

'I think that in effect we were a witch hunt', Briggs said stiffly, 'as somebody remarked. The lot of us. Or a pack of jackals. I do think that. And I was part of it all frivolously. As for yourself, since you ask, I would say such cool attentions as yours kill.'

'Concetta wept', Mechtild told her father. She walked to the fading window – to beside the cello that was transparent through to nature – and stood looking out.

'"Bad faith" all round?' Vogt taunted Briggs.

'Among other things', Briggs said.

Vogt shrugged his contempt.

'But they will certainly find something', said Mechtild.

'A "pack"? Oneself as part of a "pack"?' Vogt was considering the word with amusement, turning it in the light to appraise it. 'Now that is, or rather that would be, a strange thought!'

Mechtild plucked the bass string of the cello, high up on the neck.

'They are very, very competent people', she said.

Briggs turned and looked at the back of her head and then out past her into the dusk. The gruesome clarity of the day was gone. Points and smudges of light were coming out below around the lake, signs of distant things, begging interpretation, flattering the mind.

But he owed Kaspar some sort of a vigil he could not observe here. He got up.

'I think I must go', he said.

'Yes', said Vogt.

Publisher's note

The final manuscript of this book was approved by Michael Baxandall before his death. A few small emendations have been made for publication.

The original typescript and a partial manuscript draft are in the Cambridge University Library with the Baxandall Papers.